DAISY DOES IT ALL

KYLIE GILMORE

Daisy Does It All: © 2014 by Kylie Gilmore

Cover design by Sweet 'N Spicy Designs

Published by: Extra Fancy Books

ISBN-13: 978-0-9912665-3-1

Reality is overrated. Escape into a book!

1
_____

The blog post that went viral…

Daisy Does It All
   Mom, wife, domestic diva

Valentine's Day with Baby

I know what you're thinking, Valentine's Day with a baby in
tow? Not romantic. But I'm here to tell you it can be. Here's
what Darling Husband and I have planned for our very
special first Valentine's Day with Baby Delight. Let me set the
scene at our charming Victorian home: fresh red roses in a
crystal vase on the foyer table, a pink paper heart chain
hanging from the fireplace mantel, and the scent of cinnamon
in the air. (No-bake solution: simply boil some hot water and
drop cinnamon sticks in for the scent that's a proven aphro-
disiac for men.) I'm wearing a little red dress—cue dramatic
music—that I picked up on sale at Target. Ladies, I'm telling
you, you don't have to spend a lot to look good. The flowing
A-line covers any pregnancy weight that might be lingering,
but Darling Husband never notices my waistline because his
eyes are fixed up top, thanks to a red lace push-up bra and

peek-a-boo draping neckline. Now you see them, now you don't.

Okay, back to baby. Yes, your adorable baby can get into the spirit of the day. For Baby Delight, I knitted him these darling heart booties. I also found an adorable red long-sleeve onesie with an embroidered heart, added matching red leggings, and voila! Baby Delight is our chubby-cheeked Cupid. Because isn't the beautiful child you have together—with all your love, hopes, and dreams attached—the best thing about marriage? I say yes.

Now on to the big day. This year it's on a Sunday, so we can celebrate all day. First, we'll visit a nearby horse farm for a family sleigh ride. (If you don't have a horse farm nearby, take a drive through a beautiful area. Baby might even fall asleep, leaving time for intimate conversation.) Then on to my parents' restaurant for a Valentine's Day brunch with heart-shaped waffles, eggs, and bacon. Bring along baby's home-made organic pureed food. Or let baby try some scrambled eggs if he/she is old enough. Of course, you can make a delicious brunch at home too. Cooking for your family is another way to say I love you.

Back home, I'll light some candles, put on soft jazz (or whatever silky, slow tunes make you feel loose), and Darling Husband and I will slow dance with our little Cupid until he falls asleep for his afternoon nap (the baby, not the husband, LOL). Tuck baby into his crib, then it's just me and Darling Husband, holding each other in the living room by very flattering candlelight, surrounded by roses, hearts, and the scent of cinnamon. Now this is important: just as your sweetie starts to get ideas about taking this upstairs, make him hold that thought. Anticipation is the best part.

No afternoon delight here, folks.

To distract him, tell him you have a surprise for him. He must sit, eyes closed, waiting for your gift. Which is...lacy, racy, black lingerie.

For you, of course.

But also for him. And his pleasure.

Hopefully, Darling Husband will take the hint and give

you his gift. I'll keep you posted on that, though I did find a Bermuda travel brochure tucked away in the computer desk!

When Baby Delight wakes from his afternoon nap, we'll bundle him up and visit the relatives. Have I mentioned the positively frigid winter we've had in Connecticut this year? Anyway, our little Cupid will give each of them a fresh-baked heart cookie wrapped with pink ribbon. Then it's time for a family dinner back home, just the three of us with Chinese takeout. Darling Husband won't let me cook on Valentine's Day. He wants me well rested for...other activities. And, ladies, this is the best part, please do share this with your Darling Husbands—he takes over baby duty for the night. I'm talking bath, pajamas, lullaby, tucked in for the night. Is there anything that melts your heart more than seeing your husband lovingly care for your child?

Finally, Baby Delight is asleep. And I'm in my bed. Waiting in black lace. It's not quite our bedtime, and that's okay, 'cuz this could take a while. Fade to black, Darlings. Some things are private.

XOXO!

Daisy

Daisy Garner hit Post on her blog and stood, stretching her sore back, still aching from serving customers during her long dinner shift at Garner's Sports Bar & Grill. She shuffled to the kitchen in her thick wool socks, sweatpants, and ancient NYU sweatshirt, and surveyed the mess. The tiny one-bedroom apartment had once been her sister Liz's place. Back then, the kitchen, hell, the whole place, was neat and sparkling clean. Now—sink full of dishes, bottle sterilizer that needed to be refilled, garbage can overflowing with takeout containers and an old pizza box. *Tomorrow I'll tackle the kitchen,* she promised herself for the zillionth time.

She poured a glass of water as quietly as she could, tilting the glass so the flow of water was silent, desperate not to wake her fussy six-month-old son. Bryce of the power lungs was blessedly sleeping. She just hoped he slept long enough for her to stretch out on the sofa and watch at least one rerun of *Law & Order: SVU*. She turned for the sofa.

WAAAAHHHH!!!!!

Her milk released, soaking the front of her sweatshirt. *Dammit.*

"I'm coming," she muttered.

Too bad there wasn't any Darling Husband in the picture to take baby duty. *Just me, myself, and my imagination.* Though she actually did have Valentine's plans. She was going to the first annual Jorge Chavez Valentine's Day Dance at his dance studio. Jorge was practically family. He'd recently married Travis O'Hare's grandmother, Maggie. Trav was Bryce's father. And Trav's brother, Ryan, was engaged to Daisy's younger sister, Liz. So, family, in a tangled web of relationships.

Daisy was happy for Liz and Maggie in their giddy, slightly nauseating lovey-dovey states, but for herself, she didn't have the energy for a relationship on top of being a mom. She couldn't even make this little man happy; she certainly didn't want to work on making a full-grown man happy. She scooped up her red-faced son, settled into the cushioned glider with a few sweaters thrown over the back, and began to nurse. He sucked vigorously as if he hadn't just nursed two hours ago.

She sighed. At thirty-three, she really should have her life in order. The fact that she was still deep, deep in debt was never far from her thoughts. That's what she was working on. The late nights of interrupted sleep combined with long shifts waitressing at her parents' restaurant were exhausting. Working for her parents wasn't all ice-cream-with-a-cherry-on-top either. On the plus side, they bent over backwards to be flexible with her schedule. Her mom even took care of Bryce a few days a week while Daisy worked. (She had a babysitter for the other days.) On the minus side, they treated her like a screwed-up flake that needed to be taken care of. She couldn't blame them. Classic example of her many screw-ups: Fifteen-year-old Daisy standing on the doorstep with Police Chief Bailey at her side.

Her dad had answered the door. He took one look at Daisy in her usual outfit—oversized sweater, ripped jeans, and combat boots—and shook his head. "Again?"

Her mom appeared behind him and asked tiredly, "What'd she do this time?"

Daisy had stared at the officer's handcuffs. She knew she'd really screwed up this time. She'd probably be grounded forever. Never allowed out of her room. Put on bread and water.

Chief Bailey had said she could've been put in *jail*. A girl named Daisy would surely be someone's bitch within minutes. She shuddered.

The police officer hitched his thumb in the direction of her parents' empty driveway. "She took your car out for a spin." He enumerated her offenses on each finger. "Driving without a license, speeding, reckless endangerment." He put his hands on his hips and gave her a hard look. She winced under his harsh scrutiny. "Tell you the truth, she was easy to spot. She had the hazards going, the left blinker on, wipers on, trunk popped open, and a flat tire."

The flat tire had happened when she'd swerved to miss a squirrel and ended up on the sidewalk running over a broken beer bottle instead. She'd immediately swerved back to the road and pressed what she thought was the hazard lights and somehow popped the trunk open. The rest of the stuff had turned on while she looked for the button to close the trunk.

"Dorothy Marie Garner, what were you thinking?" her mom demanded.

Daisy groaned at the full-name treatment. She *hated* her real name, a tribute to a great-grandmother she'd never met. Her dad had nicknamed her Daisy as a kid because he'd said she was always bright and sunny like a daisy.

Her mom continued. "You could've been killed or hurt someone. You don't even know how to drive! I can't even wrap my head around this. It's just wrong in so many ways. Have I taught you nothing about right or wrong?"

Daisy remained silent at the officer's side. It was almost

better to stand with the chief than to go inside and face her parents.

"The car was towed to the impound lot," Chief Bailey said. "You need a lift to pick it up?"

"No, my car is still in the garage," her dad said. "Thanks."

Chief Bailey rocked on his heels. "Look, this is her first offense with the car, so I'm leaving her punishment up to you, but if it happens again, there will be penalties."

"Oh, she will be punished," her mom said. "I'm sorry you had to deal with her. It'll never happen again."

Her dad looked at her and shook his head in disappointment. He was forever shaking his head at her. "Go inside, Daisy."

She'd bolted to her room, avoiding her parents, but they'd come in to talk a few minutes later.

"Turn off that music," her dad said. "Now."

She turned off Eminem and sat on the edge of her bed, playing with the frayed edges of her jeans, making the hole in the knee bigger.

Her parents looked at her, disappointment clear in their eyes.

"First of all, you're grounded," her dad said.

"For three months," her mom put in.

"Three months!" Daisy cried. "That's insane! I can't stay home for three months. I'll die!"

"We've been very patient with you over the years," her mom said. "But it's always something with you. If you show up here with a police officer at your side one more time, I'm just going to let them throw the book at you."

"You'd let them put me in jail?" she asked, horrified.

"You'd go to juvenile detention," her dad said.

Daisy pounded a fist on the mattress. "I can't believe you'd sell me out like that!"

"We're afraid it's the only way you'll learn," her mom said solemnly.

In the three months she'd been grounded, she managed to sneak out and drive their car five more times. She craved speed, the thrill of danger, the freedom of the open road.

She'd been caught speeding twice, but no juvie. When push came to shove, her parents just couldn't throw her to the wolves, though they grew weary of dealing with her. She felt the weight of their mistrust and their resigned expectation of her failures.

She spent the rest of her high school years hanging out with older, bad boys—they had attitude, liquor, and a driver's license. And they never judged her.

But that was all before Bryce. For the first time in her life, she wasn't listening to impulse and seeking the next adventure; she was planning ahead, doing everything she could to ensure a stable bright future for her demanding son. She loved the little screamer.

She stroked her son's sweaty wisps of blond hair. Did she miss living in the city? (New York City being the only city worth mentioning in this part of Connecticut.) Traveling wherever the wind took her? Running on pure instinct, jumping with both feet into the new and exciting? Yes. But she'd resigned herself to her new life back home in Clover Park and was doing her best to make it fit. She could change. Grow up. Be the daughter her parents always wanted her to be. Be the mom her son deserved.

It didn't help that every struggle she had with Bryce, her mom had a similar story that featured her own motherly accomplishments and successful solutions to everyday problems. Baby crying? Rock them with a lullaby. (Never worked for Daisy.) Colic? Put them on your lap and rub their back. (Nope.) Won't take a nap? Play classical music in a dimly lit room. (Double nope). Next to her mom, Daisy felt like the most inadequate, fumbling mess of a mother. And her mom always looked so cool and collected, even as she'd held down a full-time job, running Garner's with Daisy's dad, and raised a family.

Was it any wonder in the face of such perfect motherhood that Daisy had needed some fantasy accomplishments of her own?

The blog had started as a way to share her new experiences as a mom with other moms—dressing up her baby, soothing baby (or not), celebrating firsts. But the more her perfect mom grated on her nerves, the more perfect her life became on the blog. Everything was wonderful in her fantasy world—a charming house, a devoted husband, a baby who didn't scream all the time.

And thousands of blog followers loved her fantasy life.

2

"Daisy Garner, will you marry me?"

She bit the inside of her cheek to keep from screaming. Not this again. Travis O'Hare down on bended knee, in a suit no less, holding up a diamond ring. Of course he would do this to her at the Valentine's Day dance in front of all of their family and friends.

Heat crept up her neck. "Get up," she hissed.

"Not until you answer." His hazel eyes, usually dancing with good humor, were dead serious and locked on hers.

She sighed. Tango music carried on in the background, but no one was dancing. Her parents, Trav's brother Shane, his grandmother Maggie, Jorge, Jorge's daughters, and all of their friends stared, waiting for her to say yes. Too bad her sister Liz had left early with Ryan. *She* would've taken Daisy's side.

"No," Daisy said, clearly and loudly enough for all to hear. She turned to face her audience. "Dance, people, nothing to see here." She turned to Trav. "You can't peer-pressure me into a marriage."

He rose from bended knee in one smooth gesture. The man was all lean, sinewy muscle, thanks to his job. He was a landscape architect, but didn't hesitate to jump in and do the hard manual labor of shaping the landscape.

"Daze, come on." Trav took her hand, and a familiar

warmth shot up her arm. She ignored it and pulled her hand from his. The days of falling headlong into lust were done and gone.

"I have to check on Bryce."

She turned away, and he stepped in front of her. Too close. His piercing eyes gazed into her own. She blinked. It was like he was trying to look into her soul.

"He's fine," Trav said. "Your mom's got him."

She looked over to where her mom was lifting Bryce into the air while he let out adorable squeals of delight. He *never* laughed like that for Daisy. She turned back to Trav. "Okay, fine. Listen up. This is the third time you've proposed. I don't want to marry you. Please stop asking. You're embarrassing us both."

His face flushed red. She hadn't meant to be harsh, but *come on*. She stepped to the side to pass him, and he stepped with her. She stepped the other way. He stepped with her again and grinned.

She gave him a little shove. "Stop it."

His eyes danced with mischief, his usual humor back. "We're dancing."

She bit back a smile. He did make her laugh. She just didn't want to encourage him.

She forced a straight face. "No, we're not. I'm trying to walk, and you're in my way."

A corner of his mouth kicked up in a charming, lopsided smile. "Dance with me. It's the least you can do for the man who gave you the sperm you so desperately needed."

"So desperately needed?" she blurted way too loud. She lowered her voice. "More like drunken—"

"Bliss," he said, spinning her into his arms. He began an exaggerated tango, leading her one way only to pivot suddenly and lead straight-armed the other way.

She burst out laughing. "You're nuts. Did you take lessons from Jorge?"

"Not a one. I'm good, though, aren't I?"

"Sure," she managed to say before he whirled her around. The song ended and changed to a slow dance that could've been a waltz, but he pulled her close, swaying slowly. She told herself she should pull away, but the heat coming off him was intoxicating, and it felt so good to relax into his arms, to just be held. She rested her cheek on his chest and breathed in his clean scent. He always smelled like he was fresh from the shower. She sighed.

He stroked her long hair and murmured close to her ear, "Daisy, Daisy, Daisy, I'll get you yet."

She looked up into his gorgeous face, with sparkling hazel eyes, perpetual stubble along his jaw, and a ready smile. "Now why do I feel like Little Red Riding Hood?"

He flashed a toothy smile and lunged for her neck. She squealed and squirmed, but he held on and chomped gently down her neck.

She smacked his arm because she liked that a little too much. "Back off, Big Bad Wolf."

He continued their dance as if nothing had happened. Trav used to be big and bad. He'd been an angry rebel, a year behind her in high school. As a teen, she'd admired all the trouble he managed to get in and out of with hardly a mark on him. She hadn't hung out with him then, preferring older guys with cars. Now he was very special to her for one six-month-old reason. But that didn't mean she wanted to marry him.

Trav spoke softly in her ear. "What's it going to take for you to say yes?"

She stiffened. He just wouldn't stop pushing her for more. Her track record was horrible in the relationship department. Her head hurt just thinking about all that pain and heart-break. The bad boys who cheated on her, the men who left her, and the worst, Max, who took off after she lost their baby. She pushed that pain down. She had Bryce now. And he couldn't be part of her relationship wreckage. She wouldn't let that happen.

She tried to pull away from Trav, but he held onto her arms, forcing her to stay. Fine. Clearly at marriage proposal number three, it was time to be blunt.

"You don't love me."

He looked confused. "You're the mother of my only child; of course I love you."

She shook her head. "You love Bryce. You don't love me. We did this all backwards, and you can't change that. I barely remember the night we hooked up. Do you?"

He hesitated. "Parts of it."

"See? And now you can't separate me from Bryce. I'll never know if you love me for me or because of the baby."

He cocked his head to the side. "You want the truth? Love is something made up by corporations to sell more cards."

"If you really believe that, then you've never been in love."

"So you'll say yes if I give you some sappy declaration of love?"

She pursed her lips and thought very hard, *You are an idiot.* She only kept it to herself because she didn't want to fight.

He dropped his hands and released her. "Dammit, I want him to have my name. He's an O'Hare. I want him to have a family, *two* parents that live with him."

"He does have family; look around." And with that she made her escape, overheated as usual from Trav. He was always too close, too demanding, too…sexy. She was listening to her brain nowadays, not her libido.

She stopped at the refreshment table for punch. A few minutes later, she searched the room for her mom and Bryce. Her mom was handing Bryce over to Trav. Daisy sighed. Trav did have a way with Bryce. Her son slapped both hands on either side of his daddy's face and gave a delighted two-toothed smile. His daddy smiled back. She instantly forgave Trav for his pushiness. She loved him for loving Bryce. Just not the in-love kind of way.

She headed over to the happy pair. Love was overrated anyway.

Her mom blocked her path before she could get to Bryce. The older woman with long, wavy blond hair and blue eyes resembled a more polished version of Daisy plus twenty-something years. Daisy braced herself.

"Dorothy Marie Garner, what were you thinking?" her

mom demanded. "Turning Travis down cold in front of everyone. Couldn't you at least have said maybe?"

Daisy threw her hands up. "I'm not going to pity marry him."

"Pity. Ha! He's a good man. He's Bryce's father. You can't ask for better than that."

"Mom, it's none of your business. Seriously."

"Why do you have to make everything so difficult?" her mom asked. "Let Trav take care of you and Bryce. He owns his own business that's doing very well, I hear. You won't have to work unless you want to. You can live in a house instead of that mess of an apartment. He'll help smooth out your edges."

Daisy nearly choked on her anger. "My edges? What's that supposed to mean?"

"Just that…" Her mom paused, choosing her words carefully. "It's no secret that you've always needed a little help to keep the road smooth. I mean, you have no career to speak of. If only you'd finished college or at least held down a job for more than two years. When I was your age—"

"I know I haven't always had my life together," Daisy said through clenched teeth. "I've made some bad decisions." She took a deep breath, her chest aching with the knowledge that her perfect mom had no faith in her firstborn. "I'm trying very hard to make a good life for Bryce. And I don't want Trav or anyone else to do that for me. I want to do it on my own."

Her mom's brows drew together in a concerned look. "But, darling, are you sure you know how?"

Daisy saw red. "I'll figure it out!"

She stormed off to Trav, collected Bryce and the diaper bag that doubled as her purse, and headed for the door. She stopped, realizing she had to bundle them both up, and went to the coat rack for her down parka and his bunting. So much for the dramatic exit.

"Let me help," Trav said, appearing at her side.

Without a word, she handed him Bryce, and he slipped the baby's legs into the bunting and maneuvered in his arms.

His fingers deftly did up the snaps faster than she ever could. He was a whiz with the baby gear.

She zipped up her coat and held out her arms for Bryce.

Trav handed him over and pulled the hood over Bryce's head. "You okay?"

She blinked back tears of frustration from the fight with her mom, from sleep deprivation, from the relentless pursuit by the guy she impulsively, drunkenly hooked up with one sad and lonely Thanksgiving weekend. Lust, liquor, and a rebound hookup—she'd just been dumped the day before— not her finest hour.

She'd immediately left town. Trav had called her, repeatedly, but she let the calls go to voicemail. He just didn't get that it was a one-night stand. It had to be; she wasn't ready for more, not then, not now. She'd gone from regret over her impulsive nature to terrified with the surprise pregnancy. She'd freaked over the pregnancy all the way until she held her beautiful baby in her arms.

Daisy called over her shoulder to Trav as she headed toward the exit. "I'm fine. Night."

A moment later, she heard footsteps behind her. She sped up.

"Wait," Trav said.

She didn't slow, but knew her fate was to deal with him over and over and over again. Bryce tied her to him forever. She unlocked the tomato red station wagon. She still couldn't believe she drove a station wagon. It was a gift from Trav for Bryce's safety.

Trav caught up with them.

She wiped away a tear that had managed to escape and turned to Trav. "Can we talk later? I'm having kind of a shit night."

He held Bryce's blue blankie with the embroidered teddy bear on the corner in one hand. "Well, I got a loud 'no' to my marriage proposal, so I know a little something about shit nights."

His tone was light, but she knew she'd hurt him. He handed over the blankie.

Bryce relaxed into her shoulder; the boy was worn out from his busy night. She cuddled him close. "I had a fight with my mom."

"We need to talk," he said flatly.

Completely out of patience, she snapped, "Make it quick. Bryce needs to get to bed."

He didn't react to her tone. He never did. Calm, steady, always in good humor. It made her want to shake him. That was the problem with Trav. He always felt distant, like the real Trav, the Trav who was an angry, rebellious teen raising hell had been buried so deep that all that was left was this pleasant but distant guy.

"This won't take long," he replied.

Trav's chest ached as he watched Daisy tuck their son into his car seat. He'd never get tired of that sight. Mother and child, so close like that. He didn't know if he'd had that with his mom as a baby, but, as a kid, they'd watched *Peter Pan* together, and every night when she tucked him into bed, he would say, "I wish I could fly right out that window to Neverland." And she'd say, "Me too," then she'd sprinkle pixie dust over him and say, "Think happy thoughts and fly in your dreams." It was his best memory of her.

The only gaping hole in his son's life as far as Trav was concerned was not having his parents together. Like a family should be. Like he'd always wished his own family had been.

Daisy shut the car door gently and turned to him.

"I'm not giving up on us," he informed her.

"There is no us," Daisy said.

The woman was maddening. He hadn't missed the tears. He knew she was exhausted. If only she would let him in. He wanted to make life easier for her. Get rid of those dark circles under her eyes; get some of that bubbly personality back.

He held his palms up. "You won't give us a chance. What are you afraid will happen?"

She heaved a long-suffering sigh that pissed him off, but

he tamped down the anger, knowing it never got him anything but trouble.

"I'm not afraid of anything," she said. "Okay, say we got together and it didn't work out. Bryce would suffer."

"And what if it did work out? Then Bryce could have a normal family."

She pushed her long, blond hair out of her face and blew out a breath that left a puff in the cold air. She was beautiful even when she was tired, frustrated, and on the verge of anger, like now. Always so beautiful. He'd had a thing for her since he moved to Clover Park sophomore year. Not that she'd ever noticed the skinny kid a grade behind her. Junior girls didn't give sophomore boys the time of day. Now it was different. They were responsible adults with a child. Bryce was all that mattered now.

"Bryce doesn't know any different," she said. "This is a normal family to him."

"I want more for him. A real family. Two parents that live with him."

"I just...don't want to be in a relationship with anyone right now. I'm on my own for the first time in my life. I'm working hard to get out of debt and provide a good life for Bryce. I need to show everyone, including myself, that I can do this. I've spent too much of my life letting other people fix my problems. If I take the easy way, I'll never know what it feels like to be independent."

"I never said being with me would be easy," he said, keeping the tone light. "I leave the cap off the toothpaste, and you really don't want to see this bedhead in the morning." He pulled his hair up and snarled.

"*Trav*, you know what I mean. Be serious."

He paused, serious now. "You could still be independent. We can do this on your terms. I'd never stand in your way." His voice came out raspy over the tightness in his throat. Annoying. He cleared his throat.

She frowned and looked at the ground. "No one has faith in me, with good reason. I've made some bad decisions." She met his eyes, and he read the pain there. "Impulsive, spur-of-the-moment decisions that ended with me out of a job, home-less, penniless. Seriously, up until Bryce, my life has pretty much been a disaster. If it wasn't for my family, I hate to think where I would've ended up."

She's too hard on herself. It wasn't like she'd been into drugs or drinking. She just hadn't found her niche. Hadn't yet found the right person to share her life with. But he knew this was it. He was her person. Their little family was her niche. You couldn't have a miracle like Bryce and not know that *together* was where their family belonged. But he didn't say any of that. He knew when to let up. That didn't mean he was giving up on her.

He peeked in the back seat at his sleeping son. "Good-night, little man." He turned to her. "Night, Daze."

She looked relieved that he was leaving, which left a sour note.

"Night, Trav."

He stepped back while she got into the driver's seat. He usually had an easy way with women. Flirt, get a laugh out of them, enjoy each other for a while. But now…now when it really counted and his son's future was at stake, he struck out. He was starting to feel like a loser. But, as his big bro Ry used to coach him, *Winners never quit.*

Daisy turned on the car and powered down her window. "No more marriage proposals. Okay?"

He winked. "Not unless you're the one asking."

She laughed. "Fair enough."

He stepped back, his smile frozen in place, and watched her pull away with his son. He turned for his car and let out a frustrated breath. He hated saying goodbye to Bryce so much. He wanted to see Bryce's drooly, two-toothed smile every morning and tuck him in every night. He wanted him to have a rock-solid foundation. He unlocked his Toyota RAV4, bought especially for its safety and reliability when Bryce came into his life, and blasted Metallica all the way back to his empty house.

3

The next morning Trav and his crew chief and friend, Rico del Toro, drove to the supply yard to stock up on rock salt. The weather reporters were going nuts about the snowstorm likely to hit at the end of the week. His plow and shoveling service kept his landscape business going in the winter months. Rico was the only one he kept on payroll, though. The rest of the crew was seasonal.

"You're pretty quiet over there, *jefe*," Rico said from the passenger side of the truck.

Even though Trav knew Rico from back when they were kids in New Jersey, before Trav moved to Clover Park at fifteen, he still didn't want to talk about what was bugging him.

"Enough with the boss shit," Trav snapped.

"Touchy."

Trav exhaled sharply. "It's Monday. I'm not awake yet."

"I'm thinking someone didn't have such a dreamy Valentine's Day," Rico teased.

Trav snorted and glanced over. "And you did."

Women loved Rico, and he loved them right back. Not enough to stick around, but they generally knew that going into it. His rep was legendary.

Rico puffed out his chest. "I don't kiss and tell, but

someone wanted a *luscious* caramel valentine. *Bow-chicka-wow-wow.*"

"Geez, man, shut up." He stopped at a light, last night's disaster with Daisy fresh in his mind. He really did have to stop proposing to her. It was getting embarrassing. Maybe marriage wasn't in the cards for them. The light changed, and he hit the accelerator hard.

Rico grabbed the oh-shit handle. "Fuck. What is wrong with you today?"

"Daisy turned me down again."

Rico clucked his tongue. "I told you not to ask her anymore. Have some pride."

"I do have pride," Trav snapped. "I've also got a son who doesn't have my name and who doesn't have a family."

"Why are you so hung up on this? I thought you were doing the...the—"

"Coparenting."

"Yeah, that. You're coparenting. Who cares what his name is?"

"I do!" Trav hollered.

Rico went silent.

Trav turned on the radio, and they drove with hard rock blasting the rest of the way there. He parked the truck, turned off the ignition, and turned to his friend. "Sorry," he mumbled.

For all of his friend's tough-guy machismo, he knew Rico was extremely sensitive. The man wrote ballads on his acoustic guitar as a hobby. He loved to sing about love even though he claimed he'd never been in love. He just "loved love," whatever the hell that meant.

Rico's lips clamped together; then he socked Trav on the arm. "Don't worry about it."

Trav grunted in reply. They walked to the small office to put in their order. No one was there. They waited for the guy who ran the supply yard, Stan, to show up.

"Daisy's got me tied in knots," Trav admitted. "I don't know whether I'm coming or going with her."

"*Ay*, you're going about this all wrong. Women are repelled by desperation."

Trav raised a brow. "I'm not desperate."

"Sure smells that way."

"Whatever."

"Just back the hell off her," Rico said. "She told you loud and clear she doesn't want to get married. Keep cool. I bet if you back off, *she'll* come after *you*."

"Yeah?"

Rico nodded. "Yeah. You're a catch, man. Women dig the stubble look." He rubbed his own stubbled jaw.

Trav laughed. "She'd be lucky to have all this." He gestured to his bod and jutted out one hip.

Rico grinned and raised his voice to a falsetto. "You work it, girl."

Trav matched his high pitch. "Bitch, you ain't even seen what I can do."

"How can I help you bitches today?" Stan, a balding guy with a huge beer belly, asked.

Trav startled and cleared his throat. "How ya doing, Stan? We're gonna need a shit ton of rock salt for this coming storm."

Stan shook his head. "Right this way, ladies."

Rico did a monkey impersonation behind Stan, dragging his knuckles, knees bent, loping forward. Trav laughed.

Stan stopped and looked behind him. Rico immediately straightened.

Stan narrowed his eyes suspiciously, turned around, and kept going.

Rico went back to monkeying around. His friend always could get him out of a bad mood. He just hoped Rico was right. His attempts with Daisy had been complete washouts. He'd back off and let Daisy come to him. If she didn't, well, he was right back where he started from, trying to pin her down. How the hell did he get himself into this mess? It had all started with those damn tequila shots.

He'd found Daisy at Garner's bar drinking alone the day

after Thanksgiving. She'd looked miserable. He'd been miserable too. He figured she'd be good company. Not to mention she was sexy as all hell. He wanted her big time—had from the first minute he'd laid eyes on her way back in high school—but she was hard to pin down. She breezed in and out of town to visit her family, and he'd never gotten past a quick hello. Her drinking alone at the bar was a golden opportunity, and he took it.

"What are you drinking?" he'd asked, moving to the barstool next to her with his beer.

One side of her mouth quirked up. "Ironically, a Slow, Comfortable Screw."

He'd gone hard just hearing the words come out of her mouth. "Why is that ironic? You prefer it fast?"

She laughed and stirred the skinny straw in her drink. "Yeah." Then she frowned. "My boyfriend cheated on me."

"That's rough."

"You know what's rough?" she asked. "I was about to bring him home to meet the family for Thanksgiving. The night before, as I'm waiting at the train station, wondering what's taking him so long, he *texts* me that he's met someone else. Texts me! After three months!"

She took a long drink.

He took a pull on his beer in solidarity.

She turned to him. "What about you? You look about as happy as I feel."

"Sherri dumped me this morning. Said she wanted to wait for the day after Thanksgiving so she wouldn't ruin my holiday."

"I don't know Sherri, but she sounds like an idiot."

He laughed ruefully. Sherri was a client's daughter and an English professor at Yale. Fortunately, he kept the client.

"She *was* an idiot." He drank to that. "Absolutely. And so was your guy."

"Jonathan." Daisy lifted her glass in a toast. "To Jonathan and Sherri."

"Idiots," they said in unison as they clinked glasses.

Daisy finished her drink and slammed the glass down.

Eyes bright, she gave him one of her sunny smiles. "I like you, Travis O'Hare. Let's do shots."

Famous last words. The rest of the night was a blur. She'd walked home with him, and they'd slammed together like their lives depended on skin on skin. He remembered her taste, like tequila and lime and Daisy, her scent a citrusy perfume. He woke up alone with a raging headache.

Nine months later they had Bryce.

He regretted nothing.

He picked up the pace as if he could outrun his memories of her. He focused on the work ahead and pushed Daisy to the way, way back of his mind.

Where he knew she'd linger and drive him nuts.

~

The blog post that proved sex sells…

Daisy Does It All
Mom, wife, domestic diva

Bedroom Shenanigans After Baby…

I couldn't leave you all hanging with last week's fantastic Valentine's Day plans without addressing a very important element of the Day of Amore—the bedroom. Now we all know that six weeks after baby, none of us feels the urge to run naked into the bedroom, but I'm here to tell you that va-va-voom does come back, if nurtured correctly.

First, you need to explain to Darling Husband, as I did, that the fastest way to naked is helping out with the baby and around the house. Ladies, do I need to tell you that this is a *major* turn-on? The man that does this says, "Honey, I love you so much that I will care for the child born of our love and keep the house running so you can relax." If your Darling Husband isn't yet with the program, show him this post. And let him know that my Darling Husband has a very satisfied smile on his face since getting with the program, as in, several times a week.

(Your "me time" benefits him too. You'll have time to shower and shop for that lacy, satin teddy. Wash it by hand and leave it hanging over the shower curtain to dry. It'll kick-start his imagination.)

Second, men are visual creatures. I know, I know, you're thinking you'd like a little less visual on your post-pregnancy bod. This is where the teddy that covers you in just the right places can really pay off. I'm talking lots of leg, lots of cleavage, flowing fabric around the middle. Your basic A-line mini. Give him a glimpse from a distance as you do a sexy bedroom dance for him. Yes, that's right, play that slow jazz (or your favorite seduction music) that says, *I'm a sexy woman, and I know it*. By the time he gets to you, he'll be tearing that teddy off so fast he won't have time to notice a few stretch marks. (Not that you should feel bad about them. They're your tiger stripes, Mama.)

Now for us ladies, we crave talk to feel close to our man. Here's a win-win: sexy talk. Tell each other what you want to do to each other, gaze into each other's eyes as you do, and that's a recipe for steamy, soul-satisfying loving. I'll leave the exact words up to you. Only you know best what your Darling Husband craves. <wink> Plan for it, set the scene, don't forget the birth control (your bod needs rest between those Baby Delights), and have fun!

XOXO!

Daisy

Daisy scrolled through the comments on her blog post from last week as she always did before writing a new post and smiled to herself. More than fifty comments on bedroom shenanigans.

"You go, Daisy!"

"Just what we needed. Thanks, Tiger Mama!"

And her favorite: "My husband thanks you!"

Her blog was doing phenomenally well. Her post on

"Valentine's Day with Baby" had the most comments she'd ever gotten from a blog post (more than a hundred), and her stats showed more than 100,000 hits that day. Apparently, a lot of people searched the Internet for Valentine's Day with baby ideas. Her post on bedroom shenanigans had an astonishing 200,000 hits. Her new focus on love and sex after baby was striking a chord. Sex sells.

Too bad she wasn't getting any.

She exhaled sharply and focused again on the screen. What to post today, the day after Valentine's? How to top that? Her stomach growled. She hadn't eaten anything since that turkey wrap she'd had on break at Garner's more than three hours ago.

She stood, stretched, and headed to the kitchen. She grabbed a bag of potato chips she'd picked up at the health food store in town, Gary's Greens & More, and chomped on a chip as she walked back to the sofa, feeling good about the fact it said "All-Natural" in big letters on the bag. She liked to buy all of her junk food at the health food store—chocolate crème-filled sandwich cookies that were almost like Oreos, organic peanut butter cups that were sorta like Reese's. The only exception was Sno-Caps. The health store brand made of carob just couldn't compare.

She settled back at the laptop. Ooh, maybe she and Darling Husband could plan a fabulous vacation with baby. She glanced toward the bedroom, where Bryce was sleeping. Hard to imagine traveling with him. Still, she had to keep things interesting on the blog. Where could she go with baby in tow? She had mentioned in her Valentine's post that Darling Husband had a Bermuda travel brochure in the desk. She could say he gave her a trip to Bermuda as a Valentine's gift and then talk about their plans. She warmed to the idea— sand, surf, sun. Lord, how she missed the sun; the Connecticut winter dragged on and on.

She switched over to another tab and searched for family-friendly resorts in Bermuda. Her mind boggled at all the choices. And it was all so expensive. Oh, what the hell. She was already pretending to live in a beautiful house with a perfect husband and baby. Might as well pretend to be rich too. She'd throw in a bunch of sex on the beach ideas too.

She quickly typed a glowing post about her dream vacation with Darling Husband playing her Romeo at every turn. Flowers, couples massage, tropical island drinks, and lots of handsy action in the ocean while Baby Delight was with the hotel babysitter. Ahh...if only. She added a planned moonlight stroll on the beach, ending with making love on a blanket right there on the soft sand just like they had on their honeymoon in Hawaii. So what if her mysterious Darling Husband looked like Trav in all her fantasies? It was just because she saw him so much because of Bryce.

She hit post and, not for the first time, considered what her life would be like if she and Trav ever did marry. Why was she resisting? It would be a sensible, stable marriage with a sensible, stable guy in a sensible, stable small town. Sensible and stable, two words that had never been applied to her. An unwanted memory pushed in of Max, the man she'd once loved in an open-to-the-soul way that she'd never managed again. They'd had a whirlwind romance in the city, their time together an exciting adventure, until the miscarriage. Max's relief in the face of her wretched grief had devastated her. And then he dumped her.

She sucked in a breath, the memory still cut deep even after all these years. She hoped Max was fat and bald and living alone in a rat-infested apartment. She smiled to herself. Sometimes having a big imagination made life a little easier to swallow.

Marrying Trav would be good for Bryce. Trav always made that point, and he was right. How much longer could she keep up her grueling pace and still do a good job raising Bryce? She wanted her son to have a good life, a stable life. She *should* marry Trav. It was like her motherly duty or something.

She frowned, not liking the idea of duty and marriage in the same breath. She was about to shut down the laptop and head to bed when her eye caught on the email icon with a red dot indicating one new message.

She clicked on it.

That was strange. The email was from kateshaw@roguetv.com. She didn't know anyone at Rogue TV. Probably some sales pitch for a product they wanted her to buy. She opened the email. *Okay, what're ya selling?*

Dear Daisy,

The producers at *Mornings with Jessica* have read your blog with great interest and would love to interview you at your home at your earliest convenience. Jessica Larsen's viewers are your target audience and would boost your blog following significantly. Please call at 212-555-5623.

Sincerely,

Kate Shaw

Talent Booker

Daisy slapped a hand over her mouth and silently squealed in delight. *Amazing!* She did a little happy dance in her seat, stomping her slippered feet on the floor. She couldn't believe it. A national talk show? That meant major press. She might even start making money doing what she loved! Sponsors for her blog! TV appearances!

She could pay off her debt!

She'd show everyone she could stand on her own two feet!

She grabbed her cell and dialed the number. It went to voicemail. It *was* ten o'clock at night. Who cared? She grinned into the phone, waiting for the beep.

"Hi, it's Daisy Garner. I'd love to do your show! I'm so excited. Call me!" She nearly hung up before remembering to leave her phone number. She hit end and jumped around her living room.

"Bryce, this could mean the start of something great!" she said aloud, though not too loud, since he was sleeping. She hugged herself, her smile stretching ear to ear.

Slowly, she lost her smile and sank to the sofa as a feeling of dread came over her. Problem. She didn't *exactly* live in a charming Victorian home.

Or have a sweet Baby Delight (more like a Red-Faced Screamer).

Or have a Darling Husband.

Or any husband at all.

Trav!

He could play her Darling Husband. He'd do it for sure. And she could borrow Maggie's Victorian home. That had been her inspiration anyway. Hopefully Bryce would nap through the interview. He did look angelic and sweet when he slept.

It could work. Right?

She felt a little shaky as a greater terror took hold. Omigod, she could be exposed as a fraud, ruining her reputation and all future career prospects. No one would ever take her seriously. She'd be doomed to work for her parents forever while they quietly judged her for her mess of a life.

She grabbed her cell and hit redial. She had to cancel immediately.

WAAAAHHHH!!!!! WAAAAHHHHH!!!!!!

She hung up and raced to Bryce before he could work himself into a state that forecast a long period of wakefulness. She scooped him up and settled into the glider. Her head dropped back in exhaustion on the sweaters thrown over the back of the glider. She'd worry about that talk show business tomorrow.

She yawned. A short while later, she tucked Bryce into his crib and climbed into bed.

She woke to the sound of the phone ringing the next morning, still exhausted from her night with Bryce. She grabbed her cell before it woke him. The last time she'd gotten him back to sleep was at six, and he was going on three hours sleep now. Her shift at Garner's didn't start until four, and she'd hoped to get a little more sleep before she had to deal with her day.

"Hello?" she whispered.

"Hello, Daisy, this is Kate Shaw from *Mornings with Jessica.*

We're so happy to have you on board. I've moved some things around so we can do a location shoot this Friday. We want to get you on while your blog is at its peak. Does that work for you?"

Daisy looked wildly around her messy apartment as if someone else would jump in with the right thing to say. But it was just her. She should call it off. Right? Before things got out of hand, and she was outed as a complete fraud.

"I think so," she said slowly, "but—"

"Great! We'll be there by eight a.m. with our crew to set up for a ten a.m. interview. I'll email you our standard release and some tips for being your best self on camera. Look for it. Thanks!"

"Wait! I have a question."

"Shoot."

"Is the interview just me? The baby probably wouldn't do well on camera, and my husband…he has to work."

"We want the whole family. Jessica is looking forward to meeting you on Friday. Buh-bye."

Rewind! I have to cancel this whole crazy thing! What was I thinking?

"Me too," she said weakly to the dial tone.

4
_____

Daisy's stomach churned with anxiety as she drove to Trav's grandmother's house with a sleeping Bryce in the back seat. She was grateful for the quiet, but she would've liked it better if he napped when she wasn't driving too; then she might actually get a break. She pulled into the driveway and fetched Bryce. He woke instantly from the movement and the cold wind hitting his face. She tucked him close, shielding him from the gusting wind, and hurried to Maggie's door. She rang the bell and bounced her fussy boy.

The door sprang open a moment later. Maggie stood there smiling in an off-the-shoulder orange and white polka-dotted shirt with leopard print leggings and bunny slippers. A diamond tiara was perched on her head. "Come in, come in!"

Daisy stepped into the cozy living room, where a fire was crackling in the fireplace. Maggie's laptop sat on the coffee table. The older woman loved being online and spent a good amount of time searching for new knitting patterns on Ravelry, planning weekend trips for her and Jorge, and updating Facebook with her adventures, which included snorkeling, go-kart racing, and ziplining.

"Let me see my great-grandbaby," Maggie cooed as she lifted Bryce from Daisy's arms. "How's my boy?"

Bryce squirmed and looked to Daisy.

"He's cranky," Daisy said. "Let me nurse him, and then he's all yours."

"Can I get you some tea?"

"No, thanks." Daisy settled with Bryce on a red velvet chair. Maggie sat across from her on a floral loveseat. "I like your tiara."

Maggie reached up, seeming surprised to find it there. "Oh! I forgot it was there from a little game of queen and servant this morning with Jorge." She giggled and set it on the table.

Daisy worked to push that image from her mind. Maggie and Jorge had been inseparable since Maggie signed up for her first ballroom dance lesson at Jorge's dance studio. They'd married only two months after their first date. But at Maggie's age, she'd seen no reason for a long engagement. The woman was seventy-two going on fifty, which was good because Jorge was twenty years her junior. The handsome Mexican-American man was a total sweetheart with a dancer's body. Quite the catch. Still, the less she knew on the senior citizen nooky front, the better.

Daisy went back to the reason for her visit. "I never told you this, but I started a blog about being a mom."

Maggie leaned forward, her blue eyes sparkling with curiosity. "Do tell."

Daisy gave her a small smile. "It started out just as a way to sort of fantasize about…a more perfect motherhood than my own."

"Bah! No such thing as a perfect mother. You're doing great with Bryce!"

"Thank you." She looked down and put her finger on Bryce's little hand. He immediately wrapped his fingers tightly around her finger, and her heart squeezed. "I don't feel like such a great mom most of the time." She looked up. "But I wanted to feel that way, so I wrote the blog." She bit her lip. "Then I started getting creative. *Really* creative."

Maggie smiled. "I like creative."

"I described my home as a beautiful Victorian. Basically yours. I mentioned my Darling Husband."

"You could have a darling husband. Trav—"

"Yes. I definitely want him as Darling Husband and—"

Maggie clapped her hands. "I knew it! I bet Jorge you two would marry before Bryce turned one." She beamed.

Daisy forced a smile. She had to let Maggie believe they were getting married. The fewer people who knew it was a fake marriage, the better.

Daisy continued. "I also said I had a Baby Delight. You know, a sweet, not screaming kind of baby that smiles a lot and makes you feel like the best mom ever just by existing."

Maggie grinned. "So not Bryce."

"Not Bryce."

Maggie spread her arms wide. "So you embellished a bit. Nothing wrong with that. Creative license, I say."

Daisy grimaced. "Just one problem. *Mornings with Jessica* is coming to interview me at my fake house with my fake family on Friday."

"*Mornings with Jessica!* I love that show. Jessica has the most fascinating people on. Yesterday she did a segment with Daniel Craig for his new movie. He is so dreamy. Have you seen him as James Bond?" She raised a brow and fixed her with a smoldering look. "Bond. James Bond."

Maggie's completely missing the point here.

"Uh, no. I—"

"I wonder if Jorge has a tux." She tapped her finger on her chin. "We'd have to rent an Aston Martin."

Daisy had more urgent concerns than role-playing; well, actually, that was her main concern. The role of a lifetime.

"I have to ask you something really important," Daisy said. "Can I borrow your house for the show on Friday morning?"

"Absolutely! How fun! This is so exciting!"

"It is exciting, but..." Daisy took a deep breath. "Do you think maybe it's wrong to pretend?"

"Nah. You have a baby and Trav already. Who cares if you're just visiting my house for the interview? It's no different than being on a TV set. Those backdrops are all fake too, you know."

"I guess," Daisy said slowly.

"Go big or go home, that's what I say. Can I stay and meet Jessica?"

"Of course. Actually I was hoping you and Jorge might babysit Bryce upstairs while I'm being interviewed. I sorta made him sound like a sweet baby on the blog, and, well, you know how he can be."

"The boy loves motion, that's all. Once he's walking, he'll be much happier, mark my words."

Daisy suddenly realized parenting him when he was mobile would require a whole new level of vigilance. "This parenting thing doesn't get any easier, does it?"

"You love 'em, and then they leave you. That's the harsh truth. But, ooh-boy"—she slapped her knee—"what a trip!"

Daisy thought about the hell she put her parents through, especially as a teenager, and the bad-boy rep that Trav had as a teenager. They were in for it.

Maggie shook her head. "It's about time you and Trav got married. It's not like you're buying a pig in a poke. You've already had a taste of the bacon." She winked.

"We-well," Daisy sputtered. She really didn't want to talk about Trav's *bacon* with his grandmother.

"What?"

"We're happy."

Maggie smiled widely. "I'm glad."

Even if we don't love each other. We can pretend.

Maggie patted Daisy's knee. "Welcome to the family! In an official legal sense, since you've been family the minute you gave birth to Bryce."

Daisy's throat tightened. Maggie had treated her like family right from the beginning. Guilt stabbed at her for deceiving Maggie with a fake marriage at the same time as relief washed through her that Maggie was helping her out.

"Awww…thank you," Daisy said. "I appreciate it."

She hoped Trav would be as understanding.

～

Trav knew something was up when he got the unexpected call from Daisy. "Hey, Trav, can you stop by on my break at Garner's? Around seven? I'll save some meatloaf for you."

Of course he'd said yes, no questions asked. She'd never asked him to stop by on break, though he'd shown up a few times to pick up dinner when he knew he'd run into her. Maybe Rico was right. If he backed off, Daisy would come to him. Course, he hadn't exactly backed off. It was only two days ago that he proposed. She must want something.

That night, he walked briskly to Garner's in the brutal cold. Temps below freezing and a lot of snowstorms had been good for his snow-plowing business, but he was looking forward to spring and all the work that meant for his landscape company Elegant Land Designs. He pushed open the door of Garner's and walked into the always busy restaurant. Daisy's parents had made it into a welcoming place for people in town to get together on any occasion. He spotted Daisy right away—who could miss that sunny smile as she chatted with a customer—her long, wavy, blond hair, her lips so full and lush. And her body, a perfect hourglass that always had his hands itching to run up and down those sweet curves. He raised a hand to signal her.

She held up a finger and pointed to the bar. He settled at the bar to wait. He glanced at the TV. The Knicks were clobbering the Grizzlies.

"What can I get ya, Trav?" the bartender Josh asked.

"Just some water," Trav said. "I'm not staying long."

Josh nodded and filled a glass, handing it over.

"Thanks." Trav went back to the game. A few minutes later, someone tapped his shoulder. He turned, already smiling in anticipation of seeing Daisy. "Hey."

It was Rico. His smile dropped.

"Not who you were hoping to see?" Rico asked with a smile.

Trav turned back around. Rico lived in the same apartment complex as Daisy on the other side of town, though not near her apartment. Thankfully. Otherwise Daisy might have been one of Rico's long line of women. Trav didn't like the idea of sharing her with his friend. Ever.

"What's up?" Trav asked.

"Not much. Watching the game. Drinking beer. Chatting up the lovely ladies." He signaled Josh. "Corona." He turned to Trav. "No beer tonight?"

"I'm not drinking," Trav said. "I'm meeting Daisy."

Rico gestured for Trav to grow a pair.

Trav gestured to his middle finger.

Rico shook his head sadly. "We talked about this. Let her come to you."

He smiled. "*She* called *me*."

Rico's beer arrived, and he took a long swallow. "Ahhh." He pointed his beer bottle at Trav. "Yeah? What'd she want?"

"I don't know. Who cares?"

"A guy with pride would care." He flashed a smile over Trav's shoulder. "*Hola, mamacita.*"

Daisy kissed Rico on the cheek. "*Hola, guapo.*"

Rico smiled widely. "Oh, *guapo*. Very good. And true. *Muchas gracias.*"

"I picked up a little Spanish one summer in Costa Rica," Daisy said modestly.

"What's it mean?" Trav asked.

"That's between me and *mamacita*," Rico said, putting an arm around Daisy.

Daisy laughed. "It means good looking."

"Hey, you never call me *guapo*," Trav said.

Daisy flashed him a sunny smile, and he actually felt his heart kick up. That's what he'd been missing seeing from her. That sunny smile aimed right at him just about made his night.

"You never called me *mamacita*," she said, handing him a takeout box with the meatloaf she'd promised. "I've only got a fifteen-minute break. Come with me."

He rose from the bar stool and followed her.

"*Cojones*," Rico stage-whispered behind him.

Trav turned halfway to slash a hand through the air in a clear gesture of *shut your trap* to Rico, but Trav never took his eyes off Daisy's hips as they swayed in those snug black pants. She headed for the back door, stopping to grab her down parka from a hook near the exit, and the enticing rear view disappeared.

She headed for her Subaru. They got in, and she turned the car on, blasting the heat.

"This is cozy," he said from the passenger seat. His breath came out in a cold puff of air.

"I needed privacy."

Be cool. Don't make a move without a sure signal. She has to meet you at least halfway, or you're going to look like a complete fool.

He set the take-out container on the floor. "What's up?"

She laughed nervously and licked her lips. His joystick perked up. *Down, boy. Nervous laughing is never a good sign.*

"I, uh, got myself into a little jam, and I was hoping you could help me out."

She bit her lip, and he stifled a groan. *Sure, I'd love to help you out...of those clothes.*

Daisy kept talking, but all he could hear was the imaginary sound of those pants sliding down to the floor. He wondered what kind of underwear she wore. It was probably black. She'd look so sexy in black. Black panties with those high-heeled black leather boots of hers.

"Trav, are you listening?"

"Mmm..." *Maybe a matching bra.* His eyes trailed down.

No, topless is better. No bra. Perky breasts, nipples at attention.

"It's a pretty big deal." She sounded annoyed.

Focus. Was this a good big deal or bad big deal?

He quickly shifted his attention back to her face. Her brows were scrunched down as she regarded him with some irritation. He had to tread carefully. "That would be..."

"Awesome."

He smiled. "Yes. And also—"

"Well, I'm a little worried. I've never been on TV before."

TV?

He went for casual. "What's the name of the show again?"

She narrowed her eyes. "I'm going to be on *Mornings with Jessica* this Friday."

He let that sink in. "For…"

"Ergh! I knew you weren't listening! You had this goofy smile on your face."

He gave her a slow smile. "I was distracted by your beauty."

"By my…" She jabbed a finger at him. "You're not getting out of this by flattery."

He leaned close to whisper in her ear. "You were wearing black panties, boots, and nothing else."

She went quiet, and he took the opportunity to gently kiss the rapidly beating pulse point at her throat. She swallowed.

Her voice came out soft. "It's because of my blog."

He played with a lock of her hair. "Do you need me to watch Bryce?"

She pulled her hair out of his grasp and shifted further away; though the car wasn't that big, he could reach her easily. "That's the thing. I have this really popular blog on being a mom, and they want my whole family on. Here's where you come in." She grimaced. "I sorta let people believe I'm married, so will you play my husband on TV?"

Trav saw his opening like a flashing green Go sign. She needed him or she'd look the fool, or worse, a fraud. This could be a win-win-win. Win for Daisy, win for him, win for Bryce.

He smiled his sweetest, most charming smile. "Of course I'll play your husband on TV."

She blew out a breath of relief. "Great! Thank you. I knew you'd understand."

She reached for the ignition to shut off the car. He placed his hand on hers. They weren't done quite yet.

"As long as you play my wife in real life."

She dropped her hand and slowly turned to him. "You want me to pretend we're married?"

"No, I want a marriage for real."

"Trav, come on."

"Those are my terms. I promise we'll look good for the

cameras. Everyone will believe we're happily married. But only if you promise we do it for real."

She hesitated. He could see the wheels turning in her head, the battle between what she wanted and what he wanted. Fact was, she was in dire need of a husband right now. He waited for her to realize his terms were the only chance she had of pulling this talk show deal off.

She stared at her hands. "I don't know." She met his eyes. "It seems sorta rushed?"

"I've waited six months," he said quite reasonably.

Her eyebrows crinkled, and she bit her lip. He played it cool, waiting her out. He could see the finish line. He didn't touch her, barely breathed, just sat there willing her to cross that line with him.

She gestured with her hands as she talked. "We've been so busy raising Bryce. I don't want to marry for the wrong reasons."

"Bryce is the right reason."

"Bryce, yeah." She stared out the front window and started muttering to herself. "Well, it is his father *something something* duty *something* should, but *something* mom. Ho, wouldn't that just be *something something*. Fucking perfect as if *something something*...never even had *something*." Sigh. "Best thing for him really *something something*." She finally ran out of steam and turned to him.

He raised a brow.

"Okay," she said with zero enthusiasm.

He grinned. Not offended at all. "Okay, then."

Should they shake on it? Kiss? He felt like they should mark the occasion somehow. He squeezed her hand, and she gave him a tight smile.

"It's not a death sentence," he said. "It's marriage."

"Yup." Her eyes darted toward the door. "I'd better get back to work."

"We'll go for the marriage license at Town Hall tomorrow morning," he said. "Ten a.m. good for you?"

Her shoulders sank. "Sure."

"I'm thinking a small wedding with a justice of the peace. Then we'll act like we've been married for…what? A year?"

She sighed. "Might as well call it a year and a half so Bryce looks like he came along after the wedding."

He couldn't help smiling. "You got it."

She turned off the car and reached for the door handle.

"See you tomorrow…fiancée."

She waved weakly and left the car.

This was the opening he'd been looking for since Bryce was born. Besides, Daisy laughed at his jokes, they agreed on parenting, and, when he pulled her close, she got flushed and flustered and all together irresistible. Sex, hell yeah, that was a good start. The rest would fall into place. He'd be a faithful and committed family man. Better than his old man. He'd never abandon her and Bryce. Daisy would soon appreciate what he offered as a husband and father.

He grabbed the takeout, exited, and made for home, a little bounce in his step.

Good talk.

5

Daisy puzzled over how her life had gotten so wonky. One minute she was looking at a first-time-ever TV appearance and a possible new career, the next she was standing in line at the dinky Town Hall with an annoyingly cheerful Trav waiting for a marriage license. Trav held Bryce, and the two of them had an unending game of peek-a-boo going on. Trav kept peeking at him between his fingers to Bryce's delighted squeals.

Things could be worse. Daisy shifted uneasily, nervous energy shooting down her legs. She fought the familiar urge to run. She *had* to stop running from her problems. That was part of the reason she never seemed to get on track. Every time the going got tough, or just uncomfortable, her fight or flight kicked in big time. Her instinct was for flight. But Bryce needed her. She had to stay and fight. Or at least just stay.

She paced a bit while her mind ricocheted from one extreme to another as they waited their turn for a license.

Just go with it. Everyone says you should be together. He's a good dad, a good man.

Then the other extreme: *He doesn't love you. Don't marry for the wrong reasons.*

The older man in front of them left with his dog license and gave them a smile on his way out.

"Next," the town clerk, Sally Phillips, called. Sally was the eyes and ears of the town. She wore a pink fuzzy V-neck sweater, jeans, and her dyed black hair teased up in a style that screamed, *I never left the '80s.*

Trav grabbed Daisy's hand and pulled her forward.

"We'd like a marriage license," Daisy whispered, though they were the only people left in the office. "But we're keeping it quiet. Okay? Out of respect for Bryce's future."

Trav nodded.

Good. Trav's playing along.

"Oh, my, my, my," Sally said, placing a hand on her heart. *Were those tears in her eyes?* "I've been praying for you. We all have. And now, look, it's come true."

"*A-men*," Trav said, his eyes dancing with laughter.

Daisy bit back a sarcastic reply. She'd just bet that Sally and her friends were praying for them. More like gossiping about them. Sally didn't hesitate to share the latest with anyone who came into Town Hall.

Sally crossed her arms over her ample bosom and continued smiling at them as if she alone were responsible for this wonderful turn of events.

"The license?" Daisy prompted.

"Of course! Coming right up!" Sally caroled. "My, aren't we in a hurry all of a sudden."

Sally spun her chair around to the wall of file cabinets behind her and scooted the chair toward a file drawer. Like standing up was too much work. Trav grinned at Daisy, evidently getting a big kick out of Sally.

Daisy saw nothing amusing in this day.

Sally scooted back to her desk with the form. She handed it to Daisy. "Fill it out in full and bring it back to me. I'll hold this sweet baby so you can work on the form without any grabbing fingers."

"Thanks, Mrs. Phillips," Trav said with sickening sweetness.

"Oh-ho-ho, you're quite welcome. Please call me Sally."

Trav gave her his charming, lopsided smile. "Thanks, Sally."

Sally tittered.

"Are you done flirting?" Daisy sniped as they walked over to a small raised shelf on the side of the office to fill out the form. She lowered her voice. "She could be your mother."

He leaned close, his hand warm on the small of her back. "Jealous?"

His voice so low and rumbly in her ear sent an involuntary shiver through her. Trav chuckled, the darn man didn't miss a thing, and handed her a pen to fill out the bride's section first.

She got to work. Name, address, birthplace, date of birth, parents' names, marriage number, and reason the last marriage ended: death, dissolution, annulment, previous civil union, or did not end. *Uh-oh.*

Daisy turned to Trav, who was intently watching her. "Can you check on Bryce?"

"Sure."

He stepped away, and she wrote quickly. Marriage number: 3. Reason last marriage ended: death.

She winced. That sounded bad. But that *was* how marriage number two ended, unfortunately. She still missed Tom. Marriage number one hadn't ended much better. Not that they'd asked, but...heartbreaking divorce. Stupid Max. That was probably called "dissolution" in legal talk. She crumpled the license form and tossed it into the nearby trash can.

"I messed up," she announced. She crossed back to Sally's desk. "Can I get another form?"

"Sure, honey. Just a minute."

Trav raised a brow. Bryce reached for Daisy, and she took him. She cooed at her son and gave him a raspberry on his chubby cheek. He grabbed her hair and shoved it in his mouth.

A moment later, Sally wheeled back, new form in hand. "Here you go."

They traded baby for form. Daisy turned to where Trav now stood at the shelf where she'd been filling out the form. He stared at her, his expression uncharacteristically serious.

An uneasy feeling snaked through her. Trav with a serious expression was a little intimidating.

She went for casual as she reached his side and grabbed a pen. "All set."

"Marriage number three?" he asked quietly, opening his hand to reveal the crumpled form now folded neatly in his palm.

She swallowed hard.

He raised his brows, waiting for an explanation.

"Yes, but the other two barely counted," she whispered. "In fact, they were so short I hardly remember them. I don't think I need to report them."

A muscle ticked in his jaw. "You might have mentioned them to me."

"You never asked."

"I'm asking now."

She glanced back over her shoulder at the prying ears of Clover Park's gossip central. "Can we talk later?"

He nodded. "Oh, yeah, we're gonna talk. My place tonight for dinner. I know you get off early on Wednesdays. Ask your Mom to watch Bryce."

It was more command than request, and she felt an unwelcome flutter of desire as Trav's usual playful tone switched to badass. Not to mention it would be the first time they were alone together without Bryce. "Sure, no problem."

His voice rumbled close to her ear. "And don't lie on the form, sweetheart. It's easy enough to check on records of marriage."

Daisy steeled herself against the weakening in her knees and went back to filling out the form. Badass was not good. She had a long history of bad boys in her past. She *loved* bad boys. But they were no good for her, especially now that she had Bryce.

Marriage number: 3.

Sure, she'd been frustrated with Trav's pleasant but distant personality and had wondered what ever happened to the bad boy in him, but now that he was making an appearance, she knew she was in trouble. Marrying a bad boy? That had disaster written all over it!

"It's official," Trav announced when he stopped by Ryan's place later that day. His older brother had just gotten off an early shift as a police officer in nearby Fieldridge. It also happened to be the town where their father lived. His old man was sober going on three and a half years. Trav had made his peace with his father, as had his brothers, in their own ways.

"What's official?" his younger brother, Shane, asked, coming in from the kitchen.

"You cooking for Ry now?" Trav asked.

"I was dropping off a crepe pan for Liz. She wanted to try her hand at it."

Ry gave Trav a pointed look. "They've been exchanging recipes."

Shane had graduated from the Culinary Institute of America and could easily have been a chef, but he'd focused on gourmet ice cream for his own shop in town, Shane's Scoops.

"Lucky you," Trav said. "Have a seat." He gestured to the leather sectional in the living room.

"'Have a seat,' he says." Ry took his time walking into the living room. "Like he owns the place."

"Shut up. This is important." Trav flopped down on the chaise end of the sofa and propped his feet up. He folded his hands behind his head. "I've got big news."

He waited for Ry and Shane to take a seat. He felt like he was gonna burst from the news. "Daisy and I are getting married on Saturday."

"Congratulations!" Shane said.

Ry grinned. "I knew if you hung in there, she'd come around. Congrats! Why so soon, though? Doesn't she need time to plan? Liz has been planning for going on six months."

He shook his head. "You should see her color-coded spreadsheet. Scary."

"It's just gonna be a simple ceremony with a justice of the peace. We need to keep it quiet on account of we're already supposed to be married." He explained about the blog and the talk show appearance coming up on Friday.

Ry frowned. "So you're getting married because of a TV show?"

Trav sat up, annoyed with his brother's tone. "No, it's not like that."

"Kinda sounds like that," Shane said.

"That's just what got the ball rolling," Trav said.

Ry and Shane exchanged a look.

"What?" Trav snapped.

Ry scratched the back of his neck. "Can't you just pretend for the show? I mean...I dunno—"

"Do you love each other?" Shane asked.

Trav couldn't honestly say he loved Daisy. Truth was, he'd never loved anyone. Except family. He didn't even know what that would feel like. And he didn't care. The only thing that mattered was his son.

"We love Bryce," Trav said. "This is all for him."

"What's the rush?" Ry asked. "Why don't you date or something first? Get to know each other."

Trav blew out an exasperated breath. "Suddenly you're the relationship expert? You couldn't even stay with anyone for more than three dates until you met Liz."

Ry just stared at him. Trav squirmed under his brother's scrutiny.

"I want Bryce to have a family!" Trav exclaimed. "Is that so hard to understand? Why can't you be happy for us?"

"We are happy," Shane soothed. "We're just looking out for you."

"Well, don't!" Trav jammed a hand in his hair. "Everything will be fine. You'll see."

Trav's chest tightened. He couldn't believe his brothers were giving him shit about this. They knew how much he wanted a family for Bryce. They knew what it meant to come from a seriously messed-up home. Their mom had suffered from depression and committed suicide when Trav was fifteen. After she died, their alcoholic father took off. Ryan, only two years older, had done his best to take care of them, but it was Gran who'd rescued them. If it hadn't been for her, he was sure the three of them would've ended up in foster homes. He probably would've landed in juvie.

He was determined to do better for his son. Bryce would have a real family.

Shane held his hands up. "Okay, okay."

Trav scowled. "I wanted you both to be my best man, but not if you're gonna act like my marriage is a mistake."

"I'm in," Shane said.

"Me too," Ry said.

The ache in Trav's chest loosened. "Okay. I'm gonna ask Rico too."

Ry snort-laughed. "Now you're being ridiculous."

Trav raised his palms. "I can't choose."

Ry socked him on the arm. "It's your wedding."

Trav smiled. "Yeah, it is."

He could finally relax. Everything would be okay for Bryce. And once Trav was living with Daisy and helping with the baby, she'd be less exhausted and go back to her usual sunny personality. She'd keep their home bright and light. The kind of place he would've given anything to live in as a kid. The kind of place Bryce would be so lucky to grow up in.

And he couldn't wait for a wedding night he could remember with Daisy.

～

Daisy heard a commotion coming from Garner's kitchen as she punched in a customer's order on the computer. Her father's low voice and her sister Liz's rising soprano. *News travels fast through the O'Hare brother grapevine.* Trav must have told Ryan about the wedding, who told Liz. They'd just gotten the marriage license this morning, so Daisy had little time to spread the word herself. After the license, she'd taken

Bryce to his checkup at the pediatrician, fed him lunch, and went to work. She told her parents when she'd started her shift. They'd been thrilled. At least Daisy didn't have any worries there. Her future husband on the other hand…

"I'm taking a break," she told one of the other waitresses.

Daisy slipped into the kitchen, where her mom was now offering Liz her usual glass of ice water with lemon and coaxing her to take a seat at one of the tall swivel stools by the side counter.

"How're ya, sis?" Daisy asked, bracing for the explosion of unrelenting concern.

Liz jumped up. "How am I? How are you?"

Liz rushed forward, studying Daisy's face, worry etched into her delicate features. Her sister was three years younger, but acted like she was the big sis. Truth? She'd let Liz play that role for far too long. Daisy had left all the worrying about rules and responsibilities to Liz. Until Bryce. Everything in Daisy's life changed once her son was born.

"I heard the news as soon as I got home from work," Liz said. "I would've been here sooner, but Ryan said I had to mellow out first." She blushed scarlet and took a long swallow of water.

Daisy beamed a smile at her sister's obvious embarrassment. Ryan had the magic touch with Liz. Her sister had softened from her previous uptight self and was much easier to deal with. Not easy, just easier. "I'm fine. No worries."

Liz blustered on. "What made you finally say yes to Trav?"

Daisy lifted one shoulder up and down. "It was time. You know? Why play hard to get? He's Bryce's father. We both love Bryce. Easy-peasy-lemon-squeezy. Happy family."

"Don't give me that crap." Liz grabbed Daisy's arm and pulled her away from their eavesdropping parents and the cook staff, who were pretending to be busy so they could listen in. They went into their dad's small office.

"Sit," Liz commanded, taking their dad's tall, leatherback chair for herself.

Daisy sat meekly in the plastic chair opposite her sister.

She knew Liz wouldn't let her off easy on this one. Her sister had understood perfectly Daisy's reluctance to marry because of the baby. Now she'd want a good explanation.

"Tell me the truth," Liz said. "Why the change of heart? You said Trav didn't love you. That you didn't want to marry just because it was convenient." She paused, and a light of realization slowly dawned on her face. "Did he say he loves you? Have you been seeing each other?"

Daisy's lips formed a straight line. "No and no." She got up and shut the office door. "This doesn't leave the room. Not even to Ryan."

Liz crossed her heart and silently nodded, the gesture a solemn callback from when they were kids and confided their deepest, darkest secrets. Sadly, the deep, dark secrets had all been Daisy's. Liz was an open book, but also a really good secret keeper.

Daisy explained about the interview and Trav playing her husband.

Liz looked relieved. "Oh, it's a pretend marriage. Now that makes more sense." She crinkled her nose. "But Ryan said he and Shane were going to be best men. Are you sure Trav knows it's pretend?"

Daisy twirled a lock of her hair. "Well…Trav will only go along with it if we make it a real marriage."

Liz stood, bright spots of color dotting her cheeks. "That's blackmail! He can't do that! I'm calling Ryan. He won't let Trav do this."

"No, I said this doesn't leave the room," Daisy said patiently. She went for a surefire distraction. "Besides, we don't want any bad blood between brothers before your wedding. It's only four months away."

Liz sat down again, a dreamy smile on her face. "That's really soon, isn't it? I can hardly wait. I've got everything planned, though I was rethinking the flower girl's head-piece…wait, you're trying to distract me from the real issue. Daisy, are you sure you want to marry Trav?"

"Sure. Who knows? Maybe we'll grow on each other. You know, learn to love each other." Her mind flashed to tonight's dinner, and she wondered which Trav would greet her at the door. Goofy guy or bad boy. She secretly wanted bad boy, even though she knew she shouldn't. That wasn't part of the new and improved Daisy's life.

Liz waved a hand in front of Daisy's face. "I asked you if the wedding is really *this* Saturday, as in three days away?"

"Yup."

"I just don't see why you have to rush. You can hardly plan anything good with so little time."

"It doesn't have to be a fancy wedding. We just want to get it done and move on with our lives." All of Daisy's weddings had been small, legal ceremonies at a town hall. Besides, she could hardly have her dream wedding on the beach in the middle of winter.

Liz fixed her with her classic responsible sister look—a mixture of *listen up*, and *I know best* that used to make Daisy feel secure, but now irritated the hell out of her. "It just doesn't seem wise to try to pull off lies on national television. I think you should back out of the interview. I'm sure they can find other guests. This could go very wrong. If people think you've misled them, gosh, all those moms who look up to you, you could be ruined career-wise. And I don't like this rush wedding just because Trav says so. Get rid of the interview and everything goes back to normal. No lies. No rush wedding. Marry Trav if you love each other, not because of lies."

"Are you done?" Daisy asked tightly.

Liz's eyes widened. "Don't be mad. I'm just trying to help you fix the problem."

"There is no problem. I fixed the lie by making it the truth, and I *will* go forward with the interview. This is a once-in-a-lifetime opportunity, and I'm not going to let it pass me by!" She stood. "I'd better get back to work." She almost made it out the door when she heard her sister's gentle rebuke.

"Are you sure you're doing the right thing?"

Daisy shook her head and kept going. Liz didn't believe in her. Her parents didn't believe in her. She knew why, her past haunted her through their eyes. She just wished they'd give her a chance to prove she'd changed, that she could make good choices. She knew she could pull this off.

"Excuse me," Mrs. Peters, Daisy's old first-grade teacher, called. "Can someone take our order?"

Daisy got back to work. "Coming, Mrs. Peters!"

6

Daisy Does It All
Mom, wife, domestic diva

I'm going to be on TV!!!

I'm super excited to announce I'm going to be on *Mornings with Jessica*! Thank you, ladies! I couldn't have done it without all your comments, shares, and tweets! Ahhhhhhh!!!!!!! This Friday the crew will be arriving at my house to interview me, Darling Husband, and Baby Delight. I'll let you know the air date as soon as I hear. I can't wait!

I have no idea what to wear. Leave a comment and let me know what you think. Dressy as in a dress? Business casual as in whatever-the-heck that is nowadays? My usual casual attire—sweater, jeans, boots?

Happy dance!
Mojitos all-around!
See you on TV!

XOXO!
Daisy

Trav decided he'd cook for Daisy. And that meant the one and only thing he knew how to make: fried chicken. Gran used to make it for them once a month. After he'd left for college, he'd craved it so much he forced himself to master the recipe to keep homesickness at bay. While the chicken bubbled in the oil, he dumped a bag of frozen mashed potatoes into a pot, emptied a bag of salad for Daisy, and dreamed about some biscuits to go along with the meal. Not having the skill for biscuits, toasted slices of baguette would have to do. He turned the chicken.

He wasn't one to quibble over details—he *was* getting the marriage he wanted—but it was hard to overlook the fact that he was husband number three for Daisy. What else hadn't she told him?

Just as he pulled the last of the fried chicken from the pan, the doorbell rang.

Daisy stood on his doorstep, a wine bottle in hand. "Hi," she said softly.

"Geez, don't look so nervous," he said, taking the wine. "It's just dinner. I thought we should get our story straight before we go on national TV as loving husband and wife."

She blew out a breath and brightened immediately. "Of course! Great idea."

He led the way into his apartment on the second floor of the old blacksmith place. His landscape office and equipment storage area took up the bottom floor. "Have a seat," he said, indicating the sofa. "I usually eat there at the coffee table."

"Okay." She took off her white down parka and draped it over the chair where his own coat hung. She wore a form-fitting shirt with stripes and shiny sequins, tight jeans, and the black high-heeled boots of his fantasies. *Screw dinner.* He wanted her for appetizer, entrée, and dessert.

She looked around curiously, and he tried to see his place through her eyes. The walls were white. He had one framed picture on the fireplace mantel of him with his brothers and Gran. That was it. TV, sofa, coffee table, couple of chairs he'd picked up at IKEA. The kitchen was tiny, added after the fact to the old place.

He filled a plate for her, then his own, and carried both to the coffee table.

"This looks wonderful," Daisy enthused. "I only know how to make grilled cheese."

He grinned. "I only know how to make fried chicken. Between the two of us, we're all set. Be right back." He opened the white wine and grabbed two wine glasses. He was more of a beer drinker, but he kept the glasses on hand because he'd found most women liked wine. He joined her on the sofa.

She dug into the chicken right away. "This is delicious! Wow! You should give my dad your recipe for Garner's."

He laughed. "Gran would kill me. It's a family secret."

"We're practically family," she said, licking fried chicken spices off her fingers.

His brain stopped working for a moment. *Talk first*, he reminded himself. He took a swallow of wine and regrouped. "So tell me about husband number one and two."

She waved her hand. "Not much to tell. Husband number one was freshman year of college. We were too young. It lasted two weeks." She looked away, and he knew there was more to the story. "And husband number two was a friend. He died shortly after our marriage."

Wow. A divorce and a death, and she was only thirty-three.

"What happened to the guy who died?" he asked. "Was he sick?"

She set her plate down and wiped her mouth with a napkin. "No. Tom was in the army about to ship off to Iraq. He wanted someone to come home to, something to cling to, to help get through that time. We shouldn't have married. We were good friends. Best friends. But not in love." She began to shred the napkin in her hand, lost in her memories.

He stilled her hand. "You don't have to tell me."

"No, I want to. He...his convoy was hit by a roadside

bomb. I still miss him. He was a good guy." She blinked away tears.

"Daze, I'm sorry. That's rough."

She gave him a watery smile that just about killed him. "I refused his death benefits. It just didn't feel right. We were only married for a day before he shipped out."

Not much of a honeymoon. He was glad and instantly guilty for thinking it.

"Well, you're marriage number one for me," he said with a grin. "You get to train me up on being a good husband. I already know toilet seat down."

She relaxed and went back to eating. "That's right. Don't forget, doing the laundry gets you bonus points."

"What do I get for bonus points?"

"I'll leave that as a surprise."

His mind immediately went to those luscious lips and what they could do to him. "I like laundry."

She laughed. "Yeah? It's all yours."

Trav launched into his favorite story of Ry doing laundry way back when, with Shane's clothes still covered in baking powder and flour from his latest baking experiment, and too much detergent. The soap bubbles exploded from the washer. Gran hadn't been happy, but the look on Ry's face when he skidded through bubbles and ran around like a chicken with the sky falling was classic comedy. Trav called him Chicken Little for a while.

He left out the part where Ry threatened to tell the next girl who called the house Trav's nickname, Turtle, because he was so slow getting ready in the morning. The rumpled-hair look took time. Trav had been mortified that the girls might think he was a slow dork, when he wanted to come off as too cool to care about anything or anyone.

"Any dark secrets I should know?" he asked.

"Nope," she answered right quick. "How about you?"

He raised his palms. "Open book."

His past troubles with the law weren't exactly secrets. Still, he didn't want to talk about them. He was trying to get away from that image.

She tossed back some wine. "Yeah, me too."

He wasn't so sure.

After they'd finished dinner, Daisy stood. "I'll clear the dishes."

"Don't worry about it."

She glanced toward the kitchen, which was a mess of pots with a sink piled high with dishes. "Sure?"

"Positive." *Now comes the seduction part of our evening.* "More wine?"

"Yes, please." She sat down again and held out her glass. After he refilled it, she tucked a leg under her and leaned back on the sofa, looking relaxed. Her cheeks were rosy from the drink, her full lips parted slightly...What were they supposed to talk about again?

He set his wineglass down and turned to her. "Maybe you should fill me in on this blog of yours. What did you say about your husband and our married life?"

She perked up. "Well, I call you 'Darling Husband' on the blog because you're so, well, darling. You're a great dad..."

He made checkmarks in the air. "Darling and great."

"And a wonderful help around the house, always looking to give me time to relax and recharge."

She smiled dreamily, and it occurred to him she'd created the life she wished she had, and, if he was smart, he'd make her dream a reality. That's how he'd get in with her. He could help around the house. Couldn't be that hard—stick some dishes in the dishwasher, toss clothes in the washing machine. He already liked being with Bryce.

She continued. "You appreciate all of my efforts at being a good mom. You surprise me with flowers just because." Her eyes lit up. "And we do all sorts of fun things together, like horse-drawn sleigh rides in the snow, slow dancing in front of a toasty fire—"

"Paint each other's toenails?" He couldn't help interrupting. Their life was beginning to sound like a chick flick.

She shut her mouth with a snap. "You think it's stupid."

"I think it sounds like a wonderful fantasy," he said diplomatically.

"What's wrong with a fantasy? I have tons of blog readers —moms from all over the world—who find it inspirational."

"Nothing wrong with a fantasy. But do your readers know that? Because nobody has that kind of life, except in the movies."

She raised her chin. "I'm sure some people do. And I want it. It's a good life."

"It's a fake life."

Her brows knitted together. "Can you just pretend for one day?"

"I can do better than that. Be right back." He headed for his bedroom and returned with the laptop. "Pull up the blog. I'll read every entry and make your dream a reality. I'll be your fantasy come true."

She put a hand to her throat, her face flushing. "Really?"

That flushed, breathless reaction was exactly the reason he was happy to do it. "Really."

He handed her the laptop. A moment later, the blog popped up. The title, *Daisy Does It All*, already had him thinking dirty. He began to read.

The first blog posts weren't that interesting. "The Joy of Sunday Cooking" caught his eye. Apparently she made rosemary leg of lamb with baby potatoes and steamed asparagus, and then doubled the recipe to freeze for "busy weekdays." He kept going. She talked about food a lot—spinach and leek quiche, lobster tail with saffron rice, vegetable lasagna. His mouth watered. He turned to her. "You said you only cooked grilled cheese. Here you've got all sorts of complicated recipes, and I know I've had that lamb at Garner's."

She smiled tightly. "I borrowed some from there, some from my travels."

"You'd better hope Jessica doesn't ask you for a cooking demonstration."

"Don't be silly. She just wants to interview me. Us."

He turned back to the blog. Trips to the doctor with baby, driving with baby while listening to classical music, dressing baby up for holiday pictures—Bryce had looked adorable in his Santa hat—the New Year, and keeping a journal to remember all of baby's firsts. So far, only hints of Darling Husband—he agreed with her, helped her with pictures, and reminded her of baby's first laugh. Easy enough.

Oh, hey now, things were getting interesting. Valentine's Day seemed to involve an elaborate seduction scene. Yup, he was all over that. Next was bedroom shenanigans—double yup—and a vacation with sex on the beach. *Hell, yeah.* He stopped reading and gave her a once-over.

She squirmed.

He laughed. "No worries. I got the gist. I'm your man."

She gestured to the screen. "I mean, this wasn't exactly *my* fantasy life, more like what I imagined my readers might like." Her cheeks flushed pink, giving her away.

"Sure, sure." He let her off the hook, for now. "We should have a first date story to tell everyone."

They'd never had a first date. Just one crazy drunken night.

Daisy pursed her lips, trying to come up with a story they could actually tell people about. "How about we ran into each other at Garner's one summer when I was home visiting my family? We caught up over dinner, sitting in a back booth, and ended up talking all night."

They'd never spent much time talking besides stuff about Bryce. "What did we talk about?"

She turned to him, eyes bright. "Our dreams, our hopes for the future, what we love, what we hate."

He tugged a lock of her hair, unable to resist touching her. "Kind of generic. Fill me in."

She gestured with her hands as if they helped her talk. "You know…like, I told you I dreamed of a career I was passionate about, though I hadn't yet found it. I hoped to learn French and play the guitar. Maybe travel to Australia."

"Yeah? That sounds good. So that's dreams and hopes. Tell me what you love and hate."

"Love: wine"—she raised her glass—"chocolate, and horror movies."

He sat up straighter, surprised she was into horror movies. "I'm with you on the horror movies. What do you hate?"

"Traffic, artificial sweetener, and people who don't keep their promises."

"Exactly!" The more he got to know her, the more he liked her. "Me too. Just give me the damn sugar, and do what you say you'll do. Traffic's a bitch no matter where you go."

"So what about you?" She looked at him expectantly. "What does Travis O'Hare dream of, hope for, love, hate?"

"Hoo-yah." He blew out a breath, thinking fast. This was not the kind of thing he spent any time pondering, but he knew it was important to her. "Dream: retire young and travel the world."

Her eyes widened. "Really? You want to travel? I always pictured you wanting to stay here. Have you ever left Connecticut?"

He snorted. "Of course I've left Connecticut. I've seen most of New England. And New Jersey, of course, that's where I lived as a kid."

"Have you seen the rest of the country? Europe?"

"No."

"Have you ever been on an airplane?"

"Nope. My family's here and so is my business."

She looked disappointed for some reason. It wasn't like he could just drop everything to see the world. He owned his own business. And now he had a son to raise. Besides, he loved Clover Park. Nothing he'd seen ever appealed to him as much as home.

"What do you hope for?" she asked.

He kissed her gently on the tender spot below her ear and inhaled her scent, a potent combo of citrus and Daisy. "Hope," he said softly, "that's easy. To marry you."

She blushed and ducked her head.

He leaned back. He needed a little distance or he wouldn't be able to keep his hands off her. "Loves: Bryce, fresh-cut grass, fast cars, *horror movies*." He smiled. "Hate: nothing."

She cocked her head. "Really. Nothing bugs you?"

"Nope."

"Huh." She picked up her wine and sipped. "So it wouldn't bother you if someone cheated on you?"

"That's never happened."

"What if it did?"

He didn't like where this was going. "What are you saying?"

"Nothing," she said a little too quickly.

"I take the vows of marriage seriously. I'd never break that promise."

"Me neither."

He shoved a hand in his hair. "Then why are we talking about it?"

She grinned and set her glass down. "You're mad. Something did bug you."

He tickled her. She squealed in surprise and tickled him back. He'd spent years wrestling his brothers and had her wrists pinioned in one hand within seconds. He quickly raised her arms over her head and maneuvered her flat on her back, where he'd wanted her from the moment she'd stepped into his apartment.

She stared at his mouth, breathing hard, and he slowly leaned down for their first real kiss. His lips were nearly on hers when she spoke.

"Let me up."

He released her instantly. "What's wrong?"

She sat up and smoothed her hair. "Nothing. I just...I think we should take things slow. Rushing things has never worked out for me."

That horse was already out of the gate as far as he was concerned. They'd done the deed. He wanted more.

She looked toward the door. "Maybe I should go."

"Stay. I promise not to pounce on you again. Slow is fine. Great, in fact. We can..." *What was it women always liked to say?* "...get to know each other better."

She raised a skeptical brow. "You don't sound very sincere."

He folded his hands in his lap and tried for choirboy despite his raging hard-on. "I'm very sincere."

"You think I'm weird, don't you? Asking you to marry me and then not wanting to—"

"I think you're a timid woman."

She smacked his chest and laughed. "No one has ever called me timid."

"No? The stylin' outfits, the huge laugh, all your adventures. No one ever said, 'That Daisy Garner is one timid girl?'"

She made a face. "I do not have a huge laugh."

He tossed his pretend long hair over his shoulder. "Ah-ha-ha-ha-ha!"

"Shut. Up." She picked up her wine, leaned back on the sofa, and shook her head. "You're a goof."

"Anything else I should know before we go national?"

She waved a hand toward the laptop. "Everything's in the blog."

"I'll memorize it."

She laughed.

"Oh, I just remembered something. Be right back." Trav went to his bedroom and slid open the nightstand drawer. Inside was the diamond engagement ring he'd bought for Daisy and matching gold wedding bands he'd picked up earlier today. They'd need them for both the wedding and for their TV appearance.

He slipped one of the gold bands on his ring finger. The jeweler had told him it went on the left hand because it was supposedly closer to the heart. It felt weird to wear a ring, but he'd get used to it. He brought the other two rings out to Daisy.

"We have to wear wedding rings," he told her. "Most married people do."

"Oh! I completely forgot about that. I'm so glad you remembered. Good thinking."

He took her hand and slipped on the diamond engagement ring. She admired it from all angles. "It's gorgeous."

He held her hand and looked at the square solitaire diamond set in gold under the light. He'd spent a fortune on it, so it better look good. "Yeah, it is gorgeous. Wait. The wedding band goes on first." He slipped off the engagement ring, slid on the band, and put the other ring on top. "I now pronounce you my wife."

She stared at it, her brow furrowed, like it was a spider sitting there instead of 14-carat gold.

∽

Daisy literally couldn't move. The wedding band on her hand taunted her with her failed marriages, the fallout for her son's future, Trav's expectations of her—whatever they were—that she would surely never live up to. Trav tipped her chin up, and she met his hazel eyes, feeling tangled and confused inside.

"Daze, if we want to be believable as husband and wife, we need to practice kissing so it looks real natural for the cameras."

Her jaw dropped, and her heart started pounding. Practice kissing like husband and wife? Now? When she was ready to run straight out of this apartment?

He stroked her hair. "Come on, you know I'm right."

She snapped her jaw shut. Took a long swallow of wine. Breathed in and out. She could do this. She flashed him a quick smile that she was sure neither one of them believed was sincere. "Of course."

She gave him a quick peck on the lips. He slipped his hand around the back of her head and kept her close when she would've pulled back. His lips nearly brushed over hers when he spoke. "Not so fast, Miss Speedy."

He took his time, kissing her cheek, her jaw, working his way up to her ear and down her neck. She felt herself relax as a languid warmth stole through her. She slid her fingers into the hair at the nape of his neck. His lips met hers, soft at first, then more demanding. She opened for him, and his tongue slid along hers, stroking, imitating the mating she was starting to crave as long-dormant parts of her heated and came to life again.

She slipped both hands around his neck, giving herself over to the sensations. Long, slow kisses. His large, warm

hand stroked her back under her sweater. Her hands moved
to his chest, gripping his shirt. Lord, she was already hot and
wet and aching for more. He slipped his other hand under
her shirt, and she felt her bra spring open.

She broke the kiss. What was she doing? She was
supposed to be getting to know her future husband not
sleeping with him every time he kissed her. Okay, just the one
time, but look what happened then. *Hello, Bryce!*

"That's enough for tonight," she said.

He pulled back and stared at her, his eyes hazy with lust.
She couldn't screw this up. The stakes were high with Bryce's
future happiness in the balance. Maybe if she did everything
the opposite of how she'd normally act with a guy, they might
actually stand a chance.

"What?" he asked, though she was sure he must've
heard her.

"Slow, remember?"

He stood and adjusted himself. "Sure."

She stood, grabbed her coat, and slipped it on. She
avoided his eyes. "I think we'll do fine on Friday. Thank you
for dinner."

"You're welcome."

He walked her to the door, and just as she thought she
might escape, he snagged her by the belt loop on her jeans,
pulling her close so they were within kissing distance again.
He cradled her face with one hand, giving her plenty of time
to pull back, but something kept her there, lips parted in
anticipation. He kissed her long and hard, and her knees gave
out. His hands went to her bottom, holding her up, pressing
her against his hardness. She moaned and rocked against
him.

He pulled back and looked at her, his hands still firmly on
her ass. "Daze, I want you."

Her breath caught in her throat. It was too soon. Her brain
knew that. Down under was sending different instructions.
Let us play!

"I should go," she said, pushing gently against him.

He released her, and she turned away, relieved he'd

offered no sweet words of persuasion. Or worse, another scorching kiss.

"I expect a wedding night," he said in a commanding tone that at once inflamed and irritated her. "And our wedding is Saturday."

She whirled. "I know our wedding is Saturday! But that doesn't mean we have to rush—"

"No rushing."

Good.

He held the door open for her. "Daze?"

"Yeah?"

"It could take hours."

She went stock-still, her imagination flooding her poor brain with images of Trav taking his time with those lips, and tongue, and strong, warm hands—

Get out! Get out now before you run naked into his bed.

She rushed down the stairs and heard his low chuckle on her way out. Did he think he got the best of her? She was no shrinking violet. She stopped and thought about returning to wipe what she was sure was a smirk off his face, but figured she'd better quit while she was ahead.

Brain trumped hormones.

She was almost sure that was a good thing.

7

Daisy felt like she'd fallen down the rabbit hole into Bizarro-land as she drove to Maggie's house the day before the interview. She was about to marry Trav, who was still too demanding, but also an *amazing* kisser. Why hadn't she kissed him before? All she remembered from their one night together was laughing and falling into bed. And she was about to launch what could be her dream-come-true career as a pro blogger, maybe with a paid column or sponsors. She could finally get out of debt.

She parked and got Bryce out of the car, along with a large diaper bag of baby stuff to leave at the house. They needed to make Maggie's place look like their family home before the *Mornings with Jessica* crew arrived early tomorrow. Trav promised to meet her at her apartment later to help move the baby gear.

Maggie answered the door in a red turtleneck paired with a huge knit black and purple polka-dotted cowl and red velvet pants. At least no tiara today.

"Come on in!" Maggie said, stepping back from the door. She gestured to the living room. "Do you like it?"

Daisy stepped inside. "Oh, Maggie," she said reverently, taking in the room.

Maggie had recreated the Valentine's scene from Daisy's

blog, complete with roses, a chain of pink paper hearts hanging from the fireplace mantel, and slow jazz music. It was like stepping into her fantasy life.

"I love it!" Daisy shifted Bryce to her hip so she could give Maggie a one-armed hug. "It's just like I pictured!"

Maggie beamed and grabbed her hand. "Oh my goodness, look at this diamond ring. Beautiful! Trav knows how to pick 'em. The boy must have spent a fortune on this!"

Daisy cringed. "I know. It's too beautiful." She was still getting used to the feel of the two rings and trying not to feel panicky about the wedding band. It had been a long time since she'd worn one. How long would this marriage last? She broke out into a sweat.

"Just enjoy it, sweetie. And look at that shiny gold band. So new! Ah, newlyweds. Well, not yet, but soon. I heard the secret day is on Saturday. I can't wait. I know you're keeping it small, so your mother and I just invited Jorge, your parents, of course, Liz, Ryan, Shane, and Rico."

Daisy had left the planning up to her mom with the only rule being: keep it simple and small. Her mom had been thrilled to have at least one daughter that let her fuss over the details. Liz planned her whole wedding herself. It was still more people than Daisy would've liked for a secret wedding, but she couldn't uninvite anyone.

"That sounds like the most people we should have. No more, okay?" Daisy unzipped Bryce from his bunting. "And keep it hush, hush. We're supposed to already be married according to my blog."

"I love your blog, by the way. Wait here. I have something for you." Maggie disappeared into the dining room.

"Okay." Daisy looked to Bryce quizzically. "What could it be, Baby Delight?"

He shoved a fist in his mouth, keeping his thoughts to himself.

Maggie returned with a purple gift bag. Daisy reached for it, but Maggie shooed her hand away.

"Just a minute. I have to do this right." Maggie reached

her hand in the bag and pulled out a crocheted daisy pin. "Something old…"

Tears sprang to Daisy's eyes. It was just like Maggie to do something thoughtful like this. "It's so cute. I'll wear it for the interview."

Daisy handed over Bryce and pinned the daisy to her pink, striped V-neck sweater. Maggie handed Bryce back and reached into the bag again. "Something new…"

A black satin and lace teddy. Oh, Lord, it was the A-line mini she'd described on her blog. She felt herself flush. It was one thing to describe bedroom shenanigans to faceless blog readers, a completely different thing to know Trav's grand-mother read all the gory details.

Daisy touched the satin with one finger. "It's beautiful."

Maggie smiled and set it on the coffee table away from Bryce's grabbing hands. "Something borrowed…"

A romance novel—Kathleen Woodiwiss' *The Flame and the Flower*. "To get your juices cooking," Maggie explained. "I know after having a baby—"

"Thank you!" Daisy said before Maggie could get into any *juicy* details. *Ai-yi-yi*. The book joined the teddy on the coffee table. "Anything blue?"

"Of course!" Maggie fished the last item out of the bag. Daisy sucked in an audible breath of surprise.

Edible underwear. Blueberry flavor.

"These are lots of fun," Maggie said, holding up the box. "We've tried all the flavors."

Daisy snatched it from her and tucked it face down on the loveseat. *Not better*. Just a picture of the rear view. Her cheeks heated. She looked up. Maggie was grinning, her blue eyes dancing with mischief. Daisy was starting to see where Trav got his mischievous side.

"Thanks so much," she said as graciously as she could to the gift of edible underwear from her fiancé's grandmother. She was pretty sure this wasn't covered in any of the bridal etiquette guides.

Daisy handed over Bryce and stuffed all the gifts back in the bag. She'd quietly hide it in her closet when she got home.

"I'm just so happy for you and Trav," Maggie said.

Daisy grimaced, instantly feeling guilty. She felt like a fraud agreeing to marry Trav when they didn't love each other. Tomorrow she'd feel like an even bigger fraud in front of millions of *Mornings with Jessica* viewers. Adrenaline shot down her legs.

"I'd better run." She avoided Maggie's eyes and pointed to the diaper bag she'd left on the floor. "He's got a change of clothes, diapers, and milk." She pulled out the insulated bag with two bottles of expressed milk and set them on the coffee table. "Trav and I'll be back soon with all the baby gear." She kissed Bryce. "Bye-bye."

She headed out.

"Say bye to Mommy," Maggie said.

Bryce let out a wail of protest.

Daisy cringed and shut the door behind her. It was never easy to leave Bryce. She got in the car and headed back to her apartment. Her stomach pitched just thinking about the charade they were about to begin.

Fraud, fraud, fraud.

The end justifies the means.

She had a nagging feeling that she'd gotten herself in too deep. As usual. But this time she wouldn't ask her family to dig her out. She'd handle it herself.

Even if that meant she was forced to admit she'd made up her perfect life.

Even if that meant her reputation was in tatters and she'd never work again.

As long as she had Bryce, it would be okay.

She pulled into the apartment parking lot and spotted Trav right away, leaning against his car like he didn't have a care in the world. She instantly felt annoyed. Here she was about to make a complete fool of herself on national TV, and he didn't even care.

She stashed the gift bag under the front seat and got out of the car.

"Hey, wifey," he said, picking up a toolbox from the ground. "I'm practicing for tomorrow."

"Don't call me wifey," Daisy snapped, marching upstairs to her second-floor apartment.

"What do you want to be called?" he asked, keeping pace with her up the stairs.

"I don't know…honey or sweetie." She jammed the key in the lock and burst into her apartment. She snatched a baby rattle, some blocks, and a stuffed rabbit off the floor. "Just grab everything."

Trav stood there, doing absolutely nothing.

She glanced back at him. "Why aren't you helping?"

He set down his toolbox. "Are you okay, honey-sweetie?"

She knew he was joking with the endearment, but it still made her throat go tight over the caring she heard there. She threw the baby toys on the sofa. "I really screwed up."

"How so?" He stepped closer, but didn't touch her, for which she was thankful. She didn't want to cave and sob in his arms, letting him take care of everything. Still, she couldn't help sharing her misery.

"I'm pretending to be happily married with a beautiful house and a darling sweet baby on TV. It's all a lie! I'll probably crack under the pressure and admit I'm a fraud. Everyone will hate me."

"No, they won't," he said firmly. "It'll be fine. Besides, we'll be happily married the next day."

She shook her head. "This is my worst one yet."

"You're really doing a number on my ego here."

"Nothing personal," Daisy rushed to say.

He cocked his head. "It's a little personal."

"I'm sorry. You've been a dream through all this. I'm fine. Let's pack up."

She turned and gathered the toys off the sofa, yelping in surprise as Trav scooped her up. He settled on the sofa with her on his lap. She dropped the toys and gave him a good glare over her shoulder. "Trav, stop fooling around. We've got to get everything set up."

She leaped off his lap. He grabbed her and put her back in place.

"We're gonna take a little trip in the ol' Trav time machine."

She fought to get up, but he had her hips clamped firmly in his strong hands.

"Stop wiggling, honey-sweetie, or we're gonna take a very different kind of trip."

She stilled. "Don't call me honey-sweetie."

He rested his chin on her shoulder. "What would you like me to call you? Fiancée?" He lowered his voice to that shiver-inducing range. "Lo-oo-ver?"

"Daisy! Just call me Daisy!"

He straightened up. "Okay, Daisy-just-call-me-Daisy, let's go for a ride. Close your eyes."

She did.

"Vrrrr…putt, putt. It's slow to warm up," he told her.

She smiled a little in spite of her dark mood.

"Rrrr…okay, now we're cooking." He rocked her crazily side to side.

Her eyes flew open. "Trav!"

He stopped. "Time travel's a little rough. We're going back to the day after Thanksgiving at the bar."

She stiffened.

"Hang in there. We've only had one drink, and now I ask you out. Our courtship begins," he said grandly.

She relaxed again.

"We have the requisite number of dates before we do the deed. And I'm spec-tac-u-lar."

"Of course you are," she said, trying not to laugh.

"Naturally. And so are you, of course. And, in the heat of the moment, I propose. Two months later, we're happily married. How do you like that story?"

She leaned her head back against his warm chest and sighed. "I can't tell Jessica Larsen that you proposed in bed."

"Might be good for ratings."

"Be serious."

She shifted off his lap. He took one of her hands in his, and she felt the rough calluses of a man who worked with his hands. Her mind flashed to those hands on her bare skin. She snatched her hand back.

"How would you like me to propose?" he asked.

She thought back to the two proposals she'd had from her ex-husbands that were nothing special. More like spur-of-the-moment ideas. Then Trav's proposal at the Valentine's Day dance had been pretty nice, if she'd actually wanted to marry him. They needed a story for Jessica. One that put Bryce on the map after the wedding.

"You're going to have to start the time machine again," she said. "Go a little further back."

He pressed some imaginary buttons. "Boop-boop-boop. Where we headed?"

"Fourth of July two years ago. We're at the town fireworks."

He was uncharacteristically quiet. Their eyes met, and she felt something deep inside flutter a bit in hope.

"Go on," he said in a husky voice.

"So just as the last firework display fires in the air, you go down on one knee and propose. I say yes, and we celebrate later with champagne."

Nerves ran through her as she remembered telling him no the last time he proposed. She had no business marrying him. This could be a disaster. She'd screw up Bryce for sure.

"Then what?" he prompted.

Her attention snapped back. "We marry in October. Bryce is conceived over Thanksgiving. So we've been married almost a year and a half."

"I like that version even better," he said, gazing into her eyes.

She fidgeted under his attention. Her past relationships gave her little faith she'd do any better with this one. And now that Bryce was part of the deal, a relationship scared her. She never wanted Bryce to suffer because of one of her screwups. She wasn't so sure she could go through with a wedding.

"We'd better get packing," she said.

He stood and retrieved his toolbox. "I'll start with the crib."

She picked up the toys again and paused. "Thanks, Trav. For everything."

He gave her a jaunty salute and headed to her bedroom for Bryce's crib.

Please don't let me mess everything up for Bryce, she said in silent prayer. Then she got to work.

8

The crew of *Mornings with Jessica* ran through Maggie's house like a pack of rambunctious puppies destroying everything that was charming about the place. The red velvet chairs, floral loveseat, antique end tables—gone. All of it shuttled to the basement. At least they left the paper heart chain and roses on the mantel. In went Jessica's cushioned, white leather swivel chair and a pair of smaller matching swivel chairs for Daisy and Trav, along with lights, cameras, and a slew of wires that ran everywhere.

"Now be careful with that!" Maggie hollered as some burly men hauled her antique coffee table to the basement.

The baby gear that Daisy and Trav had spent *hours* loading in yesterday—gone. All of it moved upstairs.

"Great," Trav muttered under his breath.

"I know," Daisy said. At least they'd given the impression a baby lived here, though they probably could have done it with a lot less effort.

Just then a tall, blond woman, Jessica Larsen, strode in wearing a blue and white checked dress with a deep V-neck and a skinny belt flaunting an impossibly narrow waist. Daisy immediately felt underdressed in her white ruffled V-neck pullover, burgundy pants, and her favorite black leather ankle boots. At least the daisy pin Maggie had given her made her feel special.

Jessica thrust her hand out to Daisy. "Hi, Jessica Larsen. So nice to meet you finally. I feel like I know you from your blog. You've got your finger on the pulse of the twenty-five to forty-year-old mom, a key demographic that we need to capture." She smiled, a plastic smile, showing off painfully white teeth. Her ice-blue eyes and sharp cheekbones gave little warmth to her expression.

Daisy shook her hand. "Nice to meet you. I'm a fan of the show."

Jessica smiled politely. "Thank you."

Daisy usually slept through Jessica's early morning show, but she'd recorded and watched it faithfully this week once she knew she'd be on it. Jessica liked to interview actors, chefs, authors, and, well, her. She always managed to get some juicy story out of her guests that they swore they'd never told anyone before. Well, not Daisy. She'd be the perfect wife and mom. Pleasant, charming, and drama-free.

Jessica turned to Trav. "And you must be Darling Husband."

Trav shook her hand. "Travis O'Hare. Nice to meet you and welcome to our humble home." He gave her the charming, lopsided smile that made most women up their flirt factor. Jessica was no exception.

Jessica leaned in and touched Trav's arm. "I wouldn't call it humble. It's lovely. Old Victorians like this fetch a pretty penny from people looking for a little country getaway. What'd you pay for it, if I may ask?"

"Well, Jessica, I don't like to talk money," Trav responded. "Ask me anything else you'd like."

"Anything?" Jessica's eyes lit up, and she smiled a predatory smile. "I'll save that option for filming."

Daisy discreetly stepped on Trav's toe. He wrapped an arm tightly around her waist and smiled. The happy couple.

Maggie approached wearing a lemon yellow Jorge Chavez Dance Studio T-shirt with skinny jeans. A cute lemon yellow bow was pinned to a lock of her short white hair. Daisy wondered if she got the bow from Babies-N-Things. It looked just like the bows she saw on little girl babies.

"How ya doing?" Maggie asked, grabbing Jessica's hand and pumping it vigorously. "Jessica Larsen, I'd know you anywhere. You rouse me and my Jorge every morning with your fantastic guests, and now you've got the best of them all —Daisy and Trav."

Jessica smiled her plastic smile. "Thank you! It's always nice to meet a fan."

"Just a minute." Maggie jammed her hand in her jeans pocket, pulled out her cell, and dialed. "Hey, hon, come downstairs. I want you to meet Jessica. Don't forget the T-shirt."

Jorge appeared a few minutes later wearing his matching Jorge Chavez Dance Studio T-shirt and carrying an extra T-shirt in his hand.

"Delighted to meet you, Ms. Larsen," Jorge cooed, kissing her hand. "I am Jorge of the Jorge Chavez Dance Studio."

Jessica took this in stride, seemingly used to men kissing her hand. "Nice to meet you too, Jorge."

Maggie grabbed the extra shirt and tried to hand it to Jessica. Jessica didn't touch it. She looked horrified, like it was just pulled from the garbage.

"We'd love it if you wore this on the air," Maggie said. "Doesn't have to be today, could be any show you want. Just to, you know, put a plug in for Jorge's dance studio."

Maggie held the shirt up to show off the front with a couple ballroom dancing; then she turned it around. The back read: Dancers do it backwards and in heels.

"Gran!" Trav exclaimed, grabbing the shirt. "Did you design this one?"

Maggie's chest puffed out proudly. "I sure did. It's just for the women. The one for men says 'Dancers do it in the ball-room.' Cute, right?"

Trav laughed. Daisy elbowed him.

"We didn't mean to overstep," Daisy said.

"Not at all," Jessica said smoothly. "I like her. Cute and kitschy. You should write her into your blog."

"Does that mean you'll wear it?" Maggie asked, holding the T-shirt out to Jessica again.

Jessica pushed the shirt out of her personal comfort zone. "I don't wear T-shirts. My stylist, Kimberly, does a fine job scouring the city for the right Jessica Larsen look. Wouldn't want to hurt her feelings. Oh, our producer is here." She turned, and her voice hit a husky purr. "Max, finally."

Jessica airkissed a tall man with jet black hair. When she stepped back, Daisy sucked in a breath. It couldn't be. He looked like…her Max. Her heart raced. She clutched Trav's arm; she couldn't seem to catch her breath. Oh, God. No, no, no. Not now.

"I've got to get some Perrier and organic lemon slices to the set," Jessica said. Hand on her hip, she said playfully, "You know I depend on it when we're on location."

"Of course," Max murmured.

Daisy stood, frozen in shock, everything in the room fading away except this man who'd left her a wretched mess. He wasn't fat and bald. He was gorgeous, even more so than he'd been all those years ago. His hair was still black, not a single gray hair, and cut short now. His eyes, that stunning blue-green with the thick lashes. He was fit and muscular.

The room slowly came back into focus, and a hysterical sob fought to get free. She wanted to pound his chest and scream at him.

"Ow," Trav muttered, loosening her grip on his arm.

Max Parker stepped forward. "Daisy, so good to see you again."

He embraced her while she stood with her arms stiffly at her sides. His spicy cologne washed over her, the memories flooding back. She closed her eyes against the remembered pain of their last meeting. He released her. She just stood there and stared. Why was he here? What did he want?

She swallowed hard over the lump in her throat. Unable to scream at him in front of the TV people, she remained mute.

Dimly, she heard Trav introduce himself.

"I've got to make a phone call," Max was saying to her, holding up his cell. "We'll catch up after."

"Catch up?" Trav asked, waving a hand in front of Daisy's eyes. She couldn't stop staring. "Who the hell was that?"

She blinked and slowly turned to him. "Husband number one."

∽

"Good morning, friends!" Jessica chirped into the camera. "Thank you for joining us for a very special *Mornings with Jessica*. Today I'm on location in the quaint town of Clover Park, Connecticut, in the lovely home of Daisy Garner from the popular blog *Daisy Does It All*. How are you, Daisy?"

"Great, I'm thrilled to be here," Daisy said stiffly. She tried not to fuss with her hair as she sat in the swivel chair, legs crossed at the knee in a perfect mirror image of Jessica. Two cameras focused on them, one on Jessica and one on her. They'd attached a small microphone to her shirt, and she was afraid to move in case it fell off.

Trav and Max watched off-camera. There'd been no time to catch up with Max, what with the hair and makeup guy fussing over them and the crew setting them up, but she was positive that his being here today was no coincidence. She couldn't believe he showed up now when she was trying to get through what could be the most important career-changing event of her life.

"Your blog has followers in the six figures as well as a high share rate on social media." Jessica dropped her voice conspiratorially. "So, tell us, what's the secret to creating such a wildly successful blog?"

Jessica sat, eyes wide, riveted on Daisy, waiting for her reply. Daisy made the mistake of looking at the camera focused on her, with its huge lens and red light that meant it was filming. Time seemed to slow down. Sweat dripped down her back. She opened her mouth, but nothing came out. Seconds ticked by.

"Cut!" someone said.

The red light went out. Daisy blinked and looked around.

"Sweetie, don't look at the camera," Jessica said. "Just look at me. We're just talking." She smiled, more like a baring of teeth. "Just having a little conversation, okay?"

Daisy wiped her clammy hands on her pants. "Of course. Sorry. Can I get a drink of water?"

"Got it," someone said.

Daisy turned her chair away from the view of Max and the cameras and focused on the fireplace. She had to think of a good answer to Jessica's question. Why was her blog popular? She had to make it sound like it was more than just dumb luck. Which it was. A guy returned with a glass of water. "Thank you."

She sipped, trying to cool down. The makeup guy returned to blot the sweat from her face.

"We good, Daisy?" Max asked.

No, we are not good, asshole. What are you doing here?

Geez, she couldn't blow this interview before she even answered one question.

She turned her chair back in position. "I'm good."

"And rolling…"

Jessica asked her question with the exact same tone and expression as the first time.

Daisy focused on Jessica when she answered. *Just having a little conversation.* "I wouldn't say there's any secret to it. I try to talk about things I think my readers would be interested in. Like keeping the romance alive after baby. Having fun as a family. Things like that."

"Let's have your husband come on over here." Jessica motioned Trav over. The camera followed him as he took the few steps to sit in the chair next to Daisy.

Daisy broke into a sweat again. This was the hard part, coming across as a happily married couple. The lights made her sweating even worse. Jessica looked cool and dry.

"This is Darling Husband, everyone," Jessica said, addressing the camera directly. "Isn't he a hottie? Travis, what do you think of your wife's success?"

"I'm extremely proud of her." He squeezed Daisy's hand

in a show of husbandly support. Daisy tensed at his touch and forced herself to relax. It all felt so fake.

"Any secrets you'd like to share for a happy marriage?" Jessica asked, turning back to Daisy.

Daisy glanced at Max off-camera and suddenly found it hard to breathe. She snapped her attention back to Jessica, sucked in a breath, and exhaled slowly. "Yes."

"What would that be?" Jessica prompted.

"A happy marriage is good. No secrets." *Brilliant, Daisy. Any brain cells working up there?*

"Interesting." Jessica turned her attention to Trav. "Would you agree that it's important to have no secrets in a happy marriage?"

"Absolutely. And some lacy nighties don't hurt either." He grinned and kissed Daisy's cheek.

Jessica laughed heartily while Daisy forced a smile. Trav had remembered the details of her blog. And look at how relaxed he was on camera. She took another deep breath. Trav was playing his part perfectly, and she could do the same.

Just don't look at Max.

Jessica tipped her head to the side. "Did you always want to be a blogger, Daisy?"

"It was something new for me." Daisy focused on Jessica, relieved to find the words came more easily now. "I just needed to write about my experiences as a new mom. The blog was an easy way to share that with other moms."

Jessica turned to Trav. "And I understand you're a big help around the house and with baby."

"That's right," Trav said with a straight face. He was good. This was going to be fine. With Trav at her side, everything would go smoothly.

Jessica leaned forward. "Would you agree with Daisy that your baby is the best thing about marriage?"

Trav glanced at Daisy, and she smiled, silently begging him to agree. "One of many great things about being married to Daze. She's also fantastic in the sack." He waggled his eyebrows.

Daisy gasped. "Trav! That's private!"

He patted her arm. "Sorry, honey, you're right. Change that to fantastic in the kitchen."

Daisy groaned.

Jessica tittered. "You guys are so cute together. Tell us about your first date."

"It was at Garner's," Trav said at the same time as Daisy said, "It was at the town Fourth of July fireworks."

Shit. The *proposal* was at the fireworks. Trav had it right. The first date was supposed to have been at Garner's.

Jessica looked from one to the other. "You don't seem to have the same first date. Which is it?"

"Fireworks," Trav promptly said just as Daisy confirmed, "Garner's."

Daisy rushed to explain their contradicting stories. "I mean, first we went to Garner's and had dinner, then we went to the town's fireworks show." Except Garner's was closed on the Fourth of July because they set up shop at the concession stand at the Clover Park High football stadium.

Jessica pursed her lips in a serious expression. "Do you always agree on parenting?"

"Mostly we do," Daisy said, looking with genuine affection to Trav. In this one area, they were in perfect accord.

"We follow an attachment parenting philosophy," Trav said. "It's about meeting your kid's needs when they're very young so they grow into confident, independent kids."

"Can you give us an example?" Jessica asked.

Daisy spoke up. "I breastfeed; he sleeps in a crib in my, er, our room so I can respond to his cries right away—"

"We never let him cry it out," Trav added.

Daisy nodded. "We'll often carry him around in a sling or Baby Bjorn carrier so he can be close to us."

Jessica stared at them like they were crazy hippies. "Okay, let's go back to the blog. Your post on 'Bedroom Shenanigans After Baby' has gone viral with a million views and thousands of retweets. In that post, you advocate sexy talk to get things started. Care to elaborate?"

Um, no? Daisy laughed and went for a casual breeziness she was far from feeling. "I could, but my sexy talk only works for my husband. It's very individual, so I leave that to the imagination."

"Good answer," Trav said, patting her leg.

"Thank you," Daisy replied. She wished he would stop touching her. It was making her more nervous. She was sure the cameras would pick up on their charade. Though it was nice that Max got to see her as a happily married woman. *Take that, ex-husband. I did just fine without you.*

"Any plans for baby number two?" Jessica asked sweetly.

"No!" Daisy said at the same time as Trav said, "Yes."

Daisy turned to him in alarm.

"We talked about it," Trav said smoothly. "When the time feels right. No rush."

Daisy reached for composure, extremely aware of Max studying her with an intensity that made her want to jump up and scream, *What do you want?*

"Exactly, when it feels right," Daisy said. "But one of the things I emphasize on my blog is giving your body a break between babies. So that's why my answer was no. Bryce is only six months old."

Right on cue, Bryce's throaty scream rang out from upstairs as he woke from his nap. WAAAAAHHHHH!

"Excuse me," Daisy said. "I need to check on him. He's usually hungry after a nap."

"Cut!" Jessica yelled. She turned to Daisy, eyes flashing. "We're in the middle of an interview. Couldn't his grand-mother take care of it?"

"His great-grandmother and no," Daisy said, unclipping her microphone and standing.

"Great," Jessica muttered. Her tone changed from sour to sweet in a flash. "Bring the baby in here. Our viewers would love to see the happy family together."

Daisy and Trav exchanged a look. Bryce was unpre-dictable at best. How would it look on camera to see the two of them struggling to calm their screaming son?

"Maybe later," Daisy said.

"Sure," Jessica purred. "I can wait." She smiled up under her lashes at Trav. "Tell me more about yourself."

Daisy barely held back an urgent warning to Trav, *Say nothing. Don't trust her.* Instead, she bolted from the room, knowing it was urgent to get Bryce calmed down quickly before he went to full throttle. Hopefully they'd pulled off covering up their little first-date slipup.

~

Daisy settled back into the guest chair for more questions. The makeup guy touched up her face while the sound guy reattached her mike. Bryce was happy for now with Maggie and Jorge entertaining him upstairs. Now that she'd gotten through the first few questions on-camera, she was feeling more comfortable. All she had to do was avoid looking at Max and pretend she was happily married.

She nodded at Jessica. "I'm ready."

Jessica merely rotated a finger in the air. The crew picked up her signal.

"And rolling," someone said.

Jessica leaned forward eagerly. "Daisy, we've all enjoyed reading about the delicious, healthy meals you prepare for your family. Would you make one of your specialties for our viewers at home?"

Daisy's mouth opened and closed. *Shit.* Not only did she not know her way around Maggie's kitchen, she didn't know how to cook. She glanced over at Trav, where he stood off-camera. His brows went up in concern.

"I, uh, wouldn't you rather—"

"Maybe that rosemary leg of lamb you mentioned?" Jessica looked to the camera and nodded, as if a live studio audience would back her up.

Trav grimaced.

"I'm sorry, I'm unprepared," Daisy said. "I planned on going to Garner's for lunch today. It's my parents' restaurant and very popular here in town. Would you like to have lunch there?"

Good job. She mentally patted herself on the back. *Deflect and showcase your parents' place.*

"I think our viewers would really love to see you in action at home," Jessica said. "There must be something you can make here. Let's go to the kitchen." She stood, and Daisy followed slowly behind her.

There was a flurry of activity while the crew set up cameras and lights in the kitchen. Jessica spent her time getting touched up by makeup.

Trav appeared at her side and slung an arm around her shoulders. She leaned into his side, grateful for the support. "What am I going to do?" she whispered in his ear.

"Grilled cheese," he whispered back.

She closed her eyes. Grilled cheese wasn't even close to the kind of dishes she'd described on her blog. Was she really going to show millions of viewers how to make grilled cheese?

A short time later, the crew was all set up.

"And we're good here, people," Max said.

"And...rolling."

"So..." Jessica asked in a coaxing way. "What are we having?"

"I make a mean grilled cheese," Daisy found herself saying. "High quality, organic cheese on fresh-baked multi-grain bread."

Jessica's brows shot up. "Grilled cheese? From your blog, it seemed you were always whipping up some gourmet dish. I seem to remember saffron rice and, of course, that lamb dish." She looked at Daisy expectantly.

"Sometimes simple is best for lunch," Daisy said. *Like now.* "It's important to have healthy meals for your family, but that doesn't always mean they have to be fancy or take a long time. Trav loves my grilled cheese too."

The camera swung to Trav. "Love her grilled cheese."

"Well," Jessica huffed. "I suppose. There are some gourmet grilled cheese places in the city. Could you make some of that homemade cream of tomato soup to go with it?"

Why did I spend so much time describing food on my blog? Probably because I wrote late at night when I was getting the munchies, but too tired to make anything. My fantasy food life.

Daisy pretended to think about that. "Soup, well…"

"We're all out of tomatoes, honey," Trav said.

"Yes, that's what I was just about to say," Daisy said, nodding vigorously. "We're all out. Sorry, no soup."

Jessica stared at her blandly. "Okay, let's see this famous grilled cheese."

"Sure," Daisy said. "I just need to get the bread."

She opened the breadbox on the counter and found a collection of Pez dispensers all lined up inside. She slammed the lid down and heard the clatter of *Kiss*, the Simpsons, and what appeared to be the Founding Fathers taking a dive to the counter. She turned to Trav. His eyes darted to the refrigerator.

Daisy opened the fridge. "I forgot I moved the bread to the refrigerator to keep it fresh longer. Yes, here it is. And the butter and cheese too. Perfect!"

She pulled half the loaf from the store bag, grabbed the package of sliced cheese and butter, and set it all on the counter next to the stove.

Jessica stared at the cheese. "I didn't know they made organic American cheese. Isn't that processed?"

Daisy snatched the cheese off the counter, hiding the label. "Not this kind. We get it from a health food store nearby, Gary's Greens & More." She decided to put in a plug for her dad's friend Gary. "That's also where I buy natural grape soda and the most delicious chocolate cookie sandwiches."

"You think soda and cookies are healthy?" Jessica asked.

"They are at the health food store," Daisy said as she spread butter on some bread. She glanced around the kitchen, trying to decide where Maggie would keep the frying pan. There were a lot of cabinets. Well, most people kept it in a cabinet near the stove, right?

She opened the cabinet to her right and quickly shut it.

Troll dolls. Each one next to an empty beer bottle. Little troll party in there.

She tried the cabinet to the left. Tin baking molds—camel, pig, chicken, weird doll-like people. Her eyes widened. Was that a giant—she slammed the cabinet. What was wrong with

Maggie? Didn't she own a frying pan? Her heart kicked up, and energy shot down her legs. She would not bolt. She could still pull this off.

"Looking for something?" Jessica asked.

"As a matter of fact, yes." Daisy turned to Trav. "Honey, did you put the frying pan in a different place the last time you washed the dishes?"

Trav leaped forward. "Yes. I stuck it in the oven to dry since the oven was still warm." He fetched it from the oven and handed it to her. She never would've thought to look there. She was very afraid to find out what else lurked in Maggie's cabinets.

"Thank you," she said.

He surprised her by giving her a quick hard kiss. "You're welcome."

She stared at him, momentarily forgetting her grilled cheese mission.

He smiled widely. "I'm a huge distraction. Let me step out of the way."

Jessica wagged her finger. "Oh, I think I know what's going on here."

"You do?" Daisy asked.

Trav stood, frozen in place.

"Your Darling Husband is the secret chef around here, isn't he? That's why you don't know where things are."

"He is," Daisy agreed immediately. "He helps out a lot. It just makes me love him more."

"Thank you." Trav kissed her hair. Thank goodness he didn't kiss her on the lips again. It left her mind a complete blank. "But the grilled cheese is her specialty. I'll leave her to it."

He made a fast exit.

"You have him trained well," Jessica said with a sly wink for the cameras.

"No training needed when you have a solid marriage based on mutual respect," Daisy said, surprising even herself with that statement. She was starting to believe she was in some perfectly dreamy marriage. *Lie long enough and it starts to feel like the truth.* Trav played the part so well. Was this what marriage to Trav would be like? She had to admit it was kind of wonderful. It almost made her forget the man who stood silently off-camera bringing her troubled past front and center. Almost.

She focused on the task at hand and cooked up a very respectable grilled cheese on store-bought whole wheat bread.

Jessica only ate one bite.

9

Trav watched off-camera as the interview continued. Daisy was telling Jessica how she enjoyed making every day special, like a holiday. People actually believed this shit? They sat at Gran's dining room table drinking tea, a plate of Milano cookies untouched in front of them. He'd done his part playing the adoring husband. They'd just finished the longest lunch of his life while the cameras rolled. He'd kept busy feeding Bryce chicken and rice while Jessica kept asking Daisy questions about "small-town life." Daisy grew up in Clover Park, but she'd lived in the city for years and traveled a lot too. He knew she'd lived in Israel for a couple of years and spent a summer in Costa Rica. Daisy said none of this, instead letting Jessica paint her as just a small-town girl.

If she wanted to come off that way, fine. But that guy Max...not cool. Max watched Daisy the whole time, looking like a lovesick cow. *Bastard*. Didn't the fact that Daisy was married *with a kid* register? Trav didn't know exactly what went down between Daisy and Max, but from Daisy's reaction to seeing him today, he knew Max must have done something really bad. Something that fifteen years later could still shake Daisy up. He couldn't wait to kick the asshole to the curb.

"Cut," Max said.

Jessica raised an eyebrow and turned to Max. "What's the problem?"

"Fifteen-minute break," Max said, rotating his hand in a gesture to the crew to break. "Daisy looks like she's getting tired."

"Seriously?" Jessica demanded. "She's fine. Aren't you fine?"

Daisy stood. "I would like to stretch my legs a bit and check on Bryce."

"Fine," Jessica said with a fake smile that reminded him of a kid getting underwear for a birthday present. She stood and hissed something at Max that Trav didn't catch before she walked like she had a pole up her ass from the room.

Daisy stretched her arms over her head, arching her back. Damn, she was so hot.

"You okay, Daze?" Trav and Max asked at the same time.

Trav glared at Max. The man was slippery. He didn't trust him one inch.

Daisy looked only at Trav, which suited him just fine. "I'm just going to take a little walk."

"You can't," Trav and Max said at the same time. They stared at each other.

"Go on," Max said. "You're the husband."

"Damn right," Trav said. "Daze, it's starting to flurry. The wind is picking up, and it promises to be a world-class blizzard. You should stay indoors."

Daisy took a step toward the door, plainly ignoring him.

"It could mess up your hair and makeup," Max said. "We'd have to redo it, and that would put us behind schedule."

That got her attention.

"Okay," Daisy said. "I'll just check on Bryce, then." She left.

Max watched her go. "You're a lucky man. Hold onto that one."

"I plan to," Trav said with enough bite to make his position clear. "This storm is gonna be bad. If you don't hightail it back to the city, you could get stuck on the road."

Max lifted one shoulder up and down. "We can always take the train. Anyway, I know Jessica, and she likes to really dig deep with her interviews. Get to know the person."

"She's been digging deep for more than two hours already. What's there to know? She's a *wife* and mother living the small-town life, making a good home for her family."

"That she is," Max said quietly. "We'll be out of your hair soon. Just a little longer."

"I get the feeling you had something to do with getting Daisy on *Mornings with Jessica*," Trav said. "What do you want from her?"

"Nothing," Max said quickly. "Daisy's blog caught our attention just like any newsworthy item."

Trav narrowed his eyes. "I didn't see it in the news."

Max's eyes darted to the side. "We watch trends. Excuse me. I have to check in with the office."

Trav lifted a hand in the air. "Please do."

Max headed off to the kitchen. Trav decided to go upstairs to see Bryce. He met Daisy already on her way down.

"Your grandmother got him to nap," she said.

"That explains the quiet." He turned and followed her to the kitchen.

Max sat at Gran's table, staring at his cell.

Daisy helped herself to some water and looked out the window at the snow, which was starting to stick now. No way was he leaving the two of them in here alone. He wouldn't let Max hurt her again. He joined her at the window and slipped an arm around her waist. She elbowed him. *Dammit.* He was trying to play the perfect husband.

Max spoke up. "You've made a nice life for yourself here, Daze. I envy you."

Daisy turned in surprise. Trav nodded. *She does have a nice life, not that it's any of your concern, ex-husband.*

"Don't envy me," Daisy said. "I'm living a life no different than millions of women. Do you have a family of your own?"

Max shook his head. "Never met that special someone. But you two. Wow. You look good on camera together."

"We are a good match," Trav said. "Daisy and I knew each other as kids. Back then—"

Gran walked in and pulled a bottle of milk from the fridge and popped it in the microwave. "Bryce woke up a little fussy. I think some milk will settle him right down."

"Should I go up there?" Daisy asked.

"No need," Gran said. "I've got this. You just keep on being the fabulous TV star."

WAAAHH!!!!

"I should go," Daisy said.

"I've got it," Trav said. "Finish the interview." He gave Max a dark look. "Wrap things up before the snow gets worse out there."

"It's fine," Daisy said. "I'll go."

WAAAHHH!!!

Jessica appeared in the kitchen. "Can someone quiet down the noise from upstairs?"

Daisy's mouth formed a straight line. "It's not *noise*, it's a baby."

"Relax, you two," Gran said, pulling the bottle from the microwave. "I can handle the boy."

"Good," Jessica said. "Max, let's get the crew and get back to work."

"I'll take him," Trav said. He knew he could get Bryce calmed down quickly. Daisy could go back to her interview, and then Max and all of the *Mornings with Jessica* people could get the hell out of town.

"He'll calm down faster with me," Daisy said, turning to go.

"What do you think I do when it's my day to have him?" Trav asked in pure exasperation.

Daisy stilled.

"*Your* day?" Jessica asked. She exchanged a look with Max. "Are you two separated?"

Shit.

"Of course not," Daisy said.

Trav rallied. "I'm talking about when I have him for daddy-son day so Mom here can relax."

Daisy smiled and nodded.

WAAAHHH!

"Coming, Bryce!" Trav hollered. He grabbed the bottle. Max gave him a mock salute as Trav walked by that made him want to slap his pretty-boy face. Then he jogged up the stairs to quiet the bellowing little man.

"Can we please continue?" Jessica asked, gesturing for them to get out of the kitchen and back to the dining room, where the cameras were set up.

Daisy twisted her wedding band around her finger. She was ready to end the interview—she could only hope to keep up the charade of perfect wife and mother for so long. And she wanted Max out of this house.

"We'll wait for Trav and Bryce to get back," Max said.

"I can work on Daisy in the meantime," Jessica said, her lips forming a pout.

"Take five, Jess," Max said.

Jessica's ice-blue eyes flashed at him. "Five minutes. No more. I didn't come all the way to this podunk town just to sit around waiting on other people."

She stormed off.

"I don't know where she thinks she's going," Maggie commented, watching Jessica go. She turned to Daisy. "How's it going? I know Jessica can get some spicy confessions out of her guests. I still remember when Justine Baxter admitted she used to be a man. What a shocker!"

Daisy cringed.

"That was a big show for us," Max said.

"But good for Justine, I say." Maggie patted Daisy's shoulder. "Don't you be like that." She glanced at Max. "Don't worry, Daisy's all woman."

Daisy sputtered, unable to think of a suitable response to Maggie's assurance that she was indeed a woman.

"I never doubted," Max said with a huge smile.

Maggie crossed to the breadbox. "Now what happened

here?" She righted the Pez dispensers and pulled out two *KISS* members—the Demon and the Starchild. "We're fans," Maggie explained. "Of both the band and the candy. I'll be upstairs. Jorge's got on a show about the Greek Islands. Might be our next trip!"

Silence fell after Maggie's departure, and Daisy felt the kitchen shrink around her as Max crossed the room to her side. It was just the two of them for the first time. They had nothing to say to each other. Why couldn't he look horribly lonely and aged? Instead age had only sharpened his appeal. He'd grown into his lanky six-foot frame and filled out with muscle that was clearly defined through his black mock turtleneck and jeans.

Why are you here? The question throbbed over and over in her mind. He must know she'd moved on. She had a son, an almost husband. Even if it wasn't official with Trav, even if Trav didn't love her, Max didn't know that.

"I missed you," Max said in the deep, husky voice that used to make her go damp just from the sound. Of course she'd been a horny eighteen-year-old the last time she'd heard it. Today, nothing.

"It's been a long time." She busied herself refilling her glass.

He rested his arm on the counter, barely grazing her hip. "It's no accident that I'm here."

Yeah, I'm getting that.

"I saw your blog and convinced Jessica that you'd be a boost to the show."

She turned to him. "You read my blog?"

He flushed. "I Googled you. Wanted to see what you were up to. Then I couldn't stop reading." He smiled, showing some laugh lines around his eyes.

Good, he has wrinkles.

"You're very entertaining. When I saw it rise in popularity, I knew we had to have you on the show." His voice lowered back to that scraping, rough register. "Plus I'd get an excuse to see you again."

Did he just turn that husky voice on and off to charm the

pants off women? Well, it wouldn't work on her now. The way he'd dumped her was something she'd never forget. She considered bolting, but didn't want him to know how much he affected her. She sat at the table with her water.

"I know you must've been surprised to see me," he said, pulling out a chair next to her.

She didn't reply.

"I'm a producer now," Max said. "Worked my way up from production assistant."

Was she supposed to be happy for him? Proud?

"Congratulations," she said flatly.

He laughed softly. "Lately I've been feeling like I want more. Settle down, have a family."

She felt his intense stare and finally met his eyes. *Those eyes. They used to look at me with total adoration.* She couldn't tear herself away. Then he hit her with a heart-wrenching bombshell.

"I just never met anyone that compared to you."

Anger flared within her at his blatant attempt to get close to her again. She was practically *married*. "*You* left *me*, not the other way around."

He exhaled sharply. "I'll regret that for the rest of my life. You didn't deserve the way I treated you—"

"The way you left me, you mean, *after* you found out I lost the baby." Her lower lip trembled, and she looked away. The double loss of the baby and the man she'd thought was the love of her life still hurt. When she'd miscarried and gone into a deep state of grief, her only consolation had been the thought that Max would be there to help her through.

She'd told him, in the privacy of the dorm's empty lounge, practically choking over the words.

"I lost the baby."

Pure relief had washed over his face. His words were even worse. "I'm sorry for your loss; I think we should get a divorce." All in the same breath.

"*My* loss?" she'd asked through the haze of tears. "Divorce?"

He stood stiffly. "We're too young to be married. I'll take care of the paperwork. I guess this is goodbye."

Her voice came out small. "I thought we were soul mates."

"We'll find each other again. Promise. In ten years. When we're twenty-eight, if neither of us is with anyone, we'll be together. It's just not the right time."

She'd yanked off her engagement ring and threw it at him. "Take your stupid ring and your stupid self and get out of here! I never want to see you again!"

The next week, Daisy took off for a kibbutz in Israel. College without Max, without the baby, was meaningless. She stayed on the kibbutz, working cooperatively on a farm, for two years. Her parents had tried to convince her to return to college. She'd refused.

But that was then, this was now. Now she had Bryce.

Max took both her hands in his and held them in a warm grasp. "I didn't come here to fight. I came here to ask your forgiveness."

She met his eyes, read the regret, the sincerity there, and felt herself weakening. She'd never had any backbone when it came to Max.

"Daze, I am very, very sorry."

The words were too much, far too late. She pulled her hands away. "It doesn't matter. It's old news."

He pushed a lock of her hair back, stroking her temple gently. "It does matter. I hurt you. And I'm sorry."

Daisy blinked back tears. The wind picked up, roaring through the trees. The kitchen lights flickered. Mother Nature seemed to pick up on Daisy's turmoil. She remembered everything about Max. About them. How much she'd loved him. She'd truly believed they were soul mates.

Bryce was her life now, and that meant Trav too.

"I've moved on," she said softly.

He leaned toward her, his eyes searching hers. "I just need to know if you forgive me."

She stood abruptly. "Fine. You're forgiven."

She'd almost made it out of the kitchen when she heard Max say quietly, "I never stopped loving you."

She paused, her heart racing, and shook her head as if she could shake off the words. She forced herself to walk away, one foot after the other, all the way upstairs to Bryce and the man she'd promised to marry.

10

Daisy sat in the guest chair set up in the living room for the afternoon interview, already drooping. How many more questions could Jessica come up with? Daisy wasn't that fascinating a person. Just a mom living the small-town life.

Jessica settled into the host chair and adjusted her mike. "Lovely lunch."

"Glad you liked it," Daisy said evenly, unsure if the remark was sarcastic or not. It was hard to tell with someone whose expression dialed from insanely interested to blank.

"Let's get Trav back for this next segment," Jessica called.

A crew member went to fetch him. Daisy shifted in her seat. Couple questions were the hardest to fake. She and Trav knew each other biblically, it was true, other than that, not much one-on-one time.

Jessica sat riveted to her cell while she waited. A few moments later, Trav appeared.

"I'm ba-ack," he said, leaning down to give Daisy a quick peck on the lips.

She felt herself flush. Geez, you'd think she was a teenager. She really had to get her libido under control. It was just so hard to be disciplined and responsible all the time. But that's what her mom was like. If she wanted to be a good mom, she had to at least try.

"Great!" Jessica beamed at him. None of her smiles for Daisy went beyond polite. Clearly, she favored dealing with men. Especially good-looking men. "Let's get moving, people."

A flurry of motion while the crew went back to work. Max appeared again. He avoided looking directly at Daisy, instead watching the monitor. What did Max think would happen between them? He'd show up at her house, declare his love, and wait for her to abandon her family and ride off into the sunset with him? He was seriously delusional.

"And...rolling," someone said.

Daisy sat up straighter and pushed Max to the back of her mind.

Jessica smiled brilliantly at Daisy. "One of the things that makes your blog so popular is the loving marriage at the heart of it. What makes Daisy and Travis work?"

Daisy sat, tongue-tied. What made them work? What made any relationship work? People either clicked or they didn't.

Trav filled the silence. "I think a good sense of humor goes a long way. We laugh a lot."

"Absolutely!" Daisy exclaimed. "Trav's always making me laugh. Laughter is the best medicine!" She laughed a little too heartily.

Trav stared at her.

"How long have you been married?" Jessica asked.

"One and a half years," Daisy responded immediately, happy to remember the right answer.

"Awww, you count the half years, that's adorable!" Jessica looked at the camera. "Isn't that adorable?" She turned back to Daisy and Trav. "Still newlyweds, then?"

"Yes," Daisy said with a smile.

"Very much so," Trav said huskily. He grabbed Daisy's hand and held it warmly.

Daisy's gaze lingered on him, his tone was so...happily married. She almost believed him, and she knew the truth. He winked. She grinned.

"How are things in the bedroom?" Jessica asked suddenly.

Daisy blinked. Jessica must have been holding that question for the shock factor. She looked to Trav, who set his mouth in a tight line. Should she say it's private?

At their silence, Jessica pushed on. "You did blog about bedroom shenanigans after baby and vacation intimacy. Any special tips you could offer moms who might not be feeling their usual sexy selves?"

"Daisy never stopped being sexy," Trav said.

"Aww…you too, honey." Daisy ran her tongue over her upper lip just to tease him. Trav's eyes widened, and she laughed. "Even after you didn't push out a baby."

"I did my part," Trav said.

"Yeah, the easy part," Daisy replied.

"I can see you two have a nice repartee," Jessica said. "Care to share how that carries over into the bedroom?"

"Would you get off the bedroom?" Trav muttered.

"Come on, just one juicy tip for your loyal blog readers," Jessica pushed. "Something that no one else has heard yet from Daisy who *does it all*. Or does she?"

Daisy narrowed her eyes. "What exactly would you like to hear?"

"We've all heard about your lingerie, the candles, the slow jazz…ooh, I know! Show us the sexy dance you do that has him ready to rip your teddy off before he has a chance to see your stretch marks."

"She doesn't have stretch marks," Trav said.

Obviously he hasn't seen me naked since I had Bryce.

"He's just being kind," Daisy said. Not that she wanted to bring Trav's attention to her flaws, but she had mentioned them in her blog.

"So, the dance?" Jessica prompted, lifting her arms and doing a sensual wave in her seat.

No, thank you. That's not happening on national television.

"I don't think so," Daisy said. "Maybe you'd like to hear about our vacation plans?"

Jessica turned her attention to Trav. "What would you say was your biggest turn-on to really combat that post-baby fatigue?"

Trav stood and ripped off his mike. "Enough. Our sex life isn't open to discussion."

Daisy tugged on his arm to make him sit down. The cameras were still rolling. "Trav, honey, just sit down."

He pointed at Jessica. "Do you get off on what other people do? Watch some porn."

Jessica's fake smile stayed in place as she said pleasantly, "Your wife is the one who put it out there for the world. I'm just following up on what she already shared."

"I did mention it on my blog," Daisy said, yanking Trav forcibly back to his seat. "But I also said some things are private."

Trav crossed his arms. "Yeah, private."

"I suppose you've quietly crossed over into old married couple," Jessica said dismissively. "Nothing special. Your usual Saturday night appointment."

"That's enough!" Trav roared. "This interview's over!" He rushed the camera and put his hand over the lens.

Jessica stood. "Max, get him off that camera." She turned to the other camera. "Roy, you keep rolling."

Roy gave her the thumbs-up.

"Trav, stop it! You're making a fool of yourself!" Daisy hollered, trying to peel him off the camera.

Trav set Daisy to the side, turned, and jabbed a finger at Jessica. "She's making a fool of us."

"I'm just trying to get a good story." Jessica framed a headline with her hands. "We're all happy in small-town America isn't a story. Daisy's the one who put your sex life out there."

"Don't blame Daisy for sharing on her blog!" Trav barked. "That was on her terms. Not needled out of her."

"How dare you!" Jessica huffed. "I'm a professional!"

Max pitched his voice above the noise. "Everyone calm down here!"

"Why don't *you* calm down?" Trav said, getting in Max's face.

Max glared at Trav; they were eye to eye. "Watch yourself."

Daisy rushed over. "Trav, please."

"Daze, butt out!" Trav said.

"Don't talk to her like that!" Max yelled.

He shoved Trav, and Trav shoved him back.

"STOP IT!" Daisy yelled at the top of her lungs.

The lights went out.

The house fell silent.

"What the hell?" Jessica yelled in a shrill voice.

11

"Oh, no," Daisy muttered.

"You broke the house," Trav said.

"What the hell?" Jessica shrilled again.

"Power outage," Trav said. "It's this storm."

"I'd better check on Bryce," Daisy said. She hurried from the room, nearly knocking over one of the crew's lights and catching her elbow on the banister on her way upstairs as her eyes adjusted to the sudden lack of light. Her parents had mentioned power outages in the area happening more frequently, but this was her first time experiencing it. Did she have enough diapers, baby food, fresh clothes for Bryce? Would they have heat? Food for the rest of them? She'd never thought of surviving a power outage with a baby in the middle of winter. The city hardly ever had lights out. She just prayed it didn't last long.

She burst into Maggie's room. Bryce was napping in his crib. Jorge was reaching for something on the high shelf of the closet while Maggie was sitting on the bed, pillows propped up behind her.

Daisy looked around wildly. "I thought you were watching TV."

Maggie smiled and nodded. "We were."

There was no TV in the room. "On what?"

Maggie pulled an iPad off the bed. "There's lots of TV on the Internet. Connection went down, though."

"Okay. I don't want you to panic, but the power's out."

Maggie nodded slowly. "Yes, we know, dear. Jorge's digging out the emergency radio."

"Emergency radio," Daisy repeated numbly. "Good, good." She glanced at Bryce sleeping through this nightmare. "Bryce is good. We have a radio. Okay."

She bolted again, heading for the stairs. They needed food, water, heat. Maybe not in that order. Maybe heat, water, food. Bryce would survive. She'd get him through this. At least she knew he could nurse; that was food and water combined. Okay, heat. They needed heat.

She'd find an ax and chop wood and build a fire in the fireplace. They'd huddle around the fire just like in pioneer days. She suddenly wished she'd paid more attention when Liz went on and on as a kid about Laura Ingalls Wilder and her family surviving out on the prairie.

Her baby's survival was all that mattered. Funny how all that worry about the blog and the TV show and Jessica and Max faded away the instant the lights went out. Without power, it all came down to the basics.

WAAHHHH!

Daisy raced back to get her baby.

Trav stared out the front window at the snowstorm, ignoring Jessica's rantings over the impossible weather. Visibility was bad. The wind was gusting, and the snow was still coming. There was at least three inches on the ground already. Roads weren't clear. A huge tree branch had come down across the driveway. Several more branches were strewn across neighbors' lawns. The snow on the trees made the branches heavier. Combined with the wind, it meant massive tree damage throughout the area. It would take time to clear things out.

Jessica finally ran out of steam. Trav turned and faced the

crew of *Mornings with Jessica*. "It looks like we'll be stuck here for a while."

The crew grumbled.

"You've got to be fucking kidding me!" Jessica exclaimed with fresh outrage. "Max, this interview is over. We can't do shit without power!"

Trav didn't like to say *I told you so*, but hell, he had told them to get out more than an hour ago. He wished fervently that they had. These were the last people he wanted to be trapped with in Gran's house.

"I want a car to take me back to the city," Jessica said.

"I'm on it," Max said in a soothing tone.

"You can't drive in this," Trav said. "It'll be a few hours before the roads are passable. I'm sure there's live wires down and tree branches. They might not even plow until the snow stops, and it's supposed to go well into the night."

"We'll take the train," Max said.

"Sure," Trav said. "You can walk to the station. It's about five miles away due east." He pointed the right direction.

"Great! Just great!" Jessica shrieked. "Like I'm trudging through a blizzard in my Manolos."

"We could find some boots somewhere around here," Trav offered.

"I don't do blizzards," Jessica said. "So we're basically stuck here." She turned to Max and stuck her lip out. "I didn't even get to ask the hard-hitting questions. I was so well prepared for this. And now I've got some fluff lifestyle piece."

Max put an arm around her and guided her to sit in the large host chair. He sat next to her, hands on his knees, while they continued a quiet conversation. As far as Trav was concerned, the storm ended the interview right where it should have ended. Jessica prying into their sex life had really pissed him off. Sure he joked about Daisy being good in the sack, but he'd never share details with anyone. What was even worse about her prying questions—they didn't have a sex life.

Yet. Soon, very soon. Tomorrow night was their wedding night. But now with this damn storm...he wouldn't wait to make a move. To hell with slow. These were desperate circumstances—trapped in a blackout with her ex. Trav wanted Daisy in a constant state of arousal, focused only on him. It was a good plan, one that would bring them both pleasure and make her forget about her ex.

And if that asshole hurt her again, he'd kick him out, blizzard or not.

Daisy walked downstairs with Bryce in her arms.

"Hey," Trav said, crossing to them. He kissed Bryce's cheek, and his son grabbed hold of his hair and yanked. He gently extricated his hair. The boy was going to make him bald. "I'll get a fire started. It should stay warm in the living room for a while. I'll start the backup generator once the wind settles down."

"A backup generator," Daisy said under her breath. She beamed a grateful smile that made him feel like a hero. "Thanks, Trav."

He kissed her gently and pulled back, looking into her eyes. She looked surprised. *Get used to it, honey.*

"No problem," he said.

"Wait, you have a backup generator?" Max asked. "Then we can continue the interview."

"We don't have enough wattage for that," Trav replied. "Just enough to run the essentials. We'll get by, but I'm not blowing out the circuit just for some camera equipment."

Jessica stood abruptly and paced across the room, muttering to herself.

"Okay," Max said. "Hopefully we can drive to the train station in a few hours."

Awesome plan, but doubtful. Either way, Trav was sticking to his seduction plan. Now that he'd thought it up, he was way into it.

"You're all welcome to spend the night," Daisy said. "I don't want you guys to have to go out in this."

Trav had no idea where they were going to put ten people, but they were stuck. Gran and Jorge could stay at his place across the street, but that still left him and Daisy, Jessica and Max, plus a crew of eight guys.

"My cell isn't working!" Jessica hollered. "What is this, the apocalypse?"

"Sometimes storms affect the tower," Trav said gently before the woman lost it completely. "It'll come back soon."

"Does this happen often?" Jessica asked.

"There's been some powerful weather the last few years," Trav said. "We've had at least one power outage a year for the past five years. Usually lasts about a week. That's why—"

"A week!" Jessica shrieked.

Gran and Jorge came downstairs with their emergency radio cranked up.

"Looks like the trains stopped running," Gran announced.

"Aaaah! Unacceptable!" Jessica shrilled. "Unacceptable!"

Bryce started fussing. His son didn't like all the hysterics in the room either.

"It's simply a fact," Gran replied. "Screaming about it won't help."

"I can't believe this!" Jessica said, storming into the other room.

"That woman needs a Valium," Gran pronounced. "And maybe some action under the sheets."

Jorge and Gran exchanged a loving look.

Trav rolled his eyes. His grandmother as a newlywed was still a little hard to stomach. "I'll go get the firewood."

"Thank you so much," Daisy said, bouncing Bryce. "I was worried about keeping Bryce warm."

He grabbed his jacket from the coat rack. "No worries. I got this. Heat and then some power. The pantry is fully stocked."

Relief washed over Daisy's face. It surprised him how much she'd worried. He always made sure his family was set for the winter. Plus he had to make sure he could get out and help with his own plow and shoveling service.

He left through the back kitchen door, passing Max, who was punching numbers on his cell phone and listening for a nonexistent connection. Useless jerk.

∽

Daisy settled on the living room floor in front of the fireplace, Bryce in her lap. Her son seemed mesmerized by the dancing flames. *At least I didn't have to chop wood*, she thought wryly. As if she'd ever done such a thing in her life.

It wasn't the best of circumstances, but Trav seemed to know what to do. It was comforting.

If the *Mornings with Jessica* crew were still here tomorrow, they'd have to cancel the wedding. Her mom and Maggie had decided to have the wedding ceremony right here in Maggie's living room to keep it quiet and intimate. The delay lifted some of the tension off Daisy. She hadn't wanted a rush wedding. She still wasn't sure it was the right choice. She needed Liz to make one of her pros and cons list. Daisy was terrible at those. She always found additional reasons to make each side balance out.

Maggie appeared and scooted a swivel chair toward her. "Want a chair?"

Daisy shook her head. "I sat in that long enough today. The floor's fine."

Maggie took the chair for herself. "You might need to reschedule the wedding tomorrow. Justice Fleming is getting up there in age, and she lives way out by Grand Lake. I doubt she'll want to chance the roads."

"I know," Daisy said. "We can reschedule."

"Aren't you worried someone will find out before this goes on the air?" Maggie whispered. "Maybe I could get one of those Internet ministry certificates and marry you myself."

Daisy laughed. "Well, you said the Internet line went down with the power, so I guess Reverend Maggie will have to wait."

"If I did marry you two, I'd make sure your vows were kosher," Maggie said. "No obey in there. And he'd have to promise to cook for you too. A man that cooks is a keeper. My Jorge can make paella, melt-in-your-mouth enchiladas, salmon cooked to perfection, and firecracker shrimp that will clear your nasal passages. Ooh, I'm hungry." Maggie stood. "Let me see what food I can round up for everyone."

"Thanks, Maggie."

Daisy kissed Bryce's hand and rocked him side to side.

Max appeared from the direction of the kitchen. "Mrs. O'Hare kicked me out of the kitchen. Okay if I join you?"

Daisy tensed. "Uh…yeah, sure."

Max settled on the floor, sitting cross-legged next to Daisy. "This is nice." He smiled at Bryce. "Can I hold him?"

"He's a little picky about who he goes to," Daisy said just as Bryce reached for Max with open arms. She smiled ruefully. "Sure." She handed him over.

"How ya doing?" Max asked Bryce, who stared at him. "You like peek-a-boo?" He covered his own eyes. "Peek-a-boo."

Bryce smiled his gummy two-toothed smile.

Daisy rolled into a tight ball, knees bent close to her chest, arms wrapped around her legs. Her voice came out hoarse. "You like kids."

"Sure," Max said. "Thought I'd have a couple of my own by now." He changed to a sing-song voice and spoke to Bryce. "But I haven't met the right woman, have I? Not like your mommy."

"Stop," Daisy snapped. "I'm married now."

Bryce jammed his fist in his mouth and stared at Max.

"Where'd you go after college?" Max asked.

She was quiet. *Now you care where I went?* Not one word from him to see how she was doing after she lost the baby. Not even an email.

"Daze?"

She couldn't let him know how much she still hurt over that. "I lived on a kibbutz in Israel for two years."

He laughed. "You? The city girl? You're not even Jewish."

She glanced sideways at him. "Doesn't matter. It was nice. Communal living combined with hard work. I needed that."

"What else?" Max asked. "Catch me up on your life."

She exhaled sharply and stared into the fire. "Not much to tell. I traveled a bit, worked, lived in the city for a while, though living in the city isn't much fun when you don't have money. I racked up serious credit card debt trying to keep up with my friends who had real jobs."

"What job did you have?"

"You name it. Dog groomer assistant, hostess, telemarketer, retail at a high-end boutique, assistant to a bestselling author, receptionist, waitress."

"Wow." She glanced over just as Max pried Bryce's fist out of his hair and substituted his finger. "Rogue TV was my first job after college. I got an internship and worked my way up to producer."

Despite herself, she was curious about his life. "Travel?"

They'd always talked about the travel they wanted to do —shouting at the top of Machu Picchu, snorkeling the Great Barrier Reef, getting their picture taken in front of the Seven Wonders of the World.

"A bit," Max said. "On vacations. Florida Keys. California to visit a friend in L.A."

She crinkled her nose. "That's it? You had total freedom. So disappointing."

Max played a silent peek-a-boo with Bryce a few times before speaking. "I can help you get rid of that debt and have a real career."

She looked at him warily. "Doing what?"

"You were great on camera. I can help you go further. Get you a few more talk shows, some endorsement deals, national commercials."

She raised a brow. "Yeah? I was pretty nervous at first."

"You took to it like a duck to water. Could you just picture you and Bryce in a Huggies commercial?"

She smiled hugely over that possibility. Bryce would be adorable in a diaper commercial. As long as he wasn't red in the face from crying.

Max went on. "We could make the Daisy name into a brand that says charming and fun mother does it all. Just say the word. I'd love to work with you."

Daisy shifted uncomfortably. Something about his tone implied he'd like more from her. But she couldn't deny the appeal of what he offered—money, a real career. "That's kind of you. I'll think about it."

He turned to her. "It's not kindness. You could really go

places. Parlay something big out of this blogging deal you've got going. You ever in the city?"

"Not much anymore."

He fished a card out of his pocket and placed it in her hand, his fingers touching her hand longer than necessary. She snapped her fist shut around it. "Stop by my office. We'll have lunch and talk."

She bit her lip. "It sounds tempting."

"I really think you've got what it takes. You could have a future in TV. I could make it happen."

"You really think so?" The idea was so far-fetched, but she'd be a fool to turn it down.

"I know so." He tousled Bryce's fluffy blond hair and handed him back. Then he was gone, leaving her to marvel over the possibilities for her and Bryce.

12

Trav held Bryce on his lap while he and Daisy sat in front of the fire. He felt content for the first time in a long time. Until Daisy came out with, "Max says I could have a future in TV."

"And you believe him?" Trav asked, keeping his voice low. He knew when a guy was making moves on his woman.

"Why wouldn't I?" she asked, her voice rising in agitation.

He lowered his hand to remind her of the nearness of the crew.

"He says I'm great on camera," she whispered. "My blog has a huge following. He says I could do more talk shows, maybe even commercials." She gasped. "Can you imagine if I got my own talk show? How cool would that be?"

"That would be cool, but unlikely. He just wants to get in your pants."

"Thanks a lot," Daisy huffed. "Obviously you don't think I have what it takes. Max believes in me."

He raised a brow. "Why did you break up again?"

Daisy stroked Bryce's hair and stared into the fire for a moment. "We were too young. Too much, too fast. Getting married at eighteen was a huge mistake. He realized it first and called it off after two weeks."

He winced. "Ouch."

"No, it's fine. He did the right thing. Can you imagine? I'd already be married for fifteen years by now. I could have a teen…" She lifted her chin. "It was for the best."

Rage poured through him. He wanted to wring that slimy bastard's neck. "Were you pregnant?" he asked softly.

"I lost the baby," she whispered. "Max left right after. Guess he didn't actually love me after all."

Realization hit Trav like a hammer. This was why Daisy was always pushing him away. She feared he'd walk out too.

"I'd never abandon you and Bryce," he said. "No matter what. You can count on that."

Her eyes searched his. He gazed steadily back. She looked away, chewing on her bottom lip.

She didn't believe him. Fucking Max had really screwed things up for him. Trav didn't know how to show her he meant what he said. He was already marrying her. Only time would prove him right.

"I just wish you believed in me," she finally said. "It would help if my husband was supportive of my career."

"It's not you I don't believe in, it's Max. Do what you want. Just don't expect much."

She stood and said frostily, "I'm going to see if your grandmother needs any help."

What did he say wrong? Max was the one who walked out on her, and suddenly *he's* the bad guy?

～

The storm gave Daisy a much-needed delay from her wedding. By five o'clock, it was clear no one was going anywhere. The crew took down their equipment and stashed it to one side of the living room. Then they went to the basement and hauled all of Maggie's furniture back into place. Jessica insisted that her host and guest chairs remain in the room.

It was getting dark outside. The house had only a few working lights in the kitchen, bathrooms, living room, and Maggie's bedroom. A few flashlights were lit and strategically placed, along with some candles.

"Looks like we're stuck here," Jessica said as everyone congregated in the living room. "Daisy, could you heat up one of those prepared meals you make for dinner? I'd love to try it. Maybe we could work that into the piece. You could give us the recipe to share with our viewers."

Daisy worked for a poker face. She had talked about making dinners ahead on her blog, rhapsodizing about the time savings and the more leisurely weekday, family meals. She'd stolen the idea from her mom, but hadn't actually done it herself. It had sounded like a perfect mom kind of thing to do.

Daisy stood. "Sure, let me just check what I have left in the freezer."

Jessica, Trav, and Max followed her into the kitchen.

Daisy opened the freezer. *Oh, Maggie.* Looked like hers at home. Mostly empty, except for some ice cream, ice cubes, and what looked like a slice of Maggie and Jorge's wedding cake. She turned. "Looks like we already went through our prepared meals."

Jessica narrowed her eyes. "I thought you did that every Sunday."

"Yes, and it's Friday," Daisy said. "We already ate my vegetable lasagna and extra meatloaf with mashed potatoes."

"Her meatloaf is awesome," Trav chimed in.

Yes, and it's homemade from Garner's.

Jessica studied them for a moment and turned to Max. "So what do we feed everyone, Mr. Producer?"

"Daze, do you have enough food?" Max asked.

"More than enough," Trav said. "The pantry's stocked. We'll come up with something."

"I'm beginning to think Trav is the secret housewife behind *Daisy Does It All*," Jessica said.

"We prefer the term homemaker," Trav said, batting his eyes.

"Domestic diva," Daisy said. "That's what I say on my blog."

"Guys can't be divas," Trav said. "What would you call me? Divo?"

She snorted. "Yes, you're the domestic divo."

"No, you are, honey."

She leaned in, hands on his chest, and touched noses. "No, you are, sweetie."

Trav kissed her gently. Daisy pulled back, surprised he'd kiss her so sweetly in front of Jessica and Max. It wasn't like they were still performing for the interview.

Jessica rolled her eyes. "Save it for the cameras."

The doorbell rang.

"Now who could that be in a blizzard?" Jessica asked, heading for the door. Max followed closely behind.

"Good save," Daisy said under her breath to Trav.

"I'm good for more than just a quick lay."

She gave him a playful shove. "Trav!"

"What?" He tipped her chin up. "Let me show you what else I'm good for."

He dipped his head slowly. She closed her eyes. *What am I doing? Hello, lust never got you anywhere.*

She pulled back and turned to go. "You're trouble."

He snagged her around the waist and pulled her close so her back was to his front. His voice vibrated in her ear. "Trouble used to be my middle name, but now I like to go by Magic Fingers. For obvious reasons."

Her laugh died in her throat as his large, warm hands slowly moved over her hips, her waist, the sides of her breasts. She didn't move, her breasts aching for his touch, when Maggie's voice rang out from the living room.

"Hey, you two! Come on in. You look like popsicles."

Daisy leaped away from him and went to see who it was. Trav trying to seduce her was a major distraction at a time when she really needed to focus on being the perfect Daisy from her blog. She didn't want to slip up. They were supposed to be married for a year and a half. Did married people touch and flirt so much in front of other people, or were they so used to each other it was more casual? She suspected it was the casual thing. She'd have to talk to him about it.

Liz and Ryan stood in the living room, their faces red from

the cold. They must have walked over from Ryan's house only a few blocks away. Bryce immediately reached out for Liz from where he sat in Maggie's arms.

Liz scooped him up and kissed his cheek.

"It's bad out there," Ryan said. "We just wanted to see if you were good to go. Looks like you got the generator running."

"We're good," Trav said. "How's yours working?"

"Great. I tested it last week when I heard the forecast and doubled down on fuel."

The brothers talked fuel supplies while Daisy went to give her sister a hug. Liz handed Bryce over, who promptly tangled his fist in Daisy's hair.

"How're you doing for food?" Liz asked. "We're stocked enough for the whole family, right down to the toilet paper. I'm so glad I've been preparing extra meals on Sundays. Now that I'm cooking for two, I have to plan ahead."

Daisy smiled. It was so cute how Liz took cooking so seriously now that she was living with Ryan. Her sister had probably been preparing extra meals since the first day of winter for just such an occasion.

Jessica thrust herself between them and pumped Liz's hand. "Hi, Liz, I'm Jessica Larsen from *Mornings with Jessica*. I couldn't help but overhear that you also prepare extra meals on Sundays. Were both of you sisters raised to do that?"

Liz's eyes widened in surprise. She turned to Daisy and caught her quick nod. "Absolutely. Our mother spent every Sunday cooking a few healthy meals ahead. We didn't always want to eat restaurant food."

"Family tradition," Daisy said.

Jessica raised a brow. "Interesting."

Maggie joined them. "Liz, now that you're here, would you mind if we sent some of the crew your way for the night? Trains aren't running, and the roads are bad. We've got ten people, not including the four of us and Bryce, and only four beds."

Jessica stalked off to where Max stood at the other side of

the room, holding his cell up to the window. Probably trying to get some bars to make a phone call.

"Absolutely," Liz said. "We've got three empty bedrooms and a sofa bed. I can set up some air mattresses and sleeping bags."

Trav piped up. "I'll get the extra sleeping bags out of Gran's place."

"We're calling Trav's place mine," Maggie whispered. "Jorge and I will stay there."

"Hey, everybody!" Daisy called over the chatter from the crew. After they quieted down, she asked, "Anyone want to spend the night at my sister's place a few blocks from here? They've got air mattresses and sleeping bags."

"We're staying here," Jessica announced, hitching her thumb in Max's direction.

Max gave Daisy a little wave. Daisy's stomach dropped. *What does Max want from me? I already said he was forgiven. Move on.*

The crew talked amongst themselves, working out who would go where.

"I've got s'mores," Liz said.

That settled it for the crew.

The doorbell rang again. This time it was Shane. Daisy smiled and went to greet him. She loved Shane. He was a total sweetheart, a little shy and prone to blushing red enough to match his hair. He was a big guy, like Ryan, but with a belly from all the ice cream taste-testing he did as a gourmet ice cream maker.

"Cold enough for ya?" Shane asked cheerfully. "Hey, little guy."

Bryce bounced excitedly in Daisy's arms.

"Good to see you," Daisy said, reaching up on tiptoe to kiss his cheek.

Shane smiled, revealing dimples. "You too."

Trav clapped him on the back. "I was wondering when you'd show up."

"Can I camp out here?" Shane asked. "My apartment is

freezing. I brought cinnamon ice cream." He held up two bags.

"I told you to get a generator, doofus," Trav said.

"It's not that easy to set up a generator on a second-floor apartment on Main Street," Shane replied. He lived in the apartment over Shane's Scoops.

"Of course you can stay," Daisy put in.

Trav took the bags. "You've got to be kidding about the ice cream. It's freezing out."

"We can make ice cream cookie sandwiches," Shane said. "One of the bags has pumpkin cookies. I got those bad boys out of the oven just before the power went."

Daisy's mouth watered. She gave Shane a smacking kiss on the cheek. "You are a dream. Some girl's going to snatch you up and be very lucky she did."

Shane blushed scarlet. "Thanks, Daisy," he mumbled.

Trav rolled his eyes.

"Too bad the talk show people got stuck in this," Shane said, raising a hand in greeting to them.

"Most of them are headed to Liz and Ryan's place," Daisy said. "We'll definitely have room for you."

Shane smiled. "Great, thanks."

Arrangements were worked out. A few of the crew wavered between ice cream sandwiches or s'mores, but then Liz's offer of hot chocolate cooked over Ryan's camp stove tipped the scale in her favor. The entire crew went with Liz and Ryan. Maggie and Jorge headed to Trav's place with a bottle of merlot, and Trav left to get his generator running for them. That left Daisy with Bryce, Shane, Max, who refused to leave, and Jessica, who informed them she wouldn't trudge three blocks in a blizzard no matter what food was involved, and she refused to share a room. How cozy.

While Shane whipped up ice cream cookie sandwiches for them, Max sat with Bryce in the dining room, where Bryce was happily playing with a spoonful of ice cream, smearing it all over his high chair tray. Daisy got stuck in the kitchen with Jessica.

"You're supposed to be the queen of healthy family meals," Jessica said. "Surely you have something I can eat in here that doesn't have a thousand calories of sugar and fat."

"Of course I do," Daisy said, forcing a cheerful tone. Shane turned from where he was scooping ice cream across the room and gave her a sympathetic look.

Daisy opened the pantry with Jessica at her side.

"This is what you eat?" Jessica asked. "Prunes, prune juice, All-Bran…Milano cookies?"

"High fiber is very healthy," Daisy said. "And we also have lots of canned fruit. How about some peaches?" She pulled out a can of sliced peaches in heavy syrup.

Jessica sighed. "I guess it'll have to do. But rinse off all that syrup. I gotta say this isn't what I expected from reading your blog. In fact, a lot of what I've seen and heard doesn't quite match your blog persona. Why do you think that is?"

"I have no idea. Maybe the difference between reading about someone and meeting them for the first time in real life." Daisy went for flattery as a redirect. "I'm sure you get that all the time. Fans who feel like they know you from your show and are totally starstruck when they meet you in real life."

Jessica stood a little straighter. "True. I have had some fans that were quite overwhelmed, but I assure them I'm just a regular Jane like they are."

"Of course!" Daisy searched through a few drawers for the can opener. "But even better than just a plain Jane. You look even more beautiful in real life than on the screen."

Jessica preened. "You think so?"

"Absolutely."

Shane discreetly pointed Daisy toward the can opener.

"Thank you," Jessica said. "You're so pretty too. Who does your hair?"

Daisy pulled out the can opener and pried open the can. "That's all me. With a little help from Pantene." She tossed her hair dramatically.

"No, really."

Shane chuckled.

"Really," Daisy said. She dumped the rinsed peaches in a bowl and handed it to Jessica. "There you go."

"Can I get a fork?"

Daisy opened a drawer, relieved she'd picked the right one. She held it out triumphantly. "Ta-dah."

Jessica's brows furrowed as she took the fork. "Thank you."

A few minutes later, they were all settled at the dining room table with Shane's fabulous ice cream sandwiches. Bryce had ice cream in his hair and all over his sleeves. Trav arrived back from his place just as Max was whispering in Daisy's ear, "I'm glad I get to spend a little more time with you."

Daisy didn't reply, instead smiling tightly at Trav.

"I saved one for you, bro," Shane said, offering the sandwich.

"I am way too cold for that," Trav said. "I need my wife to warm me up. C'mere, wife."

All eyes went to Daisy. She didn't like Trav's tone or the fact that he was putting them on display. She could feel the weight of Max's stare, and she didn't miss the cool, assessing look in Jessica's eyes. Given no choice, Daisy rose from her seat and slowly went to Trav's side.

He crushed her against his chest and whispered directly into her ear. "Tonight we share a bed."

She shivered at the intent she heard there. Goofy she could handle. Badass was much harder to resist.

He rubbed his hands up and down her arms. "I'm making her cold now. Let's move to the fire."

He grabbed her hand and pulled her with him. She followed him stiffly, still annoyed with his pushiness. She couldn't help but think about the night ahead. Bryce would sleep in his crib in the room with them. She sincerely hoped Trav didn't expect anything more from her than sleeping, especially in front of the baby. She reminded him of this fact once they were settled on the floor in front of the fire.

"He'll fall asleep at some point," he said simply. He pushed her hair over her shoulder and nuzzled her neck, his stubble scraping across the sensitive skin.

She closed her eyes over the heavenly sensation. "This isn't going to be a honeymoon," she mumbled.

His tongue traced the rim of her ear, and her entire body came to attention, heat flooding her. Who knew ears could be so sensitive? Her lips parted; she had to tell him...something. *Stop...soon.*

He pulled back, and she opened her eyes. He had a smug, knowing smile.

"We'll save the honeymoon for later," he said.

She shot him a dirty look for stopping with the ear thing and for being so smug. "Don't count on sex tonight," she said in what she hoped was a convincing voice.

He stroked her cheek. "You want me, sweetheart."

She straightened and stared straight ahead because she did. Too much. She'd promised herself not to fall in lust so easily, to listen to her brain. She wanted them to get to know each other better. That was why she'd told him they should go slow.

She was about to explain all this when he hooked one finger under her chin and turned her to face him. His eyes were hot on hers, and she waited, breathless. He moved to kiss her neck again, and her eyes closed on their own.

This is slow, she told herself. Deliciously slow.

His breath blew hot over her ear. "I could have you right here, right now."

Her eyes flew open. She swallowed hard. "Yeah, right."

Her body screamed, *Please do!*

"You could not," she added as his hands slid into her hair.

They were one room away from an audience.

His voice was husky. "I'm going to kiss you now."

He slowly leaned in. She should pull away. Now. Before— his mouth came down over hers. Lord, he was a good kisser. She gave in to it with a sigh. It was at once sweet and hot, and she never wanted it to end. Her hands fisted on his shirt as he deepened the kiss. He pulled her onto his lap, and she wrapped her legs around him, her throbbing center pressed against his hardness. She was burning up.

"Daisy," Shane called from the kitchen, "Bryce is getting fussy."

They broke apart and stared at each other, both out of breath.

He pressed the pad of his thumb to her lower lip. "Tonight you're mine."

She wished she could argue the point, but it was tough when she was plastered against him. Throbbing and panting. She nipped his thumb.

"Ow."

"I have to get Bryce before he starts screaming."

He put his hands on her hips and lifted her up. She smoothed her hair. He stood and straightened her shirt for her, one warm hand trailing down her bottom. She swatted his hand away. "Stop it."

He chuckled. "Yup. You want me bad."

"Oh, shut up."

She longed for a cool glass of water before facing the group in the kitchen. She hurried away, aggravated with herself for making things too easy for Trav. Charming men had always been her downfall. And bad boys. Trav was a terrible combination of every guy she'd ever fallen for with an unattractive dollop of demanding man. And where had it ever gotten her? Heartbroken and alone. Devastation, party of one.

She steeled her heart against him.

Her treacherous body ached for him.

Agh!

13

Right on schedule, Bryce launched into his early evening scream fest. Trav did the usual: pace back and forth with him. There was nothing else to do but ride it out with the boy. It was like he just had to have a good scream once a day.

Daisy came over to relieve him. She paced the length of the house—kitchen, dining room, living room—singing softly to Bryce. Trav took a seat in the living room, where Jessica and Max shared a low conversation on the sofa.

Jessica piped up. "Is the baby always like this?"

Bryce's howls got louder. Daisy must be getting closer.

"Nah," Trav said. "Not always. Just the witching hour."

Max cringed. "A whole hour?"

"Usually."

Daisy started her circuit around the room again. "We forgot the swing," she told him.

"Where did you leave it?" Jessica asked, looking from Trav to Daisy. "Isn't that kind of big to cart around?"

Daisy booked it out of there.

"Sometimes we take it to his grandparents' house," Trav said, quickly covering Daisy's slipup. The swing was at Daisy's apartment where it always was. "It helps him relax. You gotta get it cranking, though. He wants to really move."

A few minutes later, Daisy reappeared for another fast-paced stroll around the room.

"Trav says he's like this every night, yet you still call him Baby Delight?" Jessica asked.

Daisy stopped. "What would you call him?" she asked, an edge to her voice.

Jessica murmured something under her breath, and Daisy rushed forward, her face flushed with anger. *Damn.* Time for intervention. Trav neatly intercepted and took Bryce from Daisy's arms. He swung the boy up on his shoulders, hoping the new view would distract him. Bryce quieted down.

"You'd have to be a parent to understand why we'd still call him our Baby Delight," Trav said. "Right, hon?"

Daisy smiled at him gratefully. "Right."

"I guess biology will do that for you," Jessica said. "Excuse me while I save my hearing. Coming, Max?" She grabbed Max's arm, her manicured blood-red fingernails digging in.

"Ouch. I'm coming." Max got up and followed her out toward the kitchen.

Bryce started to fuss, and Trav pulled him back into his arms, bouncing him again.

Daisy shook her head. "I'm so tired of this screaming every freaking night. Do you think he'll ever outgrow it?"

"He'll probably outgrow it right around the time baby number two arrives."

"Very funny."

He wasn't joking. For once. He did a circuit of the room with Bryce. He was in it for the long haul. One day soon he hoped Daisy would appreciate that about him.

~

Daisy and Trav made pb&j sandwiches for dinner for their little group. Jessica ate more peaches rinsed of syrup. Just as they finished, the doorbell rang. Daisy went to answer it, wondering who it could be out there in the cold and dark.

"Look who we found on our doorstep," Maggie said. She

wore a puffy, red down parka and a purple knitted hat with a cheerful pom-pom on top. She looked like Santa with a grape for a head.

Rico pulled down the scarf that was wrapped around his face. It matched the yellow and red striped knitted hat with a pom-pom he wore. Looked like one of Maggie's creations. He carried an acoustic guitar case in one hand, a duffel bag in the other.

Jorge urged them both out of the cold. "Let's get inside."

"Yes, please come in! Omigod, did you walk here?" Daisy asked Rico.

"Yup," Rico said.

Trav appeared at Daisy's side, holding Bryce, whose face and hair were freshly rinsed from the sweet potatoes he'd enjoyed. "Hey. You need a place to crash?"

"Yeah. Thanks."

"I didn't say you could stay here," Trav said with a straight face.

Rico jabbed a finger at him. "Don't joke with a man who just hiked three miles across town in a blizzard."

"It's got to be more than that," Daisy said. "It takes me fifteen minutes to drive here from that side of town."

"I cut diagonally across town," Rico replied. "And I walked mighty fast." He rubbed his palms together and blew on them. "So what's the plan?"

"And who is this?" Jessica asked, crossing the room to get a good look at their guest.

"Rico del Toro, at your service," he said, kissing her hand.

She eyed him speculatively. "Very nice to meet you. I might have need of your service later this evening."

"You won't be disappointed," Rico promised with a leer. "And you are?"

"I'm Jessica Larsen," she snapped. "I take it you don't watch the show."

"Oh, that's right. The *Mornings with Jessica* show. Ah, man, you guys got stuck here in this storm."

"Yeah, and no power either," Jessica pouted.

"At least you got a generator over here," Rico said. "My apartment is like an icebox."

"Let's all sit down and get acquainted," Maggie said.

They took seats in the living room, on the furniture and some on the floor as they spilled over.

Max crossed the room to shake Rico's hand. "I'm Max Parker, producer at Rogue TV."

"Rico." He pumped Max's hand.

"Hey, Rico." Shane held up a hand in greeting.

"Shane! Glad to see you here. Now I know we won't starve."

Shane grinned. "I've got one leftover pumpkin cookie sandwich with your name on it."

"Yeah? Awesome." Rico stood to get it.

"I got it. Have a seat. You just hiked three miles in a blizzard."

"Thanks." Rico sat and looked around the room.

"So how do you play into this family drama?" Jessica asked.

Rico laughed. "I'm not family. Trav and I go way back."

"You are so family," Maggie said.

"Thank you, sweetheart," Rico said.

"Way, way back," Trav said. "We were friends back in Jersey. It all started when Rico asked me to be his boyfriend in kindergarten."

"There's a space in there," Rico said. "Boy friend."

"That's what I said, boyfriend."

"I had a pack of girls that followed me around in class," Rico explained. "Plus two older sisters. I really wanted a friend who was a boy."

Trav raised his brows. "He wanted me."

Rico shook his head. "Anyway, long story short. Ten years ago, Trav started Elegant Land Designs and called me up."

"I knew I wanted Rico as crew chief."

Rico spoke behind his hand in a stage whisper. "I'm the only guy he knows who speaks Spanish. He needed someone to talk to the crew."

Jessica scooted forward on the edge of her seat. "Are they illegals?"

Rico frowned. "Everything's aboveboard. They're legal, just not great at English."

Jessica sat back and examined her nails.

"That's not the only reason," Trav said.

"Yeah, he needed eye candy for his female clients."

Trav laughed heartily. "I'm the eye candy."

"Oh, really?" Daisy asked.

He reached over and squeezed her hand. "Not since I met you, darlin'."

Damn, he's good at adoring husband.

You're falling for a fantasy.

"Okay, then," she muttered.

Shane returned with the ice cream sandwich for Rico.

"Rico, I know you didn't drag that guitar clear across town for nothing," Maggie said. "Play something for us. You have a beautiful voice."

Rico nodded, finished off the sandwich in three bites, and fetched his guitar. He strummed a few notes, tuning it. "I write my own songs." He launched into the first song.

In Spanish.

His singing really was beautiful. Even with the little Spanish she knew, Daisy had no idea what he was singing. But it was heartfelt and sincere, the music gentle and rolling along. She picked up *beso* and *corazon*—kiss and heart. She smiled. His song was about love.

Trav set Bryce on a blanket on the floor and, without a word, lifted Daisy off the chair she was sitting on and sat there himself, with her on his lap. She opened her mouth to protest when he whispered in her ear. "Shhh…don't interrupt the music."

Maggie smiled over at them. Daisy felt her cheeks flush. Trav was overdoing the adoring husband act. Really. She was sure married people didn't sit in each other's laps normally. A warm hand slipped up the back of her shirt and rubbed slow circles. It was simultaneously relaxing and arousing.

They were in a room full of people. She subtly leaned back on his arm, pinning it still.

His other hand slid slowly across her hip, inching toward her inner thigh. She grabbed that hand and held it. He resumed the relaxing/arousing massage of her back. She considered moving to the floor, but...it felt so good.

The song ended, and everyone applauded.

"Encore!" Maggie exclaimed.

Rico launched into the next love song in Spanish, then another without further prompting. Trav never stopped touching her. His hand moved under her shirt, stroking slowly up and down her back. Another song, her shoulders. Another song, her neck, then stroking her hair. Half an hour later, Bryce was asleep and Daisy was completely relaxed, leaning her head back against Trav's shoulder. His arms were around her, his hands folded securely across her waist.

Rico looked up and smiled at everyone. "I've gone on too long. I put the baby to sleep."

Daisy sat up. "No one's complaining about that. I wish we could have you over to play for him every night."

"Every night?" Trav muttered.

Rico strummed a few notes. "Thank you."

Jorge tilted his head to the side and asked Rico a question in Spanish.

Rico lifted one shoulder up and down and answered in English. "They're about no one and everyone."

"Nobody special?" Jorge pressed. "All these songs about love, yet no love in your life? How do you speak of it so deeply?"

"I'm a deep man."

Trav snorted.

Daisy elbowed him. "I'm sure Rico is very deep when you get to know him. That was wonderful."

"Yes, lovely," Jessica said. "Do you know any songs in English?"

"I write in Spanish because I feel in Spanish," Rico replied.

"I feel in English," Jessica said, subtly leaning forward to present her breasts to him.

Rico put his guitar back in its case, not bothering to reply, though he did take in her check-these-out pose.

"Be right back," Maggie said. "Help me in the kitchen, love."

"Of course," Jorge murmured. He kissed her tenderly on the lips.

Trav's voice rumbled in her ear. "As long as we're all kissing."

Before she could say *we're not all kissing*, he'd turned her in his arms and kissed her. Already primed for more from his constant touching, she kissed him back. Someone wolf-whistled. Probably Rico.

Her cheeks burned, and she pushed against his chest. "You've got to stop doing that," she whispered fiercely. "Married people don't kiss that much."

"We will," Trav said with a pleased-with-himself smile.

She leaped off his lap and avoided looking at their audience. If he thought she was just going to fall into bed with him tonight, he was sorely mistaken. They had the baby and a house full of people. No way was she doing anything but sleeping.

She lifted Bryce off the blanket and carried him upstairs to settle him in his crib, her lips still tingling from that unexpected kiss.

She stopped short when she got inside Maggie's room. "What the hell?"

The crib was gone.

Trav! That presumptuous, smug, irritating man. No way in hell she was making tonight that easy for him.

Trav sprinted upstairs, knowing what Daisy would find.

She was pacing Gran's bedroom, eyebrows furrowed. He shut the door behind him.

She turned. "There you are! Where is it?"

"I moved it to Shane's room," Trav replied.

She looked to the ceiling, clearly reaching for calm. She leveled her gaze at him. "Which room?"

He led the way. She gently deposited Bryce into the crib and shut the door quietly behind her. She gestured for him to follow her back to Gran's room.

He knew he was in for it, but he followed her anyway. Once she got used to the idea, she'd thank him. He shut the door behind them.

She lifted one finger. "First of all, poor Shane! You know Bryce wakes up at three a.m. every night!"

He crossed to her and put a finger near her lips. "Shhh."

She smacked his finger away. "Don't you shush me! Now I'm going to have to sneak into Shane's room in the middle of the night to get Bryce back to sleep, and poor Shane's going to be up for no good reason!"

He pulled her across the room and into Gran's closet, shutting the door behind them. It was a small closet, and Gran's clothes pushed at them from both sides. It was also pitch black.

"What the hell, Trav?"

"You're just too loud. Do you want Jessica to hear us fighting? The closet at least puts us behind two closed doors." He inhaled her citrusy scent. She was so tantalizingly close. He could feel her heat and one breast pushed into his arm, but he didn't dare touch her in her current mood.

"Second of all…" He imagined she had two fingers in the air, but he couldn't see a damn thing. "We told Jessica we practice attachment parenting, that we have his crib in our room so we can respond to his cries immediately. What's she going to think when she sees his crib two rooms away and hears him wailing in the middle of the night?"

"She won't see his crib. I'll keep the bedroom doors shut and show her directly to my old room."

"Which one is yours?"

"First one on the left."

"Right across from where the baby is?" she exclaimed, way too loud.

He clamped a hand over her mouth. She bit his palm.

"Ow!"

"I cannot imagine a less appealing seduction scene, which I know is what's going on in that testosterone-polluted brain of yours, than to have Jessica Larsen down the hall, along with your brother and my ex-husband."

"And Rico."

"Yes! And Rico. Not to mention our baby, who'll wake the entire house, wondering why Mommy is taking so long to get to him."

"It won't take that long," Trav said. "Just down the hall."

She jabbed him in the chest. "You're getting up to get him. And you get him back to sleep and put him back in Shane's room. Think you can handle all that?"

Bryce hadn't yet spent the night with him, since Daisy usually nursed him back to sleep at night, but Trav would do anything to get Daisy alone in bed.

"Absolutely," Trav replied.

"Fine. Can we get out of the closet now?"

"I would love to see you come out of the closet," Trav joked.

"Keep it up, Mr. Stand-Up Comedian."

"Something is standing up."

She groaned, opened the closet door, and slipped downstairs.

He stayed behind to wait out his hard-on. That could've gone worse. He congratulated himself on winning round one.

14

Daisy returned to the living room to find a radio blaring "Copacabana" and Maggie pulling a stiff Jessica out of her beloved host chair.

"Come on, honey, we've got to loosen you up," Maggie was saying.

Jorge danced in the center of the room, doing some kind of box step involving jazz hands. Rico and Shane watched from the loveseat. Max sat on the floor, looking amused.

"I'm loose!" Jessica exclaimed.

"My kind of woman," Rico said under his breath.

"You either need to dance or get busy between the sheets," Maggie said. "When was the last time you were with a man? Honey, do you at least have a vibrator?"

Jessica's eyes bulged. Daisy stifled a laugh.

"I thought so." Maggie took both Jessica's hands and moved them side to side. "Nice and slow."

Jessica moved stiffly side to side.

"Try a little shimmy. Shake those shoulders." Maggie demonstrated.

Jessica gave a little shoulder shake while staring at the ceiling.

Maggie stopped moving. "I can see this is gonna take a little more than just a dance for you. Come with me."

She grabbed Jessica's hand and pulled her into the kitchen. Daisy almost felt sorry for Jessica, but she couldn't wait to see what Maggie did next.

"Help me make room," Jorge said to Rico and Shane. They pushed the furniture to the side to create a makeshift dance floor.

Rico bobbed his head in time to the music and wiggled his fingers at Daisy.

She giggled and joined him. Rico danced like he was born to it. Daisy pulled Shane over and danced with both of them.

Jessica returned holding a martini glass. "Cheers! Maggie made martinis! Who needs olives?" She drained the glass.

Maggie set two bottles of vodka on the mantel along with some glasses. "Anyone else for martinis?"

Jessica, Rico, and Max rushed over. Daisy didn't drink hard liquor since she was nursing, but was more than happy to let Jessica get plastered. The less observant she was, the better. She kept dancing with Shane, who did an awkward shuffle, nearly bumping into her.

A short while later, everyone but Daisy was martini-happy. They all danced to "Funkytown." Maggie was dancing with Jessica. She boxed her in with her hands while Jessica did a sensuous wave. Shane must've hit the vodka too because now he was flailing like a demented Muppet.

Trav came downstairs and shook his head. "Leave the room for five minutes and there's a mosh pit."

Rico and Shane started smashing into each other. Trav joined in with a chest bump to Rico. Rico went down and popped back up.

Daisy laughed. Trav headed straight for her, tucking his shoulder low, catching her at the stomach, lifting her up. She put her arms up in a V, feeling very prima ballerina as he spun her around. He set her down and danced with her slow and close even though the beat was fast. His hands were sliding lower on her back, pressing her closer, and she was torn between swatting his hands away or climbing him like a fire pole.

Jessica started dirty dancing with Max. Shane sang into a

pretend microphone that was his thumb, with Rico occasionally stepping in to share the mike.

A Hello Kitty bra flew through the air.

"Gran!" Trav scolded. "Put that thing back on!"

Jorge picked it up and started dancing with it between his
teeth. Maggie giggled. Not to be outdone, Jessica whipped out
her bra and flung it around Max's neck. He threw it to the side.

Trav looked to Daisy. "Your turn."

"That's not happening."

He spun her and dipped her. "It will."

"You'd love that, wouldn't you?"

He pulled her up. "I would." Then he sank his hands into
her hair and kissed her breathless.

The song changed to Janis Joplin's "Bobby McGee." Trav
pulled her close for another slow dance while everyone
danced wildly around them.

He kissed her neck, and shivers ran through her.

"Don't think you outsmarted me with that crib," she said.

He moved up to her ear, and her knees wobbled a bit.
"Never," he replied.

"We're not..." She trailed off as his mouth moved to her
jaw, coming closer and closer to her lips. "Rushing this," she
breathed.

He kissed her gently and nipped her lower lip. "We'll go
so-oo-oo-oo slow. You'll be begging for fast."

Her mouth dropped, temporarily at a loss for words.

Trav smirked.

So damn smug.

"I will never beg!" she hollered over the song that had just
ended. Her voice rang across the room. Her cheeks burned,
and she couldn't bear to make eye contact with anyone.

"You tell him," Maggie said. "Unless it's sexual, then
begging is fun." She looked around the room, nodding at
everyone.

Daisy groaned.

"Who wants to have sex with me?" Jessica asked in a loud
voice.

Rico raised his hand.

"You got it!" Jessica exclaimed. Then she jumped on Shane's back and rode him like a cowgirl.

Maggie grabbed the two empty bottles of vodka off the mantel. "My work here is done."

$\sim$

After they'd worn themselves out dancing, Gran and Jorge left, and Trav found some cards for poker. Daisy had just gone upstairs to get ready for bed, so Trav played one more round to give her time to get ready, because once he got up there, he didn't want to wait for anything. He lost the round despite the fact that Shane had the worst poker face in history and always gave away his hand. His mind just wasn't on the game. He couldn't wait to share a bed with Daisy tonight. His seduction plan was working. Daisy seemed happy, and she'd been so focused on him, she hadn't given Max a second glance.

He faked a yawn. "I'm beat. Let me set you guys up in your rooms for the night before I turn in."

"Omigod, what is it, nine o'clock?" Jessica asked.

"Be nice, Jess," Max said.

"Yeah, it's nine," Trav replied calmly. "I still have to take care of the generator, put out the fire, and set you guys up, so let's move it along."

"I'll take my old room," Shane said.

"We know, Shane; you're all set up," Trav said. Why did Shane say that? He just wanted to move this night along without any more questions or slipups.

Jessica pounced, still sharp despite pounding back the vodka. "Your old room? Did you used to live here? Is this where you grew up?"

"He means he stays with us a lot," Trav answered for Shane.

Shane nodded.

Jessica poked Shane in the chest. "Why would you spend

the night when you live so close?" She leaned into his chest and looked up at him. "Hmm? Answer that, Red."

Shane smiled down at her goofily. "It's Shane."

"He babysits," Trav said simply. "Shane, can you show them their rooms while I refuel the generator? Put Jessica across the hall from you." *The furthest from Gran's room.* "Rico, you got the sofa."

"That little thing?" Rico asked. "I'll take the floor. Good for the back."

Shane gestured for Jessica and Max to go ahead. "After you."

Jessica and Max shared a low conversation on the stairs on their way up.

Shane called down to Rico. "I'll toss down a pillow and blanket for you."

"Thanks," Rico said. "Trav, you need any help?"

"Yeah, actually, can you put out the fire while I do the generator thing?"

Rico saluted. "You got it, *jefe.*"

"What's the word for 'insolent employee' in Spanish?" Trav asked.

"I do not know this word," Rico said with a straight face.

Trav chuckled and fetched his jacket. He grabbed a flashlight from the kitchen and headed into the icy cold, thinking only of the warm, sexy woman who awaited him upstairs.

Daisy scoped out the bedroom she supposedly shared with Trav. She hadn't taken a good look at it before because she'd been so focused on Bryce and, later, her shock that the crib wasn't where it should be. Okay, this was beyond awkward. This was...*bizarro.* An iron four-poster bed with pink silk scarves tied around one post. She didn't even want to think about what Maggie and Jorge did with them. A floral comforter, with matching shams on the pillows, and several knitted throw pillows with Santa and his reindeer going across them, even though it was February.

She glanced at the nightstand. No, that was snooping.

Maybe just one peek.

Strawberry-flavored lube, pink fuzzy handcuffs, foam rollers, and a shower cap. Daisy shut her eyes tightly, working to erase the vivid images tumbling through her mind of senior citizen nooky. *Rainbows, unicorns, sparkle fairies.* Not working.

That's what you get for snooping.

She was too restless to lie in bed.

Trav would be coming up soon, with all his expectations. She didn't like the way he assumed she'd sleep with him just because they had a baby and were getting married. She snorted. She was being ridiculous. What was the big deal? Sleep with your future husband. It's what people do. A shot of adrenaline ran through her, and she fought the urge to run.

She moved on to the closet and swung open the door. No wonder she'd been squished up against Trav in here, it was jam-packed with clothes. She wondered where Jorge kept all his clothes. If anyone from *Mornings with Jessica* had looked in the closet, they would've seen right away that it wasn't Daisy's house. The clothes were way too small for Daisy's five foot six. From the one light on the nightstand she could just make out the miniskirts (super mini on Daisy), blouses, and, though she hated to say it, old lady housedresses, that all but screamed Maggie.

Daisy smiled as an idea formed in her mind. A very naughty idea. She gathered the things she'd need and headed for the bathroom, giggling to herself.

15

Trav walked into the bedroom, already stripping out of his thermal Henley. He got close to the bed and realized Daisy wasn't in it. Must be in the bathroom. She'd left the light on the nightstand on. He took a moment to check out the bed they'd sleep in—Gran's bed. Wrong, wrong, wrong. Santa and his reindeer had to go. Tonight they'd be on the naughty list for sure.

He stripped the bed of the Santa pillows, weird flowery pillow covers, and flipped the comforter over so it was on the plain white side. That was better. An image of Daisy's golden hair spread over the pillow, looking up at him, had him stripping out of his jeans. He dove under the blankets. The heat was on, but it was still cold, the old house drafty. He couldn't wait to see what Daisy wore to bed.

Several minutes later, Daisy walked into the bedroom. He bit back a laugh as she approached the bed. She wore Gran's flannel nightgown, which ended at her knees, rollers in her hair, and a shower cap. This woman killed him.

He caught her smug smile before she turned off the light and slid into bed.

He reached for her in the dark. "Gran?"

She giggled.

"Oh, Gran, you turn me on so much." He rubbed his

hands up and down her back. "Is this one hundred percent flannel?"

Another burst of giggles. She buried her head in his chest, shaking with laughter, obviously trying to keep the volume down with their guests.

"Your shower cap is so smooth on my chin."

She smacked his chest. "Stop," she wheezed.

"You're the one that dressed for the occasion. If I'd known, I would've put on the yellow ruffly robe."

They cracked up. They'd seen, on more than one occasion, Jorge hanging out late in the morning in Gran's ruffled robe.

He stroked her back until the laughter subsided. She lifted her chin and looked up at him through the dim light from the moonlight filtering in the window. She was so damn beautiful even in a shower cap.

"I think a marriage with laughter is the best kind," he said. "It'll be good, Daze. I know you have doubts about us, but it'll be good."

She surprised him by putting her hand on his cheek. "You're a good man."

"Yes."

She giggled. "Yes?"

"You're good too, woman."

"Kiss me."

He cupped her cheek, his hand hitting shower cap and rollers, and met her lips in a gentle kiss. She returned it enthusiastically, her tongue delving into his mouth. That hit him like a lit firecracker. The kiss turned hot as his hands ran up and down her curves, stopping to linger at her breasts, caressing them through the flannel. Geez, the flannel. He had to get this stuff off her.

He nudged her onto her back and slipped the cap from her head. He pulled back to slowly undo each roller, watching her golden hair drop, piece by piece, into a golden wave across the pillow. Just like he'd imagined.

"You're so beautiful, Daze."

"So are you."

He grinned. "I know."

She laughed, and he kissed that smiling mouth, his hand running through her silky hair. Her hands ran over his bare back, and he couldn't wait to get her out of that flannel, to feel skin on skin. *Slow.* He nibbled and licked his way down her neck, and she tilted her head to give him better access. He inhaled her citrusy scent, his hand slowly working up the flannel nightgown. She pushed it back down.

He kissed her some more, coaxing her in the best way he knew how, with long, slow, deep kisses. She moaned. Now her hands were running over him everywhere, which he took as a go. Slowly, he worked his hand back down to the hem of her nightgown.

She tore her mouth from his. "Trav, this is a bad idea."

"It's a very good idea."

"I promised myself I wouldn't have sex again until I got to know the person."

He nibbled on her ear, ran his tongue around the shell, and blew gently over it. "You do know me."

"Not that much. We never went on a date or anything."

He stifled a groan. Like he could take her on a date now. *Slow. Patience.* He felt like a horny teenager begging for it.

"What do you want to know?" he asked. "I'll tell you anything." He couldn't stop touching her. He stroked her hair and kissed her temple, her jaw, her throat, her collarbone. She tasted so good.

She was quiet.

He looked up. "Daze?"

Her eyes were closed. "Hmmm…" she murmured, not seeming too worried about their getting-to-know-you date.

He took advantage of that, returning to that luscious mouth and taking his fill. She moaned again.

He slipped a hand under the gown and slid it up her inner thigh, massaging her over a tiny scrap of panty. She was hot and wet. He groaned and pulled back to work off the flannel nightgown.

She wore only a pink thong. He just about lost it right there.

"That's no granny panties," he quipped.

She giggled. "Nope."

He pulled her close so they lay facing each other, skin on skin, and kissed her again, pushing his leg between hers, pressing at her center. Her nails were running up and down his back, making him crazy. He pulled back just enough to caress her breast, pinching a nipple. He jolted in surprise as something wet hit him. Milk had come out.

Her hand flew to her breast.

He laughed. "I milked you like a cow."

She scowled, rolled away, and gave him her back.

Shit.

Daisy was so embarrassed. Just add this to the long list of things she'd written about in rapturous terms on her blog that couldn't compare to her reality.

Trav curled up behind her and brushed her hair back. "I'm sorry. I shouldn't have said that."

"No, you're right. I am like a cow. Moo. Just one more way my blog bites me in the ass. Post-baby sex sucks."

"I wouldn't say sucks." He rested his hand across her stomach, and she immediately sucked in her gut.

She lay there fuming, embarrassed, and so freaking tired. Where was that damn nightgown? She sat up, groped blindly for it over the covers, got really cold, and lay down again. *Dammit.* She didn't want to spend the night naked with this irritating man.

He *laughed* at her.

"Can you get that nightgown?" she asked.

"No."

She debated getting out of bed to fetch it from wherever he'd tossed it, but it was so cold out of the covers, and it was really warm lying like this with Trav holding her. His chest warmed her back, his legs tucked against hers. She could do without the hard rod jabbing into her hip, but they were practically naked.

She exhaled sharply. "I just want to sleep."

"Me too."

A beat passed. His hand crept upward.

"Don't touch my breasts."

His hand stilled.

They lay there quietly in the dark. She took a deep breath, starting to relax again. His hand crept downward. She stilled.

"Pretend I'm not here," he told her.

She giggled.

His hand crept a little lower.

A little lower.

She held her breath.

That's the spot. She sighed. His fingers stroked and made lazy circles. He really did have magic fingers.

His voice rumbled low in her ear. "Open your legs."

A tremor ran through her. She opened for him, and he took full advantage. His fingers became more demanding, massaging and circling her center, slipping inside her. She bucked, unable to stay still under the onslaught of sensation.

He just kept going, steady, relentless, pushing her closer and closer to the brink. She fought to keep from moaning out loud, moving now automatically with his hand, instinctively seeking more of his touch. She broke in a surge of sensation, crying out and shuddering against him. He slowed his hand, but didn't stop, letting her ride out every wave of pleasure. Finally she quieted, rolled to her back, and reached for him.

He smiled down at her.

She smiled back. "You're still here."

He kissed her tenderly. "I am."

She peeled off her thong, and he stripped off his briefs. He reached to the floor and snagged a condom. He must have stashed one in his jeans earlier. She had no time to decide if she was mad or thankful for that presumption because then he was back, pressing slowly inside her. Oh. My. God. It had been so damn long. And he was so thick and hot and hard.

She moaned, and he slid an inch further.

She bucked her hips, urging him on. He didn't move.

"Trav, you're making me crazy."

"That's the idea." He slid in a little more, but not enough. Not nearly enough.

"Please." She grabbed his ass and pulled. He slid an inch and stopped.

"I told you I'd make you beg."

"Don't fuck with a sex-deprived woman." She wrapped her legs tight around him and pulled hard. That got him moving.

"That's the perfect woman to fuck with," he croaked.

She closed her eyes as they moved in a slow and steady rhythm, feeling the sensation build deliciously again. His lips met hers, his tongue thrusting in her mouth, matching the thrusts of his body.

She broke the kiss. "Faster," she told him, digging her nails into his back.

"There's no rush," he told her, moving at his slow and steady pace.

He was making her crazed. She squeezed him internally as he thrust in, bringing them both intense pleasure. He groaned and slowly pulled out. She kept it up, watching him, the strain on his face from holding back, until he suddenly pumped hard and fast, just like she liked it. She hung on tight; moments later, she shuddered again, and he let go with her.

They lay there, panting, Trav still plastered on top of her.

"That didn't suck," she told him.

He groaned next to her ear.

She laughed.

16

Three a.m. came early, bringing with it Bryce's wail, but Trav didn't care that he had nighttime baby duty. It was all worth it for that night with Daisy. He tiptoed down the hallway and couldn't help the goofy grin that spread across his face. Now *that* was a night he'd remember. No question that marrying Daisy was the right decision.

He slipped into Shane's room, passed his snoring brother, and scooped up Bryce. "Let's go," he whispered.

He brought Bryce back to Daisy. She nursed him, half asleep, propped up on some pillows, and handed him back. "You have to burp him before you put him to bed," she said before she flopped back under the blankets.

He patted Bryce's back as he paced the hallway, hoping the boy kept it quiet. He glanced at the closed bedroom doors. He just had to get rid of husband number one, and he and Daisy would be golden.

A few minutes later, Bryce burped, and Trav settled him back in his crib. He shut the door quietly behind him and headed back to Daisy. If he didn't know she was already so exhausted, he'd wake her for round two. Instead, he slipped under the covers and tucked her against his side, breathing in the scent of Daisy and sex, a potent combination. Things were finally on track for them, he thought just before he fell asleep.

Only a few hours later, as the sun began to rise, Trav slipped out of bed, knowing he had to get to work clearing out the snow. Daisy slept soundly, curled on her side. He grabbed the flannel nightgown from the floor and stuck it on the nightstand in front of her so she wouldn't be cold when she got up. Even with the lack of sleep, he was practically whistling as he headed downstairs. He couldn't wait to have Daisy again. It had been good. Better than good. Fucking phenomenal. He was a lucky man.

He stopped in the living room, where Rico was sleeping sprawled on the floor, one arm and leg sticking out of the blanket. He nudged him with his foot. "Wake up."

Rico turned the other way.

Trav walked to his other side, squatted down, and sang in his friend's ear in a near perfect impersonation of Rico's mom. "Ri-co, *mallorcas* for breakfast."

Rico's eyes flew open. Seeing Trav, he groaned and gave him a shove, knocking him off his haunches. "You suck. I haven't had good *mallorca* since I left Jersey. Whadda ya want?"

Trav chuckled. Mrs. del Toro liked to buy fresh *mallorcas,* a sweet bread pastry topped with confectioner's sugar, every weekend. Least she used to before she moved back to Puerto Rico.

"Get up," Trav said. "We've got plowing to do."

Rico pushed to a sitting position and scrubbed a hand over his face.

"Looks like you didn't get your beauty sleep."

Rico eyed him. "What are you so fucking cheerful about? What time is it, six?"

"Six thirty." He grinned. "And I'm just happy to see you."

"Yeah, right." Rico pushed a hand through his hair. "Wait a minute, I know that face. You got laid."

Trav just smiled.

Rico stood and stretched. "I told you if you backed off, she'd come to you."

Trav stood and smiled to himself. He helped her along, but, yeah, she came all right.

Rico lowered his voice and glanced toward the stairs. "Jessica paid me a visit in the middle of the night."

Trav raised a brow. "Yeah, how was that?"

His friend shook his head. "She's wearing that dress, commando. Then she lifts her dress to show me her bare ass, tells me she's a very bad girl, and asks me to spank her."

Trav barked out a laugh of surprise.

"Shhhh!"

"What'd you do?"

"You know I could never hit a woman."

Trav knew it. That's why it was so funny. He could just imagine the look on Rico's face.

They headed to the front door and put their boots on.

"Even if a woman *asked* me to," Rico added. "You know my dear, sweet mama would stretch her arm all the way from Puerto Rico and smack me upside the head if I raised a hand to a woman."

"You're a mama's boy."

"Proud of it."

They grabbed their coats and gear and headed across the street for his work truck.

"So now that you gave Daisy the milk, she'll want to buy the cow," Rico said. "Make an honest man out of you."

Trav choked on a laugh. The cow had almost killed the whole thing last night.

"Let's hope so," Trav managed.

They plowed his and Gran's driveway and dropped rock salt down to prevent ice from forming. Then they cleared the way down Catoonah Street, Elm Street, and onto Park Ave, where Ry lived. Main Street would be cleared by the town early this morning. He cleared Ry's driveway, and then he and Rico got out and shoveled the sidewalk, tossing down some rock salt. They made their way to their clients in town, stopping for a few elderly people who weren't clients but needed to be able to get out in case of emergency.

He circled back around to Ry's house and stopped to check in. Liz had hot coffee and warm blueberry muffins waiting for them in the kitchen.

"You need any help with the emergency shelter?" Trav asked. He knew Ry would help out Chief Bailey with the town's shelter at the high school and, as soon as he could, get over to Fieldridge, where he was a cop, and help out there too.

"Glenn and I are setting up the shelter just as soon as the roads are clear from Main Street back to High Ridge," Ry said. "I've got the keys to the school. Generator's already on-site. Supply closet is well stocked. I'll stop by on the way there to get you guys. We could use extra hands. Then we can split up to check on the seniors and transport those that need it over to the shelter."

Trav lifted his mug in a toast. "Sounds like a plan."

Ry ran down the list of seniors that he knew needed help, and Trav filled him in on who they'd already seen on their morning plow run.

One of the crew guys came in. "Any more muffins?"

Ry looked over to the empty plate of muffins. "Nope. There's chocolate chip cookies in the freezer."

"That sounds like the breakfast of champions." The guy pulled the plastic container from the freezer and headed back to the living room. The noise level rose as the crew dug into the cookies. It sounded like a party out there.

"This coffee is making me feel human again," Rico said, getting up for a refill.

Ry lowered his voice. "Wasn't today supposed to be the day you got married?"

"Yeah. We'll have to wait. The justice of the peace can't make it through this mess."

"It'll happen," Ry said reassuringly. His bro always could read him like an open book.

Trav's voice came out hoarse. "What if she backs out?"

"She won't," Liz said, walking into the kitchen with some empty coffee mugs. "Daisy never breaks a promise."

"Good to know," Trav said.

"The guys are getting a little rowdy from all that sugar," Liz said, looking worried. "You should've given them some fruit instead."

Ry shrugged. Liz scowled and took a deep breath in and out. A ghost of a smile crossed his brother's face for some reason. He should know better than to mess with an angry woman.

"I'd better check on Daisy and Bryce," Trav said. "Thanks for breakfast, Liz."

"Yes, thank you," Rico said.

Liz smiled. "You're welcome. It's the least we can do after you cleared all that snow for us."

"Yeah, thanks, guys," Ry said. "I'll stop by in a bit." He snagged Liz around the waist and pulled her close. "C'mere, you."

Liz giggled.

Trav left before he could witness the seduction scene. Rico followed close behind.

"Your brother's got it bad," Rico said once they were back in the truck. He took a bite of cookie he must have snagged on the way out. "I've never seen him like that."

It was true. Ry couldn't get enough of Liz. Now that Trav had been with Daisy, he knew exactly how Ry felt. Funny how that worked out—two brothers with two sisters. Too bad there wasn't a third sister for Shane.

Trav revved the truck and blasted the heat. "The love stick hit him hard."

"I'd say it knocked him out cold," Rico replied.

Trav snorted. "It had to. He's got a really hard head."

Daisy woke to an empty bed and heaved a huge sigh of relief that she didn't have to face Trav this morning. Last night was an impulse, a matter of circumstances throwing them together, and she should know better by now than to act on impulse. Her whole life was a train wreck because of her impulsive nature. A surprise pregnancy, a talk show interview based on a fictional blog, sleeping with Trav (again!)—impulse, impulse, impulse.

She slipped into Shane's room, surprised she hadn't heard

Bryce awake by now. *Awww.* Shane was sleeping with one arm outstretched, his fingers through the bars of the crib; Bryce was holding his finger. She quietly backed out of the room.

She'd just grab something for breakfast really quick. She was starving.

In the hallway she passed Jessica wrapped in a towel, with another towel wrapped around her wet hair turban style.

"Thank God you had hot water," Jessica said. "The trains *have* to be running this morning. Any word on when the power's coming back?"

"I have no idea," Daisy said.

"You might want to wait on the shower," Jessica said. "I ran out of hot water at the end."

Daisy bit her tongue over the harsh retort waiting there. Jessica *would* use all the hot water during a power outage in a house full of six adults and a baby.

"*Ciao!*" Jessica breezed past, went into her room, and shut the door behind her.

Daisy headed downstairs and ran into Max in the kitchen. Her heart slammed into her throat. She did *not* want to be alone with him. On the other hand, she didn't want him to think she was bolting because of him.

Max held up his cell phone. "Still no signal. Where's Travis?"

She shrugged, then remembered she probably should know where her husband was. "He's out...shoveling snow. Plowing. His landscape business plows in the winter."

Good job, Daisy, you remembered what your husband does for a living.

She peeked in the refrigerator, grabbed some cheese and bread. Cheese sandwich for breakfast. She should probably offer him food. "Want a cheese sandwich?"

"Sure."

She made the sandwiches and joined him at the table. She wondered how long it would take Jessica to make an appearance. She'd even take that woman in the morning over breakfast alone with Max.

"Do you remember when I shoplifted from FAO Schwarz?" Max asked.

She rolled her eyes. "Yes. If you had ended up in jail for that stupid—"

"Don't turn me in!" He grinned. "I wonder what ever happened to Holiday Sparkle Tiffany."

She took a sip of water. "You didn't throw that ridiculous doll out?"

"I didn't want anyone to see me with it. I left it in the bottom of the dresser when I left for the summer."

She shook her head, reluctantly smiling at the image of Max stashing Tiffany in his college dorm dresser. "The cleaning crew probably tossed it when they cleaned your room."

He met her eyes. "You wore the just-for-you matching sparkle ring on a necklace for a while."

She lost her smile. It had been her engagement ring. Now she was a single mother with another man's child, and that ring was long gone. She went back to her sandwich, trying to shake off the unwelcome memory.

"I just wanted you to feel special since I couldn't afford a ring," Max said.

He pulled something shiny from his pocket. She slowly set her sandwich down. Oh. My. God. The sparkle ring—a giant fake emerald set on a sparkly snowflake. She'd loved it in all its gaudiness, until one day she hadn't.

Her throat tightened. "You kept it," she choked out.

"I did," he said quietly. "When you threw it at me, I held onto it. I hoped one day our timing would be better."

Dammit. Her eyes watered. She closed her eyes for a moment, lost in old memories again. The day he'd ended their marriage.

Bryce's wail carried from upstairs. Reality hit again.

She exhaled sharply. "Max, your timing sucks."

She started to leave, and he grabbed her arm. "It's not too late for us. I meant what I said last night."

Hello? She was *married*. Sort of. She didn't want to talk

about her and Max again. She didn't want to be tempted with what might have been.

Shane arrived with Bryce in his arms. The boy looked calmly around. "He's hungry," Shane said, handing him over.

"Thanks for getting him," Daisy said. "I hope he didn't wake you last night."

"Not at all. I'm a deep sleeper."

"Lucky." She turned to Max before she took Bryce upstairs. "I hope we can still work together."

"Absolutely," Max said. "Call me in a few days after things are back to normal, and we'll do lunch."

She nodded and left to take care of Bryce. After he nursed, she changed his diaper and dressed him in a spare outfit she kept in the diaper bag. She did an abbreviated infant massage session, keeping him in his clothes. At home, she would've done the massage with almond oil on his bare skin, but it was too chilly in the room to do the full treatment. Starting at his forehead, she rubbed in small circles, onto the longer strokes on his arms, down his tummy, and onto his legs. They'd taken a mommy/baby class a few months back, and it had made a world of difference with his colic, dramatically decreasing his crying sessions.

When she finished, she brushed her teeth with one finger while holding Bryce on her hip, then returned downstairs. She walked past Max sitting on the loveseat, staring at his cell, and headed to the kitchen to find some baby food for Bryce. Shane was out back. Steam billowed out from the grill.

Max walked in. She tensed. She didn't know what to say in the face of his declaration of love. He'd put her in a really awkward position. The fact was Trav didn't love her. He stupidly thought love was made up by corporations to sell more cards. Was she giving up on having love in her life?

Before she had to come up with something to say to Max, Trav was back, his face ruddy from the cold. "Woo, it's as cold as a polar bear's ass."

Daisy laughed, and the tension she felt from Max's presence vanished. That was one good thing about Trav. He was always casual, taking things in stride. She didn't have to worry about an awkward morning after with him.

"Morning, honey." Trav gave her a smacking kiss on the lips and leaned over to buzz Bryce on the cheek.

"Morning," Daisy replied, glad for his return. She didn't want to be tempted by Max. The two men eyed each other.

Max took a step back. "We'll talk soon, Daisy."

She felt Trav's sharp gaze. "Sure," she said softly.

17

"What did Max say to you?" Trav asked.

She kept her focus on Bryce, settling him into his high chair. She couldn't tell Trav that Max wanted a second chance. Trav would probably kick his ass. It was nothing. She wasn't going to give Max a second chance, and that was that.

"Nothing," she said.

Trav narrowed his eyes.

"Where's Rico? I thought he'd be with you."

He pulled off his hat and gloves. "He's upstairs getting a shower. You sure it's nothing? You looked upset when I came in."

"I'm fine." She fetched a jar of pears and a bib. "How're things out there?"

"You don't owe Max anything." Trav's voice was hard, and his hands were in fists. "If he's harassing you, I'll send him over to Ry's place."

Daisy shook her head. "He's not harassing me. It's just awkward is all. Don't do anything, please."

He exhaled sharply. "We stopped in at Liz and Ry's place. Liz had hot coffee and warm blueberry muffins."

Of course she did.

Daisy raised her brows. "Guess you're marrying the wrong sister."

He wrapped an arm around her shoulders, pulling her close. "I'm pretty sure I got the right one." He grinned devilishly. "Besides, Ry got to her first."

She pushed him away, but he didn't budge. He tipped up her chin and gave her a tender kiss. Last night's heat flooded through her.

He smiled. "Ah, I wish I could stay and follow up on that look in your eyes, but I have to head out soon with Ry to set up the emergency shelter. You gonna be all right sitting tight here?"

She pulled up a chair next to Bryce. "Sure."

"Let me," Trav said.

She handed over the bib and watched as he expertly attached it and popped open the jar of pears. The differences in Max and Trav were fresh in her mind. Trav worked hard, and got things done, but he'd never laid his feelings bare like Max had.

"How do you feel about me?" she asked.

He looked over his shoulder at her warily. "I feel good."

"Good," she echoed.

"Yeah." He gave Bryce a spoonful of pears and turned back to her. "How do you feel about me, Miss Touchy-feely?" he asked, his eyes dancing with humor.

Always with the jokes. She never felt like she got through that facade. "I feel like you're a goof."

"A goof?" He set the baby spoon down and leaned close, his voice low and husky. "That's not what you said last night." His lips met hers, one hand sliding into her hair, holding her there as he kissed her, slow and tender. She let herself go, falling into the sensation, remembering the pleasure he'd brought her last night. He slowly pulled back, and she blinked.

One corner of his mouth kicked up. "I seem to remember some begging on your part."

"I did not!"

He closed his eyes and said in a soft, breathy voice, "Trav, please, *please*, give it to me."

She tossed her hair over her shoulder and shifted away. "You're delusional."

He turned her and pulled her into his arms. "I'm damn lucky." He kissed her until she melted against him.

"Da-da-da-da!" Bryce screamed, pounding his spoon on the tray.

They straightened and looked at each other and then at Bryce. Did he really just say da-da?

Trav recovered first. "That's right, Bryce. Da-da. What a smart boy! Did you hear that, Daze?"

She smiled and leaned against his shoulder. "Yeah, I heard it. His first word. Now we just have to work on mama."

Trav stood and kissed Bryce's hair. "We'll get there. Right, Brycey boy?"

Bryce opened his mouth. "Ah-ah-ah."

Trav took the hint, sat down, and spooned in more pears. He turned back to her. "I'll reschedule the justice of the peace as soon as the power's back up."

She nodded, coming down from her momentary joy. She was tired of fighting him. And she knew it wasn't fair to compare the two men, but Max had never been demanding. Her time with him back in college had been easy, fun, exhilarating. He was her first love. Everything had been perfect, except for the way it ended. It didn't feel the same way with Trav. With him, she felt stuck. Tied by Bryce. A part of her longed for the freedom she feared she'd never have again.

She needed time to figure things out. It was easy to fall in lust, but that wasn't enough for a marriage.

Trav glanced over his shoulder. "I see steam coming out of your ears from all that thinking. What's up?"

"Nothing."

"Okay." He went back to feeding Bryce.

Trav was always so agreeable. It bugged her. She knew he used to be an angry rebel. Now he was all smooth surface.

"You ever get mad?" she asked.

He lifted one shoulder up and down. "Most things roll right off my back. And the stuff that doesn't, well, I've learned to let that go too."

"I remember you in high school. You were wild, adventurous—all those pranks. If you'd been in my grade, I would've joined you."

"Yeah? I would've liked that."

"So what happened to that Trav?"

He spooned more pears and wiped Bryce's face with the end of the bib. "He grew up. I know better than to screw up my life getting tangled with the law. My brother is a cop, for crying out loud. Why? What do you want to do, sneak out at night with your parents' liquor?"

She paused. That had been her favorite thing to do in high school. That and driving really, really fast. "No, of course not."

He held up his palms. "What you see is what you get."

"Seems kind of boring."

"Boring!" He looked seriously offended.

She put her hand on his arm. "Don't look so wounded. I know we're parents now, but some part of me still craves adventure, a little bit of freedom. I sorta feel like I lost the old Daisy. I mean, is this all there is? Living and working with the people I've known my entire life?"

"Da-da-da-da!" Bryce hollered.

Trav smiled and spooned more pears into Bryce's wide-open mouth. "What's wrong with that? You've got family and friends. It's a good place for Bryce to grow up. You want to move back to the city or something?"

She did miss the city, the nonstop action, always someone new to meet. But she couldn't afford it, and Trav's business was here. She felt so restless and stuck. And she couldn't place all the blame at Trav's door for that. He couldn't help it if he was small town and liked it that way. It was good that he loved Clover Park. They had lots of family here to help with Bryce. And she should be glad he wasn't wild anymore. Stable was good when you had a kid.

"No, I don't want to move," she finally said. "I don't know what's wrong with me. I think being stuck in this blackout is making me restless."

He turned and kissed her softly. "Whatever you want,

Daze, I'll make it happen. You want to dance on top of a bar, you got it. You want to make out in the back of the Subaru, you got it." He gave her that charming, lopsided smile.

"But what do you want? You can't just do whatever I want."

"I want what you want."

She groaned. She didn't want someone who just did whatever she wanted. She wanted a partner, one that excited her, that she could fight with and have amazing make-up sex with. Like she used to do with Max. *Shit.* Where had that come from? She wasn't eighteen anymore. Trav was the kind of husband she should want—sensible, responsible, good sense of humor.

Fantastic in bed. *There is that.*

"I just want you to be yourself," she said.

His brows crinkled in confusion. "I am."

"Isn't this cozy?" Jessica asked, appearing in the doorway.

Daisy startled. How much had Jessica heard?

"Mind if I join you?" Jessica asked in an artificially sweet voice.

"Have a seat," Trav said.

Jessica flopped down in a chair. "I'd kill for a cup of coffee."

"Liz has hot coffee," Daisy said. "Just a few blocks away."

"Oh! Could you get me some?" Jessica asked.

"I'm not up to walking in the cold with a baby," Daisy said. "You can find it. Cross over to Elm, go three blocks, and turn down Park. Number nineteen."

Jessica turned a pouting face to Trav. "Would you drive me?"

"I need to get over to the emergency shelter soon. Ry's picking me up."

"Isn't Ryan with Liz?" Jessica asked.

"Yeah."

"Then ask him to bring some coffee with him," Jessica said brightly.

"My cell's not working," Trav said.

Jessica threw her hands up. "I've got to get back to the

city! I've already missed my morning training session with Carlos. Max!"

Max rushed into the room, and Daisy had to wonder if he'd been eavesdropping nearby.

"I have to get back to the city," Jessica said. "Within the hour. Make it happen."

"There's only so much I can do," Max said soothingly. "We'll get there soon."

Jessica's nostrils flared. "I missed my morning workout. I haven't had my wheatgrass smoothie. My metabolism is off kilter as we speak. That makes for a very unhappy host. You know our show requires me to be in top shape."

Trav cracked an imaginary whip behind Jessica's back. Daisy stifled a laugh.

"Are the trains running?" Max asked Trav.

"Cells are still down, so I don't know," Trav said. "I'll ask Ry. He's got the police radio."

"Max, what about Nielsen?" Jessica asked in a small voice.

Daisy's jaw dropped, shocked to hear Jessica's voice sound so feeble after her previous tirade. "Who's Nielsen?"

"It's her cat," Max said. He turned to Jessica and spoke in a soothing tone. "I'm sure he's fine. You said you fed him before you left."

Jessica blinked rapidly. "I know it's only been a day, but if I'm stuck here…" Her lower lip quivered. "There's no one to feed him."

"Maybe a friend with a key to your place could check in on him," Daisy said.

Jessica pulled a long face. "I don't have any friends…with keys, I mean." She crossed her arms, hugging herself. "And I can't call them anyway because there's no cell service."

"Maggie has the emergency radio," Daisy said. "Maybe she could tell you if the trains are running."

"Max, go!" Jessica ordered. "Don't come back until you have an answer."

Max grimaced. "Which house is it?"

"Right across the street," Trav said. "White house on the corner, can't miss it."

Max left without another word.

Daisy sent Trav a significant look. Jessica looked dangerously close to tears. Trav sighed and handed Daisy the baby spoon.

"Come on," he said to Jessica. "Let's get coffee."

Jessica sniffled. "Thank you." She followed him out the door.

Daisy felt a little bad for Trav, but it was such a relief to have both Jessica and Max out of the house.

She gave Bryce a spoonful of pears. "Ma-ma," she told him. "Ma-ma."

"Da-da."

18

Trav drove to his brother's house with a chatty Jessica in the passenger seat. He barely heard her as he puzzled over what Daisy wanted from him. She acted like there was a hidden Travis inside of him. He *was* being himself.

"Look at me; I've just about talked your ear off about hot yoga," Jessica said just as they pulled up to Ry's house.

He turned off the ignition and scowled. He meant it when he said what you see is what you get. He didn't play games. He liked things direct and straightforward.

"Are you okay?" Jessica asked.

He turned to her. "Do you ever feel like you're not being yourself? Like there's a part of yourself you don't show the world?"

She studied him. "Do you?"

"No."

"Well," she said slowly, "some people put on their best front and hide their true feelings. Like if you were maybe jealous of Daisy and Max, but you didn't want to show it."

"Who said anything about jealousy? I don't have anything to be jealous about. She's my wife."

"It's not my place to say," Jessica said softly, "but you couldn't have missed the way he looks at her."

He frowned, pushed open the truck door, and slammed it behind him.

Jessica caught up with him on the sidewalk. "I'm sorry. I've overstepped."

He stopped on Ry's front porch. "What do you know about Max?"

"He's a great producer. He could've done on-camera work, but he says he likes to order everyone else around, not take orders." She laughed. "Who could blame him? He does very well for himself, lives in a nice place on the Upper West Side. Anything else you'd like to know?"

He blew out a breath in frustration. "Why are women so damn confusing?"

"Did you and Daisy have a fight?" Her eyes gleamed with this juicy bit.

He quickly realized his mistake in letting his guard down. Wouldn't she just love the ratings on a trouble-in-paradise angle? Hell, she'd named her cat Nielsen. "No. We're fine. Forget I said anything."

He rang the bell. She rested a leather gloved hand on his arm. "If you ever need to talk, I'm all ears."

He'd just bet she was. Ry answered the door. "I said I'd come get you in a bit."

Trav jerked his thumb at Jessica. "Jessica needs coffee."

Jessica held out her hand. "Jessica Larsen from *Mornings with Jessica,* and I would kill for coffee."

Ry shook her hand. "We met last night. Liz's got another pot going on the camp stove."

They stepped inside, and Jessica made a beeline to the back of the house.

"Can I get a thermos to go for Daisy?" Trav asked. "Gran's a tea drinker."

Ry headed back to the kitchen. "Jorge brought a coffeemaker with him. I've seen him drink coffee over there."

"Seriously? I could've avoided that awful car ride. I wonder if the circuit can take it."

"Doesn't hurt to try," Ry said.

A short while later, Trav drove Jessica and Ry back to

Gran's place to pick up Rico. He figured it was easier to take his truck through the messy streets than take a chance in Ry's Ford Taurus. Jessica, freshly caffeinated, talked their ear off about the best sushi places in the city. It was a huge relief to see Daisy answer the door, holding Bryce.

Trav just stood there, smiling at his family, thermos in hand.

She reached out for the thermos. "Bless you."

"You asked for coffee," Ry said, stepping inside. "Liz delivers."

"Thank Liz again for me," Jessica gushed. "I'd love to have her on for a segment on disaster preparedness." Then she rushed past them toward the kitchen, with a filled thermos just for her.

"Will do," Ry called.

"Ry says Jorge has a coffeemaker here," Trav said. "I'll try to hook it up tomorrow."

Daisy beamed, and all his earlier frustration vanished. "That would be great," she said. "It must be small. I didn't see it."

"Take a look through the cabinets when you get a chance," Trav said.

Daisy shuddered. "Have you seen what's in those cabinets?"

"Gran likes to tuck away appliances in the broom closet, back on the wall behind the kitchen table," Ry said. "Says the kitchen has better feng shui like that."

"Of course it does," Trav said, shaking his head. "Rico, we gotta go!"

Rico appeared a moment later from the kitchen, straightening his shirt. "I'm ready. I could use a break from the grabby hands in there. Geez."

"I'll have a talk with Shane," Trav said.

"No means no, man," Rico said, grabbing his jacket.

"We should sic her on Max," Trav said.

"I get the feeling she's already tried that," Daisy whispered.

Rico pulled his pom-pom hat on. "Look out, Shane, you're next."

"Let's go," Ry said. "We've got work to do."

Ry led the way outside. Rico followed. Trav stopped to kiss Daisy and Bryce one more time.

Daisy laughed and pushed him out the door. "Go."

Trav unlocked the truck. "Rico, you're in the middle on account of being a shrimp. You need a booster seat?"

Rico flipped him the bird. They piled into the cab of the truck.

"Dude, I hope those are keys pushing up against my leg," Rico told Ry. "Move over, Gigantor."

"There's no place to go," Ry protested.

Trav turned the ignition. "Rico's a wee thing."

"We can't all be eight feet tall," Rico said.

Trav slowly made his way down the street. "He's five nine and a half," Trav told Ry.

"I heard about that half inch," Ry said. "Used to be just a quarter inch. Somehow in his twenties he grew another quarter inch. Next he'll be five ten."

"Might as well round up," Rico said.

Trav stopped at a stop sign. "Why not round up to six foot? No one will notice." He held up two fingers about an inch apart.

Ry grinned.

"Yeah, I don't have to round up for *that*, my friend." Rico turned to Ry. "You guys have a hot shower at your place?"

"We did, until about the third crew guy. Then it ran out. Luckily, Liz and I went first."

"Ah, some shower action," Rico commented. "Nice."

Ry said nothing. Trav glanced over. His brother had a smug, satisfied look on his face.

"Your grandma's place had like one minute of hot water," Rico said, "then it was ice."

"Why don't you move in to my place?" Trav asked. "You, Gran, and Jorge."

Ry chuckled.

"I'm afraid I'll see something I can't unsee," Rico said.

"You should be afraid," Ry said.

Daisy headed across the street with Bryce to visit Maggie and
Jorge. Shane had left earlier to get fresh clothes from his
apartment and check on his shop, and Daisy couldn't bear to
spend the day cooped up with Jessica and Max.

She rang the bell at Trav's place. Maggie answered
wearing one of Trav's long-sleeved Elegant Land Design
shirts as a nightgown with thick wool socks pulled up to her
knees. "Hello! Come on up!"

Daisy followed behind with Bryce. She'd thought they
would be up and dressed by now. It was ten thirty last she
checked the time on her cell.

"Just make yourself comfy," Maggie said. "Jorge will need
a few minutes." She headed back to the bedroom and shut the
door behind her.

Daisy sat on the sofa with Bryce and stared at the white
walls. Trav's place was far from homey. If they did get
married, she'd have a blank slate to work with. That could be
fun. She'd only rented places before and had never been able
to go all-out with the decorating.

She heard Maggie giggling.

"Stop!" Maggie said, with no real force behind it. "It's
Daisy and Bryce. Now get dressed!"

A low murmur.

A high-pitched laugh.

Oh, Lord. Daisy stood and moved to the kitchen. An
empty wine bottle sat on the counter next to a bag of potato
chips, the unhealthy kind with tons of grease and salt. Her
mouth watered, and she took one. She crunched and looked
around. The kitchen was surprisingly clean. No dishes in the
sink. No crumbs on the floor. She hoped that was a result of
Maggie and Jorge's efforts and not Trav's. She couldn't live
with a neat freak. He'd end up hating her after two weeks.

Maggie and Jorge appeared from the bedroom.

"Can I get you something to drink?" Maggie asked.

"Good morning," Jorge said. "Hello, *bebé*." He kissed Bryce's cheek. Bryce bounced in excitement.

"Good morning, and no, thank you on the drink," Daisy said. "How're you guys doing over here? Have everything you need?"

Maggie poured herself a glass of water from the faucet. "I wouldn't mind some fresh clothes. You still got the TV guys over there?"

"Unfortunately, yes. I'll sneak some of your stuff out and bring it by."

"Okay, I want my purple velour jogging suit," Maggie said. "It's perfect for this kind of weather."

"Got it," Daisy said.

"And send over Jorge's black pants with the blue striped sweater I knitted him."

"Maybe just one of my white shirts," Jorge put in.

Maggie narrowed her eyes. "You don't like the sweater."

"No, I love it. Please do bring it, Daisy."

Maggie looked pleased and opened the refrigerator.

Jorge whispered behind his hand, "Bring the white shirt too. That sweater is itchy."

Daisy smiled and nodded.

"I found grapes and cheese for breakfast," Maggie announced. "Jorge, grab the chips."

They settled into the living room. Jorge and Maggie took the sofa. Daisy sat on the floor with Bryce, who was starting to sit up by himself. Occasionally, he'd tip to the side, and she'd right him before he hit the floor.

"This place could use a woman's touch," Maggie said. "Maybe I should knit an afghan to throw over the sofa. What do you think, Daisy? Would you like that as a wedding present?"

"Oh, well, hmmm. I'm not sure about the colors yet. I'd have to think about it." If she actually did marry Trav, move in here, and decorate.

Maggie gestured to the fireplace. "The only decorations he has are that picture on the mantel and the one on his nightstand. That's a great shot that Jorge took. You guys look adorable in your matching Santa hats."

He has my picture on his nightstand?

At Daisy's puzzled look, Maggie went on. "You remember, the picture Jorge took on Christmas Eve when everyone stopped by my house."

Daisy hadn't seen the picture. "Excuse me."

She walked back to the bedroom she'd never seen. Well, she had been there that one night, but it had been dark, and she'd been focused on naked. She took in a queen-size bed with a black and white comforter on top, a black dresser, and two black nightstands. One nightstand was empty; the other had a lamp and a silver framed picture. She picked up the frame.

Yup, they were wearing Santa hats. Daisy was holding Bryce and smiling into the camera. Trav had his arms around them both, with a huge smile on his face. They looked like a happy family.

This was what Trav looked at every night. This was what he wanted for them.

She instantly felt guilty. She didn't have a single picture of Trav. Just a million pictures of Bryce.

All this time he had been thinking *family*, and she had been thinking *Bryce*. No wonder they were butting heads. But was she really ready for the commitment of family? What if she screwed it up?

Trav had to take three detours to avoid downed trees and wires, but they finally made it to the high school. Ry tried the door. It was already open. Chief Bailey must have gotten there first. They walked down the hallway and to the far left to the gym. Memories of high school flashed through Trav's brain—smoking weed under the bleachers, cutting classes, the principal's office.

The time he'd almost burned down the school.

Good times. He prayed his son took after Daisy.

Chief Bailey and his fresh-from-the-academy deputy Will were wheeling out cots.

"Ryan!" Chief Bailey called. He hustled over to them. "So glad you made it, and you brought help. How're you guys making out in this storm?"

"We're good," Ry answered. "I got a generator going, so does Trav. Rico and Shane are with Trav."

"How's Maggie?"

"She's doing well," Ry said. "She's got a generator too."

"And this guy," Chief Bailey pointed to Trav. "How's your boy? You keeping him on the straight and narrow?"

"He's six months old," Trav said. "He's not getting in any trouble. He's good."

Chief Bailey turned to Rico. "Did he ever tell you about the time I hauled him in for vandalism?"

Rico grinned. "Which time?"

Rico missed the worst of Trav's crimes. When Trav hit Clover Park as a teen, Rico was still back home, playing varsity ball, in a band, staying out of trouble.

Chief laughed. Trav would never live down all these stories. The town had a long memory.

"This was the time he turned all the street corner signs so Catoonah was Elm, Elm was Park, Park was High Ridge. He did every single sign on that side of town. Must have taken hours!" He shook his head, remembering. "No one noticed at first. Everyone around here knows their way like the back of their hand. Until the governor stopped in town to award us a historic registry plaque for the old mansion. They couldn't find the place! This huge mansion, the only one in town, and Trav had them all turned around."

Rico laughed. Ry bit back a smile. Trav stifled a groan and considered moving out of town before his son heard all these stories and got some ideas of trying stuff out himself.

Chief finished up with a shake of his finger. "You keep an eye on that boy of yours. You're not the only one who took a ride in my cruiser. Daisy was in there a bunch of times."

This was news to him.

"What'd she do?" Trav asked.

Chief laughed heartily. "She never told you? Well, the worst crime was driving without a license. Fifteen and she's speeding around town in the car she stole from under her parents' noses. I must have hauled her in five, six times for that. Thank God she finally got her license."

Trav frowned. That was before he moved to town. His hopes for Bryce took a dive. The kid was doomed with their genes.

Ry spoke up. "Let's get to work."

"Sure, sure," Chief said. "Right this way."

They helped roll out cots and set out folding chairs and a few folding tables. Rico and Trav went to the supply closet several times to haul out bottled water, boxes of granola bars, and fruit cups while Ry, Chief Bailey, and Will set out small Ziploc bags of toiletries, towels, blankets, and pillows. The showers in the gym were working, though only cold water. They had a few outlets available as charging stations for cell phones for when the tower started working again. Usually, cell service came back first. No Wi-Fi, unfortunately, the cable and Internet lines went down with the power.

"I think we're good here," Chief said. "Thanks for your help. I'll get the word out that we're open for business."

"We'll take a ride and check in on the seniors," Ry said, "see if they need a lift over here."

"Great, we'll do the same," Chief said. "Hey, send over Shane too. See what he can make of the food in the cafeteria. Granola bars and fruit cups aren't much of a meal."

"Will do," Ry said.

It was a long day of driving through the still snowed-in town, helping seniors, helping people at the shelter. More plowing and shoveling. They couldn't clear the tree branches until the utility company came through and told them which wires were still live. It was a mess. Trav was running out of steam after his night of little sleep. The only thing that kept him going was the thought of getting back to Daisy.

∼

"How'd it go?" Daisy asked Trav later that night when he returned from helping with the emergency shelter. He'd stopped by at lunch to check on the generator. Jessica and Max had driven the crew's van to Ryan's place to pick up the crew. She really hoped they'd made it back to the city.

Trav took off his wool hat, jacket, and gloves, hanging them on the coat rack by the door. "Good. The shelter's well stocked. We rounded up some of the seniors without heat and drove them over there. I'll check back again tomorrow."

"Good." She paused. "Did everyone make it back to the city okay?"

"Well, they tried," Trav said.

Her stomach took a dive.

"But there's some huge trees down on the access road to the highway in both directions. I'm talking hundred-year-old trees. It's brutal out there."

"Trains?" she asked hopefully.

He sat beside her on the loveseat and leaned his head back, closing his eyes. "They're running, but not this far north."

He'd been working hard this entire blackout. And what had Max done? Nothing. He could've offered to help.

She was almost afraid to ask her next question. "Where is everybody?"

"Liz warmed meat lasagna and garlic bread on the grill. Rico, Max, and Jessica stayed with her for dinner."

Leave it to Liz to have an ample supply of prepared meals in the freezer. Her own freezer had three things, all labeled Ben & Jerry: Chocolate Chip Cookie Dough, Cherry Garcia, and Chocolate Therapy. At least Shane was back from the shelter. Now he was cooking something on the grill for their dinner.

Trav opened his eyes and peered over at her. "Chief Bailey told me an interesting story about you."

Which one? The chief had been more patient with her than she deserved. She could see why he'd asked Ryan to take over as chief when he retired. Ryan would do the same for the next crop of troublemakers.

She stared straight ahead. "I take it he wasn't telling you about the time I made the National Honor Society."

At his silence, she turned. "Don't look so shocked. I did get into NYU."

"Wow. I'm learning something new about you every day. First I hear how you got hauled in for driving without a license; then I hear you were an honor student."

She crossed her arms. "You can be smart and still make stupid decisions."

He laughed. "Geez, Daze, all this time I was hoping Bryce would take more after you, and now I'm thinking he's screwed either way."

"He is not!" She immediately defended her baby, but then she thought about it. Her own troubles; Trav's brushes with the law. She blew out a breath. "We should drop him off at Liz and Ryan's house and never look back."

They cracked up.

"So Bryce is napping?" Trav asked when they calmed down again.

"The quiet gave it away, huh?"

"Yup. Ry's dropping off Max and Jessica for another night here after dinner. Rico too, but I didn't think you needed a warning about him."

Another night with Jessica. Every extra minute with that woman made for an extra minute where Daisy could screw up her carefully constructed lie. Not to mention Max making lovesick puppy eyes at her. She wished she could wave a magic wand and all the roads would be clear, all the downed trees gone, and the power back on. She wanted desperately to get back to her normal life. She never thought she'd miss the humdrum routine of a single mom holding down a waitress job.

A short while later, they had a delicious dinner of grilled chicken and baked potato, but Daisy didn't get to relax too long after dinner before the front door opened and she heard Jessica's shrill laugh. A few minutes later, they all settled into the living room.

"So the vodka's gone, and Liz and Ryan's place was dry," Jessica said. "Anything else to drink?"

"Nope," Trav said.

Jessica tapped her fingers and took them all in. "How about strip poker?"

Daisy rolled her eyes. "There is a baby here."

Bryce sat in the backpack carrier on Trav's back. His favorite spot to get a new perspective.

"Like a baby would even notice," Jessica snapped. She glanced at Shane, then Rico, completely bypassing Max; then her eyes lingered on Trav. "I wouldn't mind getting a look at—"

The front door sprang open, leaving Daisy to wonder how far Jessica would go. *Really? Making a play for Trav?*

Maggie stepped inside with Jorge. "Who's up for Scrabble?" Maggie asked.

Shane looked up from where he'd been reading one of Maggie's old *People* magazines. "Me."

"How're you holding up over here?" Jorge asked.

"We're fine," Trav said. "You guys all set? I refueled the generator an hour ago."

"We're cozy as two bedbugs in a city hotel," Jorge said. "No complaints."

Jessica snorted. "Not at a good hotel."

Maggie kissed Jorge. "No complaints, love," she purred. She turned to the group. "Now let's get snacks."

There was a flurry of activity as Maggie fetched a bowl of Doritos and a platter full of Milano cookies for their Scrabble game around the living room coffee table. Shane grumbled about cookies with preservatives while he helped Daisy fetch the water.

"Let's play teams," Maggie said as she settled on the floral loveseat next to Jorge. "Girls versus boys. Jessica, Daisy, come sit over here."

Jessica rolled her eyes. "Four teams work better, don't you think? I'll take Max." Jessica indicated the floor at her feet for Max to sit. He did.

Must be nice to command men to sit at your feet.

"I'll be with you, love," Jorge said, putting his hand on Maggie's knee.

Maggie pouted, but still squeezed Jorge's hand affectionately. "I just thought it'd be fun to shake things up a bit with the teams. Jessica, you seem very uptight again. Did Rico not satisfy you?"

Rico spewed his water. Trav snickered.

"That's none of your business," Jessica said frostily.

Maggie shook her head. "Oh, dear. And I'm all out of vodka too."

Daisy choked on a laugh.

"Moving on," Jessica said between her teeth.

"Sweetheart, don't be afraid to ask for what you want," Maggie said.

Jessica turned bright red. "I'm not—can we just play here?"

Trav grinned. "It does work better with four teams. You're stuck with me, Daisy."

This was always true. Though she was starting to think it wasn't such a bad thing. He lifted Bryce from the carrier and settled him on his lap.

"I'll take Shane," Rico said.

"Last pick," Shane said. "I'm getting flashbacks to middle school gym."

"Aww, Shane, not everyone is talented with a ball," Maggie said. "You have culinary talents. That's why you're my favorite."

Shane beamed.

"Hey!" Trav protested. "I thought I was your favorite."

"Oh, you are," Maggie said, winking at Shane.

"Hmph," Trav muttered. He looked at Daisy perched on the arm of the chair. "Here, you can take the chair." He slid to the floor with Bryce.

Oh, look, I can have men sitting at my feet too.

"Thanks," Daisy said. "Wait, I'll get his blankie so he can have tummy time." She fetched it from the diaper bag nearby and set Bryce down on it.

"We'll go first," Jessica said. She laid out the tiles with a smirk and looked right at Daisy: FOOL.

An uneasy feeling rolled around in Daisy's stomach. What did Jessica think she knew?

"Our turn!" Maggie sang. "We've got the perfect letters." She placed her tiles next to the L. LICK. She snapped her fingers at Rico. "Pay attention. For next time."

"*Dios mío*," Rico muttered.

"There was no first time!" Jessica exclaimed.

"Gran, can we keep it rated G?" Trav asked. "I'm begging you."

"What?" Maggie asked indignantly. "It's a perfectly valid word. And some men might not think to return the favor."

Trav groaned.

"Our turn." Daisy leaned down to Trav's ear. "What do you think?"

"I think we should bail on Scrabble and sneak back to my place," he whispered.

Her face flushed. They couldn't just bail, could they? Everyone would know what they were up to. And what would they do with Bryce?

"You're as naughty as your grandmother," she whispered.

He chuckled. "She's worse. King on the K."

She'd hoped to form a word as retribution for Jessica's "fool," but "witch" and "bitch" weren't in her letters. *Don't let her get to you. She's not pure evil; she loves her cat. Probably a spoiled, prissy cat like his owner, but still.* She nodded, and Trav added KING.

Shane and Rico added two letters to spell COT. "We've got horrible letters," Shane explained sheepishly.

"No, it's good," Daisy said. "You've got a double word score, and you spelled 'go' too."

Shane brightened.

"We did that on purpose," Rico said.

Jessica added two letters without consulting Max. OUT. She hid a smile.

Jessica was messing with her, and Daisy didn't like it one bit.

"Shoot," Maggie said. "You messed up my F. I had the perfect word." She leered at Jorge.

"Hmmm...." Jorge whispered something to her and, at her agreement, added DANCE.

Trav added letters to the D in DANCE: DAD. He smiled proudly at Daisy, and her heart squeezed.

Several rounds later, Jessica had managed to add LIAR, BOGUS, and SIN. Maggie and Jorge continued their game of seduction that appealed only to them (LIPS, BLOW, HARD) while Daisy and Trav played to win, using both a Q and an X in QUIT and EXIT. Shane stopped playing once Rico nodded off. Bryce slept nearby on his blanket, the noise of the room once again soothing him to sleep faster than the quiet of his bedroom back home.

Daisy and Trav won.

"Yes!" Trav stood and raised Daisy's hand in victory. She smiled.

Jessica sniffed. "It's just a stupid game." She stood and arched her back. "Good night all. It's been...an evening." She strode upstairs.

"We're a good team," Trav said.

"I guess so," Daisy said, not wanting to admit much more. She was starting to feel more for him, now that they'd been in close quarters these past two days. He was a loving dad. He looked out for his family. Maybe one day he'd let his guard down and she'd see more than the smooth surface.

"I'll get Bryce." Trav carefully lifted the baby from the floor.

Shane stood. "Night." He headed upstairs.

Maggie eyed Max. "How about you pay Jessica a visit? That girl is wound tighter than a polka dot." She nodded. "The French knot kind," she added.

Max's eyebrows shot up in confusion. "Well, I won't be seeing her. My heart's been taken for a long time."

"You have a long-lost sweetheart tucked away somewhere?" Maggie asked. "Go to her. Don't waste time. Life's too short."

Max looked longingly at Daisy. "Good advice, Mrs. O'Hare, thank you."

"That's only good advice if the person isn't married," Trav said.

"Depends if it's a happy marriage," Max said.

"It doesn't depend on anything," Trav snapped. "Married means off limits. And what do you mean by happy marriage? You think it's not a happy marriage? Because I'll have you know it's a *very* happy marriage."

Bryce stirred in his arms.

"Trav," Daisy whispered, inclining her head toward Bryce.

Maggie took in the three of them. "Well now, we'd best be getting on home. Thank you for an enjoyable evening."

Jorge helped Maggie into her coat, and she smiled fondly at him. The newlyweds left, and then it was just Daisy with the three demanding guys in her life—husband number one, future husband number three, and the little screamer.

"After I get Bryce upstairs, I'll check the generator one more time before bed," Trav said.

"Okay, I'll clean up," Daisy said. She began gathering the bowls and leftover snacks and eyed Max just standing there. "Grab some glasses."

She headed for the kitchen and turned on the one light that worked in there. Max deposited the glasses in the sink. She busied herself putting leftover cookies back in the bag.

"Daze, I really am sorry about the way things ended between us," Max said in the silence.

Daisy turned from him and dropped the Dorito crumbs into the garbage. She was tired of his apologies. "You've already apologized."

"I have a confession."

She turned.

"I did tell someone about us being married. My parents."

Her mouth dropped open in shock. Her legs felt shaky, and she quickly moved to a chair. "We said we would wait to tell people until I was further along."

"I know." He sat next to her. "I just couldn't keep some-thing that big from them. They threatened to stop paying tuition if I didn't get a divorce. I'd have had to quit school and work at some crap job. I was so torn. I didn't want to leave you in the lurch, but when you weren't pregnant—"

"Omigod." She dropped her head in her hands. "It makes so much sense now." Her mind reeled from shock to near relief. Max *had* loved her, just…not enough. They could've worked something out even without his parents' help. It would have been tough, but they could've made it work. If only he'd talked to her. But now it was too late.

"I should never have listened to them," Max said. "Mrs. O'Hare was right. Life's too short to waste time. I've always loved you, and if you're not happily married…"

She raised her head to find Max on one knee. He held up the plastic sparkle ring to her, just like he had all those years ago.

She gasped.

"Daisy, will you marry me again?"

19

"No!" Daisy paused, because despite herself, she felt herself weakening toward him, remembering the past, the promises they'd made to each other once upon a time, that they were soul mates meant for life. He'd said he would find her in ten years. He was a little late, but he had found her again. It was his parents that had torn them apart, outside forces, not them. They might have made it. "Give me one good reason why I should divorce my husband and marry you, Max Parker."

"I love you. I always have. I always will." His voice was gruff with emotion. "Please make me the happiest man on earth. Again." His eyes held hers, and she felt the heartfelt emotion down to her soul.

And then she remembered real life. Her life. She was a mom now. And, as far as he knew, a wife.

"Oh, Max. Get up. This would never work. I've got Bryce. I'm different."

He stayed on bended knee. "I'm not. And I'll help you raise him. If you're a little different, that's okay. I love the new Daisy too."

She was so confused. How could she be melting toward two men at the same time? Were her hormones wacky?

"I'm not getting up until I have an answer," Max said.

She sighed. "Goodnight, Max."

She turned off the light, leaving him on bended knee in the dark.

"Still not moving," Max called. "You'll find me right here in this spot in the morning."

"Trav'll be through here soon to check the generator out back."

She heard him groan.

"Just think about it," he said. "I can make you happy."

She said nothing. She headed upstairs to get ready for bed, hoping for a good night's sleep. No more manly demands. They always had strings attached.

Daisy realized once she got up to Maggie's room that Trav hadn't had any time to move the crib back. Oh, well. Shane seemed to sleep through Bryce's cries, so it was probably okay. She settled into bed in another of Maggie's nightgowns, tired of the clothes she'd worn for two days now. Last night she'd worn Maggie's gown to be unappealing to Trav; tonight she just wanted something warm and comfortable. This had been a never-ending night, and she couldn't wait to go back to her quiet, peaceful life—not counting Bryce's regular screaming sessions—in her tiny apartment. Or more likely she'd have to move into Trav's house. She'd promised to marry him. But was a promise made just to cover up a lie really valid? It just seemed like throwing oil onto a fire.

Trav walked in, already peeling off his shirt. She'd left the light on the nightstand on and caught a glimpse of golden skin stretched taut over broad shoulders and lean muscle. He even had six-pack abs. Her body reacted instantly, nipples at attention while down-under primed for action. She sat up, already pulling the nightgown up from where it was stuck under her legs.

His jeans dropped. His briefs tented over an erection, and her throat went dry. Lord, she could use the stress relief. At least that was one thing she could count on from Trav.

Keeping things light. No messy emotions. Just their bodies entwined, skin on skin.

But then he had to ruin it by talking.

"I don't like the way Max is looking at you," Trav said as he approached the bed. "Tell him to back off before his face meets my fist."

She dropped the nightgown back in place. "Trav, you won't lay a finger on him."

He slipped under the covers. She felt the welcome warmth of his body and fought the urge to cuddle up against him. She couldn't let him think it was okay to beat up Max just for looking at her. What if he knew Max had just proposed to her? She lay down and folded her hands on her stomach so she'd keep them to herself.

Still, it was tough. Her body ached for him. Geez, one hook-up and she was desperate for more. Her libido was ba-aa-ck. And it was fixated on the nearest warm body. She should be glad she shared a room with Trav. What if it was Max in here? Would she sleep with him too?

"You're my wife," he said.

Her libido whimpered. *No party tonight.* If that wife comment wasn't a splash of reality-soaked cold water, she didn't know what was. Second only to Bryce waking up and wailing.

"Not really," she said.

"Daze, it's happening. You promised."

"I know I promised, but do you really want to marry someone who's forced into it by a promise given under desperate circumstances?"

He adjusted the pillow under his head. "Yes."

"Why?"

"Nothing's changed. We should still be together."

"*Should* be. That's not how it's supposed to work. You don't get married because you should, you marry because you want to."

He regarded her with the patience of a saint. "Look, I did my part of the deal. It's your turn."

"I'm supposed to commit to you for the rest of my life because it's my turn?"

"Yes. Is that so bad?" he asked in a tone of extreme aggravation.

She was about to reply when she suddenly stopped. "You're actually getting mad here."

"Damn right I am. Stop fucking with my head and marry me."

A spark of hope lit up inside her. She turned off the light on the nightstand and scooted closer to him, turning to face him on her side. He slid an arm around her.

"You're so romantic," she teased.

"I don't do romantic," he said flatly. Back to his calm, unshakeable self.

She peeled his arm off her and lay flat on her back. "Maybe if you tried a little courtship, an actual date, instead of demanding a marriage, things would go better between the two of us."

He blew out a noisy breath. "I'm offering you everything. Every cent I have, a house, a stable future for our son. What more do you want from me?"

A beat passed in silence.

"People should only get married if they love each other," she said softly.

He snorted. "I told you how I feel about love. It's fiction designed by corporations to make us spend more money. You buy beauty stuff or whatever. Men buy diamonds, flowers, cards, chocolates, dinner; it never ends."

"It's not fiction, it's real."

He exhaled sharply. "You're waiting for someone to waltz in like a white knight with flowery talk."

"It's called chivalry," she said stiffly.

"I know Max is offering you slick promises of a career with his talk shows and commercials." He propped up on one elbow, and she could see the tightness in his jaw in the moon-light. "Is that what you want? Max? Just tell me."

"No," she said quietly. "I don't want Max." She was pretty sure, though he really seemed to love her. Were soul mates forever? Was Max her destiny? Why was everything so complicated?

"You should sleep on the floor tonight," she told him.

"Why?"

"Because last night isn't going to be repeated."

"We'll just sleep."

She didn't buy that for a minute. "I need space."

She rolled on her side, scooting to the edge of the bed.

"Too bad. I've given you plenty of space, and guess what it got me? Zilch."

She peeked over her shoulder at him where he lay on his side, facing her. He looked disgruntled. Some part of her liked that he was showing his true self, not just joking around. Still, he was too demanding. She couldn't let him walk all over her. No one bossed Daisy Garner around.

She shoved her pillow between them and rested her head on her arm. He tossed the pillow to the floor.

"That was my pillow!"

"Go to sleep."

She climbed out of bed and fetched her pillow, then settled on the far edge of the mattress. He grabbed her by the hips and pulled her close, spooning her from behind.

He was very happy to see her, apparently.

She turned and opened her arms to him. "You are a stubborn man."

"Yup. And you *will* be my wife."

She threw an arm and leg over him. He wrapped an arm around her.

"No," she said.

He tucked her under his chin. "Yes."

"I don't love you," she said sleepily. The warmth of his body relaxed her, and she closed her eyes, breathing in his clean scent.

He patted her back. "Yes, you do."

"I don't believe in love," she murmured. "It's all run by corporations."

He chuckled. "That's right, wife."

They lay in the dark, holding each other. His arm became

heavy across her side. She pushed his arm off her and wiggled the nightgown up. She'd managed to get it over her hips when she stopped suddenly as she heard a soft snore.

He'd fallen asleep.

She sighed, pushed the nightgown back, and curled up next to him. She couldn't blame him after their late night last night and all the work he'd done plowing and shoveling, refueling generators, helping at the shelter.

Still, she was surprisingly disappointed.

20

Trav returned from refueling the generator at his place and Gran's in the early morning and climbed the stairs to slip back into bed with Daisy. He'd fallen asleep last night out of pure exhaustion, but he wouldn't mind a little morning action before everyone else woke up.

He stopped abruptly in the hallway at the sight before him. Max stood in front of Daisy, who wore only a towel, her pale skin rosy from a warm shower. Fury rushed through Trav, and he counted to ten. This asshole couldn't take a hint. Daisy would never be with Max.

"Did you think about what I said?" Max asked. His back was to Trav, and Trav stayed silent to hear what the man had to say.

Daisy's eyes widened as she saw Trav standing there. She took a step back, away from Max. "Please, Max, this is not the time."

Max grabbed her arm. "This is the only time. We're leaving this morning. I checked in with Ryan. The roads are clear."

Daisy wiggled free and took off for the bedroom.

Max started to follow. Trav clamped a hand on his shoulder. "Looks like it's time for you to crawl back to that fancy job of yours in the city."

Max whirled to face Trav, eyes wide, jaw dropped. "I—"

"Shut up before I kick your ass for daring to put a hand on my wife," Trav growled.

Max jabbed Trav in the chest. "She was once my wife. We're soul mates. I asked her to marry me again."

"Marry you! Soul mates!" Trav sputtered. "That's shit. You're full of it! Where'd you get that, a self-help book on what women crave? If you really loved her, you never would've left her in the first place." He shoved him hard. "You had your chance, and you blew it."

Max narrowed his eyes. "You wanna take this outside?"

"I'd wipe the sidewalk with you if it wasn't for Daisy. For some reason she doesn't want me to touch your pretty-boy face. She's too good for you."

Max got in his face. "She doesn't love you, asshole."

Trav grabbed Max's shirt and pushed him away. "You mean she doesn't love *you*."

"Stop it!" Daisy cried.

Max and Trav turned to her as one. She stood in the hallway, wearing one of Gran's flannel nightgowns.

"What's with the nightgown?" Trav asked.

She waved that away. "I had to get dressed quickly."

"You loved me once," Max said. "Do you still, even a little bit?"

"Tell me you don't still love this jackass," Trav said in a low, even voice.

Daisy turned to Max. "I'll always have a place in my heart for you. You were my first love. But I'm not in-love with you. Do you understand? You'll always be special to me."

Max's shoulders sagged. "I understand. I don't like it, but I understand." He turned to Trav. "You win, man."

Damn right.

"No, he doesn't win," Daisy said. "I'm not some prize to fight over. Trav, I love you for loving Bryce. That will never change. But I'm not in love with you either. How could I be? I don't really know you."

It felt like a stab to the heart.

"You do know me," Trav protested.

"I know your jokes, your humor, but I don't know you."

"That is me," he said, completely exasperated. He felt heat creep up his neck as Max witnessed this scene. He turned to Max. "Go away!"

Max slipped away, heading downstairs.

"I think there's more," Daisy said, "but you never open up."

"Dammit, what do you want me to do? Cry like a total wimp and get all sappy on you?"

Bryce let out his usual full-throated wail so everyone would know he was up. Daisy went into Shane's room to get him. Trav followed her. Shane was still out cold.

Daisy shooed him out the door. He waited and followed her back to Gran's room, Bryce in her arms. She climbed in bed, propping up pillows to nurse him.

Trav paced back and forth by the bed. "First I have to deal with your ex. Then you want me to be a wimp. You want me to be someone I'm not."

Daisy just looked at him and shook her head sadly, fueling his frustrated rage. He stormed from the room. This woman wanted too much.

He went outside; it always calmed him. The crisp air, the gently sloping drifts of snow as far as the eye could see, the stark trees. He stared at the snow of the front yard, perfectly smooth and untouched. He looked up at Gran's bedroom window.

Then he did something he hadn't done in a long time. Made a total crazy ass of himself.

∿

"This has been an interesting storm," Daisy told Bryce as she walked around Maggie's bedroom, patting his back for the burp, "but we're going back home soon. Maybe in a few days, tops. As soon as we've got power back at our place. Life will go back to normal."

Burp.

"Good boy." She dressed quickly, then made the bed one

handed while holding Bryce on her hip, pulling the blanket back into place, tossing all the pillows back up by the headboard. Not perfect, but it would do. She never made her bed at home. She felt like a guest here in Maggie's house. She could hear Jessica and Max moving around downstairs and decided to stay right where she was.

She set Bryce on the bed and sang one of their favorite songs, an oldie but a goodie, "Ironic" by Alanis Morissette, as she did their usual massage routine. She finished and was just starting to think about bundling him up and slipping out to her sister's house when she heard something hit the window.

Ping. Ping.

What the hell? She crossed to the window just as another pebble hit it. She looked down to a waving Trav.

He was completely and totally naked. In the snow. She looked closer. He was standing at the end of an arrow he'd drawn in the snow. And her name was there too. Like she needed her name and an arrow to notice him.

She put Bryce on the floor and yanked open the window. "What are you doing, you crazy man?"

"Isn't it obvious?"

"No!"

The cold definitely had a shrinking effect.

"I'm bared to you. I opened up."

He began posing muscleman style—biceps flexed (impressive), a side chest move (tasty), and then arms lowered into a humungo flex with exaggerated strain on his face (ridiculous). She giggled.

Uh-oh. Her parents pulled up in their Toyota Highlander and parked on the street. Trav hadn't noticed.

He pointed one hand and lifted a leg in a fountain-spewing-water pose.

"Trav, honey, come inside. It's too cold for that. Let's talk."

He stopped posing and put his hands on his hips. "No more talking. I took action. And I won't come in until you agree to do what you promised."

She really should warn him.

But it was hard to resist watching the inevitable.

She shook her head at him and watched her mom climb out of the passenger seat and head up the front walk. Dad was right behind her.

Mom looked from Trav up to Daisy. Daisy waved. Trav's head snapped around. He immediately crossed his hands in front of him—classic Adam expelled from Paradise pose.

"Daisy, you really should let him in," her mom chastised. "It's cold out here."

"Damn cold," her dad said. "Come in with us, son. We'll get you warmed right up."

Trav dashed inside. Even from upstairs she could see his red face.

She chuckled and shut the window. She didn't know what he hoped to prove with that stunt.

Yet she couldn't stop smiling.

She headed downstairs with Bryce just as Trav dashed past her on his way up.

"You might have said something," he muttered.

"Next time keep your clothes on," she called over her shoulder.

She met her parents in the living room, where they were chatting with Rico. He turned when he saw her.

"You got him good," Rico chortled.

Daisy grinned. "He's nuts."

Rico shook his head and headed off to the kitchen.

"What was that about?" her dad asked. "Did you and Trav have a fight?"

Daisy waved that away. "Just a silly bet. So what are you guys doing here?"

Her parents exchanged a look.

"We just wanted to check in to see how you and Bryce were weathering the power outage," her dad said.

"Did you check on Liz too?" Daisy asked tightly.

"We knew she'd be okay," her mom said. "She always plans ahead."

"We stopped by there too," her dad added.

She knew her parents thought she always needed

someone to take care of her. She would've made do if she had to. She'd never let anything happen to Bryce.

"I told you Daisy and Bryce would be fine, Clive," her mom said, taking Bryce from Daisy's arms. "Trav obviously took care of them. They've got heat, power." She kissed Bryce's little fingers. "How're you for food, honey?"

"We're fine. Trav took care of that too," Daisy said.

"I'm so glad you two are finally getting married," her mom said.

Daisy did a quick shushing motion. The house was quiet, but that didn't mean Max and Jessica had left yet.

Her mom slowly nodded. Message received.

"I could've handled things, even without Trav's help," Daisy said.

"You can always come home in an emergency," her dad said. "We've got your old room waiting for you."

"Thank you, Dad, but I'm fine. I don't need someone to take care of me. When the shit goes down, I'm on top of it." *Wait, that didn't come out right.*

"Daisy! Language," her mom said, covering Bryce's ears. "And don't talk to your father that way."

Her dad patted her mom's knee. "It's okay. I know what she means. She's an adult. But even adults need help now and then."

"Not if they're married," her mom said. "Then they can lean on each other."

"I don't need...forget it." Daisy fumed. She'd always be the screw-up to her parents.

Trav trotted downstairs. "How you guys doing?" he blustered. He pumped her dad's hand and kissed her mom on the cheek.

Her mom gave him a subtle once-over. *Eww.*

"Good, good." Her dad smiled. "Too bad you lost that bet."

Daisy tilted her head and looked at Trav meaningfully.

"Yup. Too bad." He took a step toward the door, obviously still too embarrassed to visit with her parents.

"Trav, that generator you recommended runs like a dream," her dad said. "No complaints."

"We're just so glad Daisy had you to help her through all this," her mom said.

Trav smiled and turned to Daisy. His smile dropped when he took in her furious expression. "Well, I'd better be going. I'm going to check in on Gran." He ruffled Bryce's hair, grabbed his coat, and headed out the door.

"We're going to get going too, sweetheart," her dad said. "We need to check on Garner's. Make sure the pipes don't freeze."

"Sure. I'll see you later." Daisy hugged her dad.

Her mom handed her Bryce. "Let us know if you need anything."

"We're fine," Daisy said between her teeth.

"Mmm-hmm," her mom said noncommittally. Then they were gone.

"Errgh!" Daisy exclaimed. Bryce startled and started crying. She sighed and patted his back. "It's okay, baby. Mama's okay."

Five minutes later, she'd gotten him calmed down, and headed upstairs to fetch his favorite blankie and the diaper bag.

She stepped into Maggie's bedroom and stopped short. Jessica was sitting on the end of the bed.

"I got cell service," Jessica sang.

21

"Good for you," Daisy said, brushing past the nasty woman.

"It is good for me," Jessica said. "I was able to find out a few things about you that I'm sure your followers would find very interesting."

"I don't know what you're talking about." She grabbed the diaper bag and looked around for the blankie. It must still be in Shane's room.

Jessica's voice rang out sharp and clear like they were in a courtroom. "This isn't your house, is it?"

Daisy scrubbed a hand over her face. "Let me hand off Bryce, and we'll talk."

"This ought to be good."

Daisy knocked on Shane's door. "Can you take him?"

Shane slowly sat up in bed. "Sure."

She handed over Bryce and returned to the bedroom, where Jessica was snooping through the closet.

"Interesting how all your clothes are a size two, when you're obviously"—Jessica looked Daisy up and down—"at least a size twelve."

She was an eight, but she kept her cool and took a deep breath. "So tell me what you learned once you could call people."

"Why don't we start with you telling the truth?" Jessica

approached, punching her hand in the air dramatically with each question. "Why are you pretending? How far does the lie go?"

Daisy regarded her steadily. She wasn't going to admit more than she had to. Jessica would just love to drag her name through the mud.

Jessica stood, arms crossed, her nasty smile triumphant. "I know this isn't your house." Her ice-blue eyes gleamed as she narrowed in on her prey. "Found that out with one call. I suspected as much when you didn't know your way around the kitchen."

Daisy exhaled sharply. "It's not my house, but it was the inspiration for the house in my blog. No one wants to read about my crappy little apartment."

"So you all played a game of musical houses to fool everyone at *Mornings with Jessica*." Jessica nodded. "Oh, yeah, I know. The city has power, and I had my assistant look up the real estate records. This is Maggie's house. That explains all the high-fiber food. And Trav lives in the house across the street. You don't even live with him; you live in an apartment."

Daisy clamped her lips tightly together. *Keep it together. Admit nothing else.*

Jessica went on, warming to her subject. "You're not even separated; you were never together. I'll bet you don't even have a marriage record. I'll find that out the minute your dinky town hall opens again. But here's what I do know." She ticked off the evidence on one hand. "Your first date stories don't match, Trav has Bryce on *his* days, and I heard you telling him you didn't even know him. Who doesn't know their own husband?"

"That was a private conversation!" Daisy exclaimed. "You were eavesdropping. You had no right!"

Jessica laughed. "And your cooking. What a joke! All those gourmet recipes you wrote about and all you can come up with is grilled cheese. And no prepared meals. Another lie!"

Adrenaline ran down Daisy's legs. She desperately

wanted to run out of this house and never look back. But she couldn't. Bryce needed her. It was time for her to fight, not take flight.

Jessica studied her. "So that's why Max is professing his love for you. He knows you're not happily married. Oh, yeah, I heard that little scene this morning." At Daisy's shocked expression, Jessica shook her head sadly. "Two rutting stags in heat over the"—she finger quoted—"*innocent* doe. Right in the hallway outside my bedroom. Really, it's just too easy."

Daisy told herself not to rise to the bait. She didn't want to give Jessica any more ammunition than she already had.

"Did you borrow the baby too? Is he a prop in your fantasy world?" Jessica tapped her lips with one blood-red talon. "That must be why he cries so much. He wants his real mommy."

Daisy lost it. "I am his real mommy!"

"But Trav's not your husband, is he? I should tell Max you're free."

"We'll be married soon," Daisy said. "We planned to marry yesterday, in fact. You can check town hall for the marriage license."

Jessica looked down her nose at her. "How could you? All those mothers who turn to you for inspiration, who *aspire* to be a fraction of the wife and mother you are, who feel *less than* because of your lies."

Daisy felt her lower lip quiver and clamped down on it. She never wanted to make other moms feel bad. Hell, she always felt like less than the perfect mother. She never should have pretended to be the perfect mom and wife.

"I'm sorry," Daisy said in a choked voice. "It just sort of happened. I made up the perfect life so *I* wouldn't feel less than. I never meant to make anyone else feel that way."

Jessica nodded slowly. "Thank you, Daisy, for finally telling the truth. This is an even bigger story than the one we have. I can't wait to expose you on the air."

Daisy's eyes widened. "I'm not going back on your show."

"You don't have to." She opened her palm to reveal a small black recorder. She pressed a button on it. Daisy's voice played back loud and clear. "I'm sorry. It just sort of happened. I made up the perfect life—"

Daisy lunged for the recorder, but Jessica was faster.

"You can't use that," Daisy said. "You took that without my permission."

Jessica smiled coldly. "People who commit fraud don't get special treatment when a journalist is investigating them. It won't take me long to gather up all the evidence against you. Then I'll get the ratings Max promised me when he lined you up as a guest. See you on TV." She brushed past Daisy.

Daisy turned. "You better get out of this house, bitch!"

"With pleasure." Jessica sauntered downstairs.

Daisy sat on the edge of the bed, staring at her hands, as a cloak of misery gathered around her.

Trav returned home in good spirits. The roads were clear, cell service was back up, and he'd seen Jessica and Max driving off in the crew's van.

"Daisy, I'm home!" he called.

Shane met him in the living room, holding Bryce. "She locked herself in Gran's room and won't come out."

"What happened?"

"I don't know. She won't say anything. She just told me to bring Bryce up when he cried. So far, he's okay."

Trav got a bad feeling. He took the stairs quickly and pounded on the door. "Open up, Daze. It's me."

To his surprise, the door sprang open. She'd been crying. He folded her into his arms. "What happened?"

"Is she gone?"

"Jessica and Max took off with the rest of the crew. And good riddance."

She pulled back. "Jessica knows. She knows everything. She's going to expose me on the air."

"How could she know everything?"

"I don't know. She said she made some phone calls, and I admitted...*shit*. She never said what she did know. She goaded me into it." She smacked her forehead. "I'm so stupid. She recorded me admitting I lied. On this stupid little recorder she had hidden in her hand. It's only a matter of time before she puts the pieces together."

He stared at her. "Why would you admit you lied after everything we did to pull this off?"

"She just kept pushing me, telling me I was the wrong size and in the wrong house. She figured out we weren't living together. And the whole time, she had this nasty smile."

"So you just told her everything?"

She looked at her hands. "She said I wasn't Bryce's real mom." She met his eyes. "I just lost it."

"Aw, Daze, you gotta control that temper."

"I can't help it!" she cried. "I'm ruined before I even began. All that career stuff Max talked about—poof! Gone! No blog, no more talk shows, no endorsements. And you want to know the worst part? Marrying you doesn't even fix it."

He didn't like where this was going. "We could just say we considered ourselves married because we've been together so long. Make it sound like we just hadn't gotten around to making it official."

"No more lies! And no quickie wedding. It's wrong. This whole thing was wrong from the beginning, and I'm just the fool who thought I could do one good thing without screwing it up."

Tears leaked out of her eyes, and she dashed them away with the back of her hand.

"Come on, we can take her," Trav said in a coaxing voice. "Jessica's a skinny thing. One gust of wind and she's toast."

She gave him a hard glare. "Not everything's a joke."

"I know that."

"I'm out." She lifted her chin. "Of everything." She raced out of the bedroom, and he followed as she flew down the stairs and headed for the front door.

She stopped, hand on the knob. Slowly, she turned around.

He watched her curiously.

She looked at the ceiling. "I'm not running away. I just wish I wasn't cooped up here."

"We'll take a walk. It'll clear your head." He met her at the door and handed her her coat.

They left the house, stepping out into the cold together.

∾

Trav was right, Daisy thought. Walking did make her feel better. Especially once they stopped at Liz and Ryan's place.

Ryan answered the door and grinned. "We finally got rid of the riffraff, and then you show up."

"Yeah, yeah," Trav said.

They stepped inside, and Liz rushed to the foyer, wearing rubber gloves up to her elbows. "Oh, hi, guys. I was just cleaning up after our guests. You wouldn't believe the state of the bathroom." She shuddered. "Men." She turned to Ryan. "They make you look like a neat freak."

"I like neat freaks." He kissed the tip of her nose.

"Ryan, I'm all gross," Liz protested.

"I'll help you clean, sis," Daisy said.

Liz's mouth dropped open. "You want to help me clean?"

"Sure."

Trav and Ryan headed for the living room with its leather sofa and giant-screen TV. Except the TV had no power or cable with the blackout. Still, they sat in front of it.

Daisy followed Liz into the downstairs powder room. "It's already clean."

"No, it's not," Liz said. "I just started. Lucky for you I already cleaned the toilet." She handed Daisy some paper towels and Windex. "Here, get that mirror."

Liz got on all fours to scrub the floor. At least she wasn't attacking the grout with a toothbrush.

Daisy squirted the cleaner and rubbed wide circles around the mirror.

"Not circles," Liz said, peering up from the floor. "Top to bottom. Got it?"

"Got it."

They cleaned a few moments in silence.

"Tell me why you're upset," Liz said.

Daisy snapped her head around. "I didn't say I was upset."

"You have never, ever signed up for cleaning duty in your life. What happened? Was it Jessica? She stopped by here and ordered the crew around. I get a bad feeling from that one. She's not perky and nice like she seems on TV."

Daisy told her the whole awful story.

"Oh, Daisy, I'm sorry."

Daisy swiped at the mirror. They cleaned in silence while Daisy berated herself for this latest screw-up. For the fallout that would no doubt fall on her and Bryce. She glanced over at her sister, who whipped a toothbrush from her back pocket and attacked the grout.

"Can Bryce and I stay with you for the rest of the power outage?" Daisy asked.

Liz stopped brushing. "Of course you're always welcome here, but don't you want to stay with Trav? I know he cares about you."

Daisy turned away and caught her sad reflection in the mirror. Her face crumpled in misery.

Liz jumped up. "Oh, no. It's okay. Forget I said that. You can stay here."

Daisy nodded. "Thank you." She sniffled. "Trav just doesn't get it. I'm ruined. All he does is *joke* about it. You can't joke about this!"

"Okay, first of all, you're not ruined. This will pass, eventually. And as for the joking...well, everyone copes in a different way. I clean."

Daisy studied her sister. "Are you upset about something?"

"No, sometimes I just like to clean to get things back in order. Sometimes I *have* to. See the difference?"

Cleaning was cleaning as far as Daisy was concerned, but she nodded anyway.

She finished the mirror and threw out the paper towels.

"I'm gonna fetch Bryce and some of our stuff; then we'll be back. I'll grab his Pack-N-Play too."

"Okay, sweetie. See you soon." Liz went back to scrubbing what already looked like a clean floor to Daisy.

She stopped by the living room to tell Trav she was leaving.

He jumped off the sofa. "Wait up. I'll walk back with you."

They got their coats, said their goodbyes, and headed out the door.

"Feeling better?" Trav asked.

"A little. Liz always seems to know the right thing to say."

"Yeah, Ry's like that for me."

She smiled, glad for him. "I'm moving in with Liz for a while. Now that Jessica and the crew are gone, we don't have to pretend anymore. Besides, I know it's just a matter of days before the press is all over me. I'd feel better staying with a cop."

"I can protect you. Stay with me."

"I don't want you to get the wrong idea."

He stopped short. "What idea is that?"

"That we're a couple." She kept walking. "We're not."

He caught up with her. "We're not a…" He sliced a hand in the air. "*Fine*! Do what you want. I'm tired of begging."

"Trav, come on. I'm just staying with them for a little while. Maybe later—"

He shoved his hands in his pockets. "Forget it."

He marched ahead of her back to Maggie's house.

Within a half hour, he had packed them up and dropped them off at Liz's house. He drove off without a word.

22

Daisy couldn't shake the deep funk of misery that hounded her. It had been three days since she moved in with Liz and Ryan, and she could barely bring herself to leave the guest room. There were no reporters yet; Jessica must be waiting for the perfect moment. Jessica's words played on repeat in her head, *All those mothers who turn to you for inspiration, who aspire to be a fraction of the wife and mother you are, who feel less than because of your lies.* And she couldn't even do anything about it. The power was still out, going on five days now. She wanted desperately to update her blog. To apologize before the show aired where Jessica dug up whatever dirt she could and broadcast it to millions.

She knew from Max that the show hadn't aired yet, though the city had power and Jessica was hard at work putting something together. At first, when Max had called her Monday morning from the studio, she'd thought he might actually be able to help her.

"I'll pull the plug on your interview," Max had said. "We'll do damage control. If you take down your blog—"

"First of all, we still don't have power. Second, even if we did, I'm not taking down my blog! It's the only thing I've ever done that I'm proud of." Besides Bryce, of course. The blog might not have been an exact reflection of her life, but the heart of it was.

"Daze, she'll ruin you. She'll do anything for ratings. That's what the network loves about her."

"Then I guess I'm screwed."

"I'll do my best to can it. But if she goes to the higher-ups, it's out of my hands."

Jessica went to the higher-ups later that day. Max let Daisy know as soon as he found out.

"I was in on the meeting," Max said. "I told them they weren't being fair to you, but Jessica made a good point. The ratings could reel in big-time sponsors. That's exactly what the network needs to stay competitive. We've already had some interest from Gerber."

"So you just let them do it?" Daisy asked.

"I really didn't have a choice. It would've been career suicide to let my personal feelings get in the way of good business."

Daisy couldn't believe Max would turn on her like this after begging her to give him a second chance. The show would go on; it was just a matter of when and how long it took Jessica to put all the pieces together.

Then Max had the nerve to try for her again. "Daze, now that I know you're single—"

"Don't even go there!"

"This shouldn't affect us. It's Jessica's fault—"

"There is no us!" She hung up.

She couldn't believe she'd been falling for his sweet talk, for nostalgic memories of their college days.

Now Liz was poking her head in the bedroom door. "Daisy?"

Daisy didn't answer, caught up in her memories. Liz must have come in because the next thing Daisy knew, the blinds were open. She blinked against the glare of the winter sun reflecting off the snow. "Honey, it's nearly noon. Get up."

Daisy pushed her messy hair out of her eyes. Trav had taken Bryce early this morning, and she'd gone right back to bed.

Liz sat on the end of the bed. "I'm worried about you."

"Everything's fine."

Liz's mouth formed a straight line. "The power company says we should get power back today."

"Good," Daisy said. She could move back to her place. She hated to impose on Liz and Ryan, who were still very much in the honeymoon stage. She felt like a third wheel around here. Though it was better than her parents' place, where she felt like a total disappointment. And better than staying with Trav, who was still mad at her for saying they weren't a couple, even though it was the truth.

Liz scooted close and took Daisy's hand. "You don't have to pretend with me. I know you're hurting. But you know what? I don't think it's so bad that you described a beautiful house on your blog. You made a lot of people happy imagining such a wonderful place."

Daisy said nothing.

"And you're practically married to Trav anyway. He is so devoted to you and Bryce. It's just a matter of time, right?"

Daisy looked away. "I don't know."

"Do you love him?" Liz asked. "Because everything he does for you and Bryce speaks volumes about his love for you. Sometimes men just can't say the words."

Daisy snorted, thinking of Trav's belief in Love, Incorporated. "I wish I could say it was that easy." She rubbed the satin edge of the blanket between her fingers. "You know I like things easy, but it's complicated. I love Trav for being so good to Bryce. And I think he loves me because of Bryce too. It's not the same as if we met each other, just us, and fell in love. We did everything ass backwards, and you can't change that." She stared at nothing, deep in thought. "You just can't."

A beat passed in silence.

"Since when have you ever done anything in the right order?" Liz asked. "The Daisy I know wouldn't let that stop her. She'd go for it and the hell with everybody else."

"This is different."

Liz pulled back the covers. "Get dressed."

Daisy yanked the covers back over her. "I know you mean well, but I just want to stay here."

Liz grabbed Daisy's arms and pulled hard so Daisy was half hanging out of bed and about to tip out.

"Okay!" Daisy slid to the floor and pulled the blanket over her head.

"I think we need to plot a little revenge," Liz said.

Daisy grunted.

"That bitch Jessica Larsen won't get away with this," Liz said.

Daisy tugged the blanket down and stared. "Liz, I've never heard you talk like that before."

"I've never had Jessica Larsen making my sister miserable before," Liz replied. "I say we egg her limo and then stand outside the studio holding signs that say, 'Jessica Larsen is a rat.' Or we start an online petition against defamation journalism!"

"Is that a thing?" Daisy asked.

"Sure," Liz replied.

"I dunno."

"We should sue her," Liz said, rubbing her hands together. Daisy's eyes widened at this new vengeful side of Liz. "For emotional distress and defamation of character."

"I don't want her to know I'm distressed," Daisy said.

Liz's face lit up. "I know! Blog about how awful she is in real life. You expose *her*."

"I don't want to stoop to her level," Daisy said. "Though I wouldn't mind slipping something into her wheatgrass smoothie."

Liz nodded knowingly. "Ex-Lax."

"No, even better, a high-cal milkshake," Daisy said. "Have you seen how skinny she is?"

Liz giggled.

Daisy gave her a small smile. "I appreciate your mad scheming skills, but it's hopeless. I lied. She found out the truth. I deserve whatever she dishes out on her show."

"No, you don't," Liz insisted. "You don't have to take this lying down."

"I'm sitting," Daisy said, attempting a joking tone. Her cell rang, and she grabbed it off the nightstand. Max.

She put up a finger to her sister and took the phone out into the hallway. "Hi, Max. What's up?"

"I'm afraid it's bad news. The piece on you runs tomorrow morning. I'm so sorry, Daze. I feel like this is my fault for reaching out to you in the first place. If it wasn't for me, Jessica never would've heard of you."

"It's not your fault. It's nobody's but mine."

"She talked to a clerk in your town and pulled your marriage license that shows Trav was husband number three and that you didn't apply for the license until after you got the talk show gig."

"Anything else?"

"She found out where you live and got a picture of your apartment building."

"That's an invasion of privacy!"

"She can't give out the address, but she can show the building."

"I hate her."

"She has footage of Bryce screaming."

"He's a baby. That doesn't prove anything."

"It all goes into her story of how you're nothing like you say you are on your blog."

Her lips formed a tight line. "Can we stop her from running the baby footage?"

"I'm sorry. You signed a release."

She blew air through her cheeks. "Okay. Thanks for the heads-up. I gotta go."

"Wait! Are you okay?"

"I'm just great."

"We can do some P.R.," Max said. "Spin things in a positive light. I can get the word out through some of my contacts."

"No, I'm done. Just let it go."

"I'll call you again to check in. Bye."

Before she could say *don't bother*, he hung up.

She returned to Liz.

"What?" Liz asked.

"*Mornings with Jessica* runs the piece on the great fraud, Daisy Garner, tomorrow."

"I'm sorry, honey," Liz said gently.

"Thanks," Daisy said weakly.

Liz brightened. "Hey, at least no one in Clover Park will see it with the power still..." She trailed off as the lights flashed on and a few beeps rang out as appliances turned back on.

"We'll boycott it," Liz said solemnly.

Daisy bit her lip. Time to face the music.

Daisy stopped by Trav's place that afternoon to pick up Bryce and head home to her apartment for the first time since the storm.

"Hey," Trav said. "You're early."

Bryce was in his exersaucer, smacking the springy butterfly and bouncing his little legs.

"I know. I just wanted to get him settled back at home now that the power's back. Get back to our routine. Would you stop by with his crib and gear from Maggie's place?"

"No problem." He studied her. "You okay, Daze?"

"No, I'm not, but I have no one to blame but myself." She pulled Bryce from his exersaucer, and he threw both fists forward in a little baby hug. She smiled. He wasn't an easy baby, but she did miss him when he was with his dad.

"Don't be too hard on yourself," Trav said. "What'd you do? Write a blog? Since when is that a crime?" He slid the diaper bag onto her shoulder.

He was back to being pleasant and nice. She was surprised after the way they'd left things.

"I lied," she said. "And *Mornings with Jessica* is exposing me on air tomorrow."

He shook his head. "What's she gonna say? Daisy only visits the house she described? Daisy isn't married? We could get married easily." He snapped his fingers. "Like that."

Daisy shook her head, knowing it was too late to fix things. She just had to get through this. "I'll see you back at the apartment."

"Sure, I'll see ya." He kissed Bryce's little fist and put his hand up for a baby high-five. "Till later, little man."

Daisy buckled Bryce into his car seat and drove back to her apartment on the other side of town. She pulled into the parking lot and immediately slowed down. News vans sat in the parking lot, along with a group of reporters with cameras and microphones lining the sidewalk that led to her apartment. *Shit.*

She turned around and headed straight back to Liz's place.

23

Daisy Does It All
Single Mom

An Apology to My Readers

Dear readers, thank you for all your support and enthusiasm for this blog. This will be my last post. I wanted to reach out before the news hits tomorrow. I lied about my perfect life. The truth is, I'm a single mother living in a messy one-bedroom apartment. I work as a waitress at my parents' restaurant. It's not glamorous or fun. In fact, my baby is both a delight (to me) and an exhausting screamer.

It was my own shortcomings as a mom and in the life I provided for my son that led me to dream of something better. I channeled those hopes and dreams into my blog, sharing my fantasy with all of you, pretending it was real.

I am so, so sorry.

If I have made anyone feel less than, like they couldn't measure up to my perfect life, I don't want you to feel that way. We're all doing the best we can with what we've got. Some of us pull that off better than others.

Tomorrow on *Mornings with Jessica*, you might see the

apartment building I live in. You might hear me admit that I lied on a recording that Jessica made on a recorder that she had hidden in her hand. You might even see some footage of my baby, Bryce, screaming (as he does every night). These were not things I agreed to when I signed up to appear on *Mornings with Jessica*. For this reason, I will not be tuning into the show.

That is not to say that I blame Jessica or her show for exposing my lies. I take full responsibility for those lies here and will not comment further in the press.

Sincerely,

Daisy Garner

∼

Trav tuned in to *Mornings with Jessica* and watched grimly as Jessica morphed from perky host to aggressive investigative journalist. Daisy had already told him she wouldn't be watching.

Jessica looked directly into the camera, an expression of sadness on her face. "I had hoped to bring you a piece today on the woman behind *Daisy Does It All*. I had hoped to show you her beautiful family. Darling Husband. Baby Delight. Their beautiful home. Sadly, I cannot. Why, you ask? Because it is all a lie. Take a look."

She turned to a screen behind her. Daisy's blog post apologizing for the lies came up.

Trav cursed. They used Daisy's own blog against her.

Jessica read the post aloud emphasizing all the wrong parts—*lied, exhausting screamer, pretending.*

"I'm afraid that's not all," Jessica said, looking into the camera. "I was not allowed to play the recording I have, but I can read you a transcript in Daisy's own words. And I quote, 'I'm sorry. It just sort of happened. I made up the perfect life.'"

Jessica raised her brows. "I don't know about you, but things don't just sort of happen in my life. If it happened, there was purpose behind it. Intention. The home that Daisy lives in is not a beautiful Victorian that she lovingly tends, instead, it's this."

The screen flashed to a picture of Daisy's apartment building. Trav pounded a fist against the sofa. "They can't show that!" he yelled at the TV. "That's endangering her and Bryce!"

"Her husband...doesn't exist," Jessica continued. "In fact, we learned that Daisy applied for a marriage license after she booked her appearance on my show. Trying to cover up her lie after the fact."

Footage rolled of the town clerk, Sally, speaking into a microphone. "Yes, it's true. Daisy and Trav applied for a marriage license on February seventeenth." She lowered her voice. "And, just between you and me, it was marriage number three for Daisy." She straightened and jutted an ample hip out. "But I was rooting for the two of them to make it. It's so sad they never went through with it."

Trav couldn't believe it. Sally had ratted them out. The woman couldn't resist gossip, but still...to talk to a reporter about them. Unforgiveable.

Jessica went on. "This is the kind of relationship Daisy really has with the man who fathered her child." She turned to the screen behind her. He watched himself rushing the camera and covering it with his hand. Daisy yelling, "Trav, stop it! You're making a fool of yourself!"

Jessica replayed Daisy yelling three times, and each time Trav felt his rage build. How dare she? This was all out of context. He'd rushed the camera when Jessica kept pushing them for details on their sex life.

"And let me show you Baby Delight," Jessica said in a stage whisper. Footage rolled of Bryce in full throttle screaming mode.

Dammit. They couldn't show Bryce, could they? Then he remembered they'd signed a release for the whole family to appear. This looked like the tail end of their interview time. He remembered when Bryce had started crying. He thought the cameras had stopped rolling.

Jessica cringed. "Ouch. And here's some footage we shot before we realized none of what Daisy Garner says is true."

On the screen, Jessica asked them about their first date, and they came up with two different answers. Trav stood, his hands in fists. Jessica had no right to run Daisy over the coals like this. He watched to the bitter end as Jessica milked the footage she already had to the fullest, commenting on the truth, comparing it to the lies they'd told. Finally, Jessica finished.

"Shame on you, Daisy Garner, for making decent, hard-working moms feel less than compared to your glamorous, yet fictional life." She shook her head sadly, then turned to the camera with a fake smile set in place. "Stay tuned for weight loss tips from Dr. Larry that really work."

Trav shut off the TV and headed straight for Shane's shop. His brother was friends with a lawyer. They had to be able to sue for this. Jessica had no right to completely humiliate Daisy like that on national television for one stupid mistake on a stupid blog.

He found his brother serving up coffee. The ice cream section of his shop was closed for the morning. No one wanted ice cream on a cold February morning.

"Shane, I need Gabe's number. I'm going to sue Jessica Larsen and Rogue TV."

Shane raised his brows and finished up the coffee order, handing it to a customer. He came out from behind the counter. "Slow down. What are you talking about? You want to sue?"

"Did I stutter? Did you see the way Jessica Larsen just destroyed Daisy on national television?"

"No, I didn't catch it. I was working." He grimaced and motioned for him to follow him to a quiet table in a corner of the shop. "How bad was it?"

Trav pulled out a chair and sat. "Bad. She showed Bryce screaming, Daisy's apartment, her apology blog post; then she kept showing the interview and pointing out the lies. Even Sally Phillips blabbed about us not being married."

Shane crinkled his nose in disgust. "Sally ratted you out? What happened to loyalty?"

"I know! We've got to sue."

"Slow down there," Shane said. "Does Daisy want to sue?"

"I didn't ask her."

"Yeah, well, ask her first. If I were her, I would want to let it die down. A long court case, that you might not even win, just makes it drag out, not to mention what you'll spend on lawyer's fees."

"I'll talk to Daisy later."

"I don't think going to court is a good idea."

"I didn't ask you what you think! Just give me the number."

The door opened, and Rachel Miller, Liz's best friend and Shane's secret crush, walked in. Shane stood and gave her a little wave. "I have to get back to work."

Trav wrapped Shane in a headlock. "Give me the number; then you can see your *friend*."

Shane broke free. "Knock it off!" His face was bright red.

Rachel approached. "Oh, are we giving noogies? Let me get in on this action." She rubbed her knuckles on Shane's head. He let her with a smile.

Trav appealed to Rachel. "Shane won't give me the number of his lawyer friend so I can sue Jessica Larsen for her exposé on Daisy."

Rachel shook her head. "I caught that this morning. I think you should sue. I know a couple of lawyers. I could hook you up."

"Thank you," Trav said. He fished his card out of his wallet and handed it to her.

"I still think it's a bad idea," Shane said quietly.

Trav was sick of Shane's let's-all-get-along attitude. "And I still think you should stop pretending you want to be just friends with Rachel and ask her out already." He raised his brows at Rachel to see how she took that news.

She cocked her head to the side, watching Shane for his reaction.

Shane flushed, opened his mouth and shut it again.

"Don't worry about it." Rachel flipped her braid over her shoulder. "We're just friends for a reason. Friendship lasts longer than the whole boyfriend-girlfriend thing. Hook me up with some caffeine, would ya?"

Trav stopped by Ry's place to check in on Daisy. She'd told him she'd be staying there a little longer. Reporters were lined up on the sidewalk and rushed toward him with their microphones.

"Are you Daisy's pretend husband?" one asked.

"What made you do it?"

"Did you think the truth wouldn't come out?"

He pushed past them. "No comment." He stopped at the front door. A couple of them had followed him to the porch. "This is private property. Back off before I call the cops."

They backed off, but the cameras were still focused on him. He knocked on the door. Daisy answered, half hiding behind the door, and let him in.

"Hi." Her voice was a monotone. She still wore her pajamas—a pair of Ry's old jogging pants rolled at the waist and ankles, and one of Ry's old sweatshirts. She'd never gotten home for more clothes. Liz was shorter than her, and she probably couldn't wear her sister's clothes without sticking out of them.

"Hey," he said. "I can stop by your place and pick up some clothes for you."

"These are fine."

"Did you catch the show?"

"No. I told you I wasn't going to watch it."

"I'm getting the name of a lawyer from Rachel. You can sue. Jessica had no right to come down so hard on you and your personal life."

"Keep your voice down. I finally got Bryce to sleep." Daisy shuffled into the kitchen, where a cup of coffee sat. "Help yourself to coffee."

He ignored the coffee and joined her at the table. "Just say the word, and we'll go after that bitch."

"No. It's done. I'm done."

Her tone. Her tangled hair, pale face. The utter resignation set off alarm bells in Trav's head. Of his mom and her struggle with depression that ended in her suicide.

"Daze, you can't just let her get away with it." He leaned forward, staring into her blank expression, trying to reach her. She turned away. "You have to fight back."

She sighed. "I don't want to fight. I screwed up. Nothing she said could have been any worse than the truth. I lied to millions of moms. Moms who struggled just like me, who felt like they had to live up to some standard I made up."

"No, you inspired them. You gave them hope."

"I gave them shit."

Panic rose up in him. The signs of depression—hopelessness, fatigue, not taking care of herself. He couldn't lose her like he lost his mother. Their son needed her most of all.

"Daze, please. Maybe you should talk to someone. You can talk to me. Or maybe a therapist. Depression is treatable."

Gran had made him see a therapist when he was seventeen as an alternative to letting the police deal with his latest fuck-up. He'd refused to speak the entire first month, but once he had, he'd learned to let go of his anger over his mom's death. Letting go of all that anger had changed his life. It didn't bring her back, but it had helped him breathe easy again.

Daisy looked at him blandly. "I'm not depressed. I'm just screwed up. Permanently screwed up."

"You're not. I swear you're not."

She slipped off the engagement ring and wedding band he'd given her and pressed them into his palm, closing his fingers around them. "Keep them. I'm done lying."

"No, Daze, you hang onto them." He set the rings on the table.

She stared at her coffee, her hands in her lap. "Please go. I want to be alone."

His gut churned. This couldn't be happening all over again. He couldn't go through that again.

"Now," she snapped.

"I'll go. But I'll be back to check on you tomorrow."

She turned and stared out the window, dismissing him.

He left and immediately called Ry. It went to voicemail. "Call me as soon as you can. It's Trav."

Trav showed up at the police station in Fieldridge, looking for Ryan. He found out he was out on a call, so he sat down to wait in one of the cold, hard plastic chairs in the front room of the station. Trav knew he shouldn't be bugging Ry at work, but no one would understand the need to treat depression better than his brother. He was the one who'd found their mother.

He dropped his head in his hands, memories of that horrific time flooding his already frazzled brain. He'd been fifteen and in no hurry to get home after school, as usual. He'd taken the long way home and joined a game of Wiffle ball on Rico's street.

His dad pounced on him the minute he stepped in the door. "Where've you been, son?"

"I stopped to play some ball."

His dad's mouth formed a grim line. Trav took a step toward the kitchen. He was starving.

His dad snagged his sleeve. "Sit down. We need to talk."

Trav figured he was in trouble again. Usually he was grounded for a week, but that didn't stop him from sneaking out late at night when everyone else was sleeping. His friend Matt's big brother kept them in beer, which they drank in the woods behind Matt's house.

They sat side by side on the sofa.

"Your mother died this afternoon," his dad said woodenly. "She died in her sleep. Peacefully."

"What? She wasn't even sick! She's not that old!"

"Sometimes these things happen," his dad said.

That's when he realized his brothers weren't around. "Where's Ry and Shane?"

"They're in their rooms."

There had to be a mistake. Any minute his mom would come out of her room.

Trav's voice came out small, barely a whisper. "Where's Mom?"

His father held back a sob that came out sounding choked. "The ambulance took her away."

"I want to see her! I didn't get to say goodbye!"

"I'm not taking you to the morgue. You'll say goodbye at the funeral." His father pinched the bridge of his nose. "I have to make arrangements. Go see Ry."

He'd run to Ry's room. His brother was lying in the dark, staring at the ceiling, in utter silence. At least Ry wouldn't fall apart on him like their dad.

Trav turned on the light. "Is it true? Did Mom really die in her sleep?"

Ry sat up, squinting his eyes against the glare of the light. "Yeah, she did."

Trav's eyes searched his brother's. "But it doesn't make any sense. She wasn't sick."

Ry looked at his hands clasped tightly together. "She's gone, and no amount of thinking on our part is gonna bring her back."

Trav broke down in tears. Ry sat in silent witness.

Shane peeked in the doorway. "I can't believe it."

"I know, bud," Ry said. "You guys can stay in here tonight, if you want."

Trav and Shane, being the youngest, shared a room while Ry had his own. They got through the week camped out on Ry's floor.

After the funeral, Trav had felt so much rage. It had been an open casket. She had looked perfect. No wounds so he crossed murder off his list. Still, he knew his dad had lied to him about his mom dying in her sleep. He wasn't stupid. It had to have been suicide. After everyone had returned to school and work, Trav had skipped out between classes and returned home to search for proof. There had to be a suicide note. His mom wouldn't have left them without a goodbye.

He'd torn apart his father's room, going through every dresser drawer, the nightstand, under the bed, under the mattress, through the closet, everything, and came up short. Had his father thrown out his wife's last message? Burned it?

He went through the trash and came up with nothing. Then he searched Ry's room. It would be just like his big bro to try to protect him from the truth. Nothing.

He'd about given up when he thought of his dad's brief-case. Would he take it to work? He waited, biding his time until his dad took a shower the next morning. He searched the briefcase, nothing. Just stupid marketing plans. He eyed the black leather wallet sitting on top of the dresser with some loose change.

The shower turned off. He'd have to be quick. He opened it, money, pictures—their wedding picture, school pictures of him and his brothers that were at least five years old—then he found it. In a small slot behind the credit cards. A folded-up note.

The suicide note.

Her last words to them: "I love you all."

How could she say she loved them and then leave them like this?

The bathroom door opened, and he faced his father, holding the note.

"What the hell do you think you're doing?" his dad snapped.

"You lied!" Trav yelled. "I hate you!" He'd dropped the note and ran, out of the house, down the street, to the far edge of town—the woods behind Matt's house where they kept a stash of beer.

Ry had found him huddled in the woods, empty beer cans all around him. "Come home, Trav."

Trav looked up, bleary eyed. "You knew, didn't you? You lied too!"

Ry looked at the ground.

Trav jumped up and shoved Ry with both hands. "Just tell me the truth!"

Ry met his eyes, a grim expression on his face. "I knew. I'm the one who found her. I wish I hadn't. I hoped you wouldn't have to have that in your head either."

"I hate you, you liar!" He pounded Ry's chest, furious with all the lies, with the unfairness of it all. Ry wrapped his arms around him, pulling him close so his arms were pinioned too tight to punch anymore. Trav stopped fighting and went limp. Then he cried, big, heaving wails of misery.

Ry let him cry until he had no tears left. Then he walked him home.

Trav thought of the night before her death often in the coming weeks. She'd been in her pajamas and robe all day, like usual. Something that was a red flag looking back. He'd been in bed reading. She'd tried to tuck him in.

He untucked the blanket from his legs. "I got it, Ma."

She smoothed his rumpled hair off his forehead. "You ever think about flying out that window to Neverland any more?" She smiled, her sad smile that didn't quite reach her eyes, and sprinkled pixie dust over him.

"I'm too old for that," he said, though he secretly liked that she remembered. It had been a long time. Years.

She leaned down and kissed his forehead, her hair tickling his nose. "You're never too old for dreams. Think happy thoughts and fly in your dreams."

His mother had finally flown. Forever young in Neverland.

Now, Ry was in front of him in his uniform. "Hey, what're you doing here? I was gonna call you back. I just had to check in on an accident."

Trav exhaled sharply. "Something's wrong with Daisy. She's...ever since Jessica figured out the lie, she's been so... depressed. She's staying with you. Do you think she needs treatment?"

Ry sat next to him. "She's not like Mom. Anyone would be upset with all this blowing up in their face. Liz says she always lands on her feet."

"Did you notice how pale she looks?" Trav asked anxiously, working hard to keep the panic at bay. "And she looks so tired. She's not taking care of herself."

"She's taking good care of Bryce, though." Ry clapped a hand on his shoulder. "She's got her priorities straight. Give her time. It's temporary, I promise."

Trav let out a breath. "Yeah, okay."

"And as long as she's living with us, Liz'll fuss over her, so there you go."

Trav smiled. Liz did cluck over Daisy like a mother hen, even though Liz was the younger sister.

Ry stood. "Those damn reporters better stop hounding her. I couldn't get out of my own driveway this morning."

"Can't we force them to stay away?"

"They're allowed to be in the street. It's open to the public. Listen, I gotta check in with the chief, but stop by for dinner tonight."

"Yeah, I will. Thanks, Ry."

"You got it."

Trav left feeling like he'd finally gotten off the roller coaster and stood on steady ground once more.

At Liz's insistence, Daisy joined them for dinner. She really wanted to stay in the guest room. As soon as the reporters left, she'd head home. She just needed to be alone with no one fussing over her. No one trying to take care of her.

"You need any help, sis?" Daisy asked, Bryce in her arms.

Liz was pulling a meatloaf from the oven. Potatoes boiled on the stove, and a steamer was heating something, probably vegetables.

"I've got it," Liz said. "I'm going to mash these potatoes, and everything else is just about done."

Ry walked in and breathed in the scent of dinner. "You spoil me. Did you make the meatloaf yourself?"

"I just warmed it up," Liz admitted. "It's from Garner's. I know it's Trav's favorite."

Daisy stiffened and turned to Liz. "You didn't tell me Trav was coming for dinner. He's gonna bug me about my clothes or keep asking me if I'm okay."

"Are you okay?" Ry asked.

"I'm fine," Daisy said.

Liz took in her oversized sweatshirt and jogging pants that she'd borrowed from Ry. "I have a dress that would fit you, just a little higher than over the knee on you. Why don't I get it?"

"Forget it. I'm comfortable." She finger-combed her hair back from her face. Her hand got caught in a knot, and she gave up. Instead she focused on Bryce. She put him into his high chair and put on his bib.

Liz went back to the stove. Ry set the table.

Daisy went to Liz's pantry, organized alphabetically. Her sister had a full stock of organic baby food kept on hand for whenever she watched Bryce. She pulled out some peas.

The doorbell rang.

Daisy shrank back. "Do you think it's a reporter?"

"I'll get it," Ry said. "It's probably Trav."

She had to calm down. Just because reporters constantly rang the bell and called didn't mean every single person was trying to rip her apart. It was just Trav. He wouldn't do anything worse than act overly concerned like everyone else in her life that had no faith in her.

Trav walked in, concern written all over his face as he studied Daisy. He quickly switched his focus to the baby. "How ya doing, Brycey boy?"

"Da-da-da-da," Bryce chanted, pounding his high chair tray and bouncing.

Trav grinned and lifted him from the chair. "That's right. Da-da." He lifted him into the air to Bryce's delight.

"He still needs to be fed," Daisy told him.

"Okay." Trav put Bryce back in the high chair. "I'll do it." He held out his hand for the jar and spoon.

"I got it," Daisy said. "At least I can do this."

"Of course you can," Trav said soothingly.

Daisy fed Bryce, ignoring the fact that Trav was staring at her like she was going to fall apart at any minute.

"Are you okay, Daze?" he asked gently.

She fed Bryce another spoonful of peas. "Fine."

"Sure?"

"I'm fine," she said between her teeth.

Liz and Ry brought the food to the table, and they all took a serving. Daisy took a few bites of meatloaf and stopped eating. She didn't have much of an appetite lately. She finished feeding Bryce and took him to the sink to wash up.

"Do you really think she's okay?" she heard Trav ask.

"She's just upset," Liz said.

Daisy ran the water so she wouldn't have to hear them talking about her. When she got back to the table, Trav studied her. She avoided his eyes. "You want to take Bryce?" she asked. "I'm not very hungry. I'm going to go rest."

Trav took Bryce. "You okay?"

"Stop asking if I'm okay! The answer doesn't change if you ask it more times. I'm fine, I'm fine, I'm fine!"

Trav's mouth dropped open. "Okay, okay. I won't ask."

"I don't need you to take care of me."

He held up a hand. "No one's trying to take care of you."

"Good! 'Cuz I'm fine." She stomped upstairs and threw herself onto the bed.

Too annoyed to relax, she got up and opened up Liz's laptop. She checked her blog to see how her readers had taken her apology from last night. There were more than a hundred comments. She started reading.

You are a lying bitch.

I can't believe I wasted my time reading your shitty blog.

Whore! Someone else should raise that poor bastard baby.

She stopped reading and shut the laptop.

She stared at the floor. It had all started so innocently. Holidays and baby's first tooth.

Maybe it wasn't all bad. What happened to all those nice people who used to comment? Surely some of them would stop by. She opened the laptop and scrolled quickly through the comments.

Honey, get yourself some professional help for your delusional state.

LIAR!!!!

You are an unfit mother.

Her hands started shaking, and she closed her eyes tight against the pain. She knew she wasn't a perfect mom, she could never live up to her own mom's example, but she'd never thought she was unfit to be Bryce's mom.

She moved the cursor to the top of the blog. Delete this blog. Are you sure? Yes.

The blog was gone.

And her perfect life with it.

24

Daisy peeked through the front window blinds. The reporters were still camped out in front of Liz and Ryan's house. Dammit. Didn't they take Saturdays off? She knew it had been hard for Ry and Liz to get to work the past few days. She hadn't been to work at all. Her parents understood she needed some time off.

"I'm doing a few errands," Liz said, coming up behind her. "You want to come along? Nothing exciting, but we could stop for lunch somewhere."

Daisy shook her head. She really didn't want to go out. "That's okay, sis. I'll just stay here with Bryce." He was taking his mid-morning nap, usually only an hour.

Liz studied her. "You haven't gone out at all or called anyone. Why don't you have some friends over?"

"That's a good idea." She had no intention of calling her friends. She just wanted to be alone.

Liz looked relieved. "Good. Okay, I'll see you when I get back. Call my cell if you need anything. Ryan should be getting off his shift by five."

"I'm sure I won't need to call you."

Liz wiggled her fingers in a goodbye, squared her shoulders, and left by the front door. Daisy heard the rush of reporters approach and her sister's voice ring out. "Wrong sister. Daisy's not home."

"I see her car," someone said.

"Her friend picked her up," Liz replied.

A moment later, she heard Liz drive off.

Daisy flipped on the TV and watched a rerun of *Law & Order: SVU*.

Bryce's wail carried through from both the baby monitor Liz had set up and from upstairs. The kid had powerful lungs. She took care of him, fed them both lunch, and went back to watching TV. She turned Bryce's swing the other way so he wouldn't see any violent images.

She heard a commotion outside and peeked out the window. Omigod. Max was striding up the front steps, brushing off reporters right and left. He rang the bell.

She opened the door, staying out of sight. He stepped in, and she slammed it shut behind him.

"Max, what are you doing here?"

He ran a hand through his thick, black hair. "Nice to see you too, Daze."

"You shouldn't have come. The press are going to pick up on who you are. They're going to say I'm seeing my ex-husband again!"

"Calm down. Nobody cares about me." He glanced over to where the TV was still blaring *Law and Order: SVU* and over to Bryce, who was smacking the star mobile that hung off his swing. "Hey, Bryce." Max spun one of the stars, and Bryce stared at it. Max indicated the leather sofa. "Can we talk?"

Daisy followed Max over to the sofa in silence. She didn't want to talk, especially with Max, who either wanted to bug her about a relationship (not gonna happen) or talk about the blog fiasco (didn't want to go there either). But he'd come all the way from the city, and there were reporters outside, so she didn't kick him out right away. She turned the volume down, but didn't turn it off.

He leaned forward, resting his elbows on his knees. "How you holding up?"

"I'm fine. You didn't have to drive all the way out here to ask me that."

"Blunt as always."

She raised a brow. She wondered how long she'd have to wait before she could send him on his merry way. "Why are you here? Just tell me."

"I can book you on *Katie* to tell the world your side of the story. I called in a favor, but truthfully Katie knows it's a ratings boon to have you on."

Katie was an even bigger show than *Mornings with Jessica*. It was an afternoon show that even her mom liked to watch. On a normal day, she would've been jumping for joy. This wasn't a normal day.

Daisy shook her head. "No more talk shows."

"I really think you should speak up. Katie won't ask any tough questions. In fact, she'll give you approval over the questions ahead of time."

"Max, no. I just want this whole thing to go away. I want those reporters out of here with no more stories to tell. Besides, Jessica was right. I'm a liar and a fraud. If I went on *Katie*, I'd just tell her the same thing."

He scooted closer and held her hand in a warm grasp. "I can fix this. Let me help you. I'll write your answers for you ahead of time, put a positive spin on things. Then you just have to memorize them and say them on air."

She took her hand back. "You weren't much help when Jessica pitched the show to the higher-ups. You said it was good business. I don't need that kind of help."

Max's lips formed a straight line. He jerked his head in the direction of the reporters out front. "What are you gonna do about them?"

"Nothing. Just ignore them. Say no comment."

"Come back to the city with me. I'm on the twenty-third floor with a doorman. No one will bother you there."

She stared at him. "You want me to move in with you."

"You and Bryce. Yes."

"And sleep in your bed."

He laughed. "That is entirely up to you. I also have a pullout sofa."

"But you're hoping."

He raised his palms. "I hope to be with you, yes, because I love you. I will never stop loving you."

She turned her attention back to the TV. "Please go."

He stood between her and the TV, blocking her view. "Daze, I don't want to go. I want to help you. Let me take care of you."

"I don't want your help." She scowled at him. "And I don't want you either."

"So you're with Trav now?"

"I'm not with anyone. It's just me and Bryce, and that's the way it's gonna stay."

He knelt in front of her and took both her hands in his. She groaned.

"Just hear me out," Max said. "Here's what I can give you —a good life in the city, a nice apartment, a fun social life. I can restore your reputation. If you want to work, I've got so many connections, I can get you started on whatever career path you want. I will take care of you and Bryce and spend every day for the rest of my life trying to make you happy. Just say the word, Daze. And all this"—he gestured to the reporters—"goes away, and your new life begins."

The old Daisy would've jumped at the offering. The easy life lay out before her. No work, no effort, but also, no self-respect.

"It's so easy," she murmured.

His eyes brightened, hopeful. "Yes. It really is that easy. Just come with me." He stood and tugged on her hand.

She stood and faced him. "I hope you find someone that really deserves you. The kind of person who understands putting ratings ahead of people's lives. Goodbye, Max."

He blinked, nodded, and pivoted to the door. She watched him stride away, tension in every step. And then the door shut quietly behind him.

She let out a breath of relief. She was alone again. No one

asking about her, no one trying to fix her, just her and Bryce. That was all she needed.

∾

Trav sat at Garner's bar Saturday night, nursing a beer, Rico at his side. The Knicks were playing on TV above the bar, but his mind wasn't on the game. He turned to Rico. "Ry says Max stopped by to see Daisy, but she sent him packing."

Rico shook his head. "He shouldn't have told you that."

"Why? You wouldn't want to know if an ex was moving in on your woman?"

"She's not your—"

"You'd better shut it."

"You guys gossip like a bunch of old ladies. So he stopped by. Who cares? She kicked him out. Do you feel any better for knowing about it?"

Trav peeled the label off his beer bottle. "No," he admitted.

Rico inclined his head and turned his attention back to the Knicks.

"He offered to let her move in with him," Trav said.

Rico's head snapped around. "Are you kidding me? That's fucking wrong. I'd kick his ass."

"See? I told you."

"What an asshole."

"I know!" Trav felt marginally better to have Rico back him up. "She should live with me."

Rico put his hand up. "Stop right there. She sent him packing when he asked her to live with him. You think you'll do any better? 'Cuz I gotta say history ain't on your side."

Trav took a pull on his beer. "Let her come to me, huh?"

Rico went back to the game. "That's my motto. And they always do."

Yeah, but Rico didn't have a particular woman he wanted to come to him. He could afford to sit back and take whatever came his way. Trav wanted Daisy. He blew out a frustrated breath. He was no closer to having them be a family now than he was the day Bryce was born.

He had no clue how to reach her.

He only knew he had to try.

On Sunday the reporters finally left, and Daisy breathed a sigh of relief. Bryce went off with Trav for their daddy-son day. Trav was really becoming a nuisance. He checked in on her every freaking day, studying her like she was going to disappear right before his eyes. She was glad he would be busy with Bryce today.

She pulled into her parents' driveway, only a ten-minute drive from Ry and Liz's place, and knocked on the front door. She could've used her key, but she'd learned the hard way not to bust in on them without warning. The image of her parents naked on the sofa was burned into her brain. Seriously, there were four bedrooms upstairs.

Her dad answered. "Hey, sweetheart, good to see you. How're you holding up?"

She stood on tiptoe to kiss his cheek. "Fine." Her standard answer nowadays. "How're you guys?"

"Good." He turned and called upstairs. "Heather, your daughter is here!"

"Which one?"

"Which one do you want it to be?" Daisy called.

Her mom came downstairs. "Daisy, just the one I hoped. Honey, we need to talk."

"About what?"

"About this." Her mom approached, lifting a lock of Daisy's hair, pulling the sides of Ryan's oversized sweatshirt. "This look is really not working for you."

Daisy waved that away. "I'm heading back to my place after this. I'll wear my own clothes again soon."

Her mother stared. "And your hair. You've got to wash your hair. And brush it."

"I will. Soon."

Her mom put her hands on her hips. "Liz says you're not leaving the house and you haven't had anyone over."

The freaking Garner police.

"I'm here, aren't I?" Daisy huffed. "I left the house. Report back to Liz next time you talk about me."

"You want some hot cocoa with marshmallows?" her mom asked, already heading for the kitchen.

The drink promised nostalgic comfort for snow days when they'd been off school. Her mom would stay home with her and Liz and have cocoa warm and ready when they came in from playing in the snow.

"Yes, please." She followed her to the kitchen and sat in the cozy breakfast nook at the round wood table. She still always sat in her old spot, facing the window, where she had a view of the side yard, trees, and, in the warmer months, blooming azalea bushes.

Her dad stopped by. "I'm heading into town to pick up a new switchplate. Need anything?"

"We're good, thanks," her mom replied.

Her dad kissed her mom on the lips. Her parents' marriage was strong. She could do with a little less PDA in front of the kids, but she was glad. It seemed like they'd always been this way. Totally in love. Working together, enjoying each other. She'd never heard them fight.

Her dad left, and then it was just Daisy and her mom.

Her mom bustled around the kitchen, preparing the cocoa. Daisy sat quietly, watching her mom work, the sight soothing her. A short while later, her mom joined her at the table with two steaming hot cups of cocoa.

Daisy took a sip. "Mom, how did you know marrying Dad was the right thing to do?"

Her mom looked surprised at the question. "Because we loved each other, of course."

"Yes, but how did you know marriage was the right choice?" She stirred the mini marshmallows in her cocoa. "Was he, like, your soul mate? Like two halves coming together to make one whole?"

Her mom looked at her like she was an idiot.

Daisy pushed on. "Because Max says we're soul mates. He wants to marry me."

"Mr. Big Shot Producer," her mom muttered. "No."

"What do you mean no?"

"I mean, no, I don't believe in soul mates, that is, one person just for you. I think people's hearts are bigger than that. You can love many times over. The person that's right for you is the person that you genuinely like and want to be with through thick and thin. And, of course, chemistry helps too." She laughed.

Daisy thought about that.

"Daisy, I also mean, no, Max is not the one for you."

"But I did love him once."

"But you don't love him now."

She shook her head. "No, I don't."

They drank their cocoa in silence.

"Honey, I still say you should marry Trav," her mom said. "He's asked you enough times."

Daisy turned bleak eyes to her mom. "I don't love him either."

"You can *learn* to love him."

Daisy shifted uncomfortably in her seat. "I don't want to marry him and hope that one day I'll love him. That's not right."

"He's Bryce's father!"

Daisy stood abruptly. "I'm going home."

Her mom narrowed her eyes with her patented steely mom look. "Sit down. You're not running out on this conversation."

Daisy sat.

Her mom took a deep breath and looked at the ceiling. "I'm going to tell you something that I swore I would never tell you."

That got her attention. Daisy sat there, riveted.

"You want to know how I knew marrying your dad was the right thing? I didn't. Not until much later. I was pregnant with you, and he asked me to marry him, which I gratefully did."

Daisy's mouth dropped open in shock. "You were pregnant with me?"

Her mom looked a little miffed she'd been forced to share this news. "Yes. We called you a honeymoon baby, and no one knew the difference. You were conceived on impulse, much like Bryce, and I never regretted it. Not for one minute." She lifted her chin defiantly.

Daisy's mind reeled with this news. Suddenly her mom pushing her on Trav made so much sense.

"Is that why you've been telling me to marry Trav? You want me to have the kind of happily-ever-after that you did?"

"Well, yes."

Daisy looked at her mom in a whole new light. She smiled at the wonder of it all. "I never knew you did anything impulsive. I thought that was my territory."

Her mom grinned. "Well, where do you think you get it from?"

Daisy couldn't believe it. All this time, she'd thought she was just a screw-up in her mom's eyes, when her mom actually saw a lot they had in common. But she had screwed up. A lot worse than her mom ever had.

"Oh, Mom, I've really made a mess of things. Did you know I made stuff up on my blog because I thought you were so perfect, and I wanted to feel like that too?"

Her mom laughed. "Really? I thought it was because you enjoyed writing fiction. You always did have a great imagination."

Maybe that's what she should've been doing. Writing fiction instead of pretending her dream life was real. She drank her cocoa, and her mom did the same, eyeing her over the brim of her cup.

"Daisy, you're a great mom. You're doing beautifully with Bryce. That's a huge accomplishment right there. You don't have to be perfect to do a good job."

"I always thought you were the perfect mom. You always tell me how to get Bryce calmed down, and it takes me forever to make that happen. You do it just like that." She snapped her fingers.

Her mom smiled indulgently. "I'm relaxed. Babies sense that. You're exhausted most of the time. I admire your fortitude. Even with lack of sleep and working hard at Garner's, you're still doing your best for him. It's more than I did. I couldn't handle the lack of sleep. Your grandmother took nights for me."

Daisy's eyes widened in surprise. "Grandma? I never knew that."

"She lived with us for your entire first year. She took nights; I did days. And I wasn't working a strenuous job. Your dad and I were just beginning to plan Garner's. We had savings from his pro career."

Her dad was the former quarterback for the New England Blazers. So it *had* been easier for her mom. She hadn't been the perfect mom. And that meant Daisy wasn't the most imperfect mom ever. A vague memory of her grandmother at the house tickled her brain. "She lived with us when Liz was a baby too, didn't she? When I was three. I remember helping her make peanut butter jelly sandwiches for lunch."

Her mom smiled. "I couldn't have done it without her." She squeezed Daisy's hand. "And now I'm paying it forward. I have been a help with Bryce, haven't I?"

She had. She hadn't moved in—too much work at Garner's for that—but she'd taken many afternoons and was always available on a moment's notice.

"Daisy, the rest of your life is waiting for you to take the reins. Are you going to stay holed up at home, or are you going to get back out there?"

Daisy straightened. "What a question. I'll get back out there."

"That's my girl. And give Trav another chance. I have a really good feeling about you two."

"You're just saying that because you want me to marry Bryce's father."

"I'd never push you if I didn't think he was a major hunk." She hid a smile by sipping her cocoa.

"Mom!"

"What? I did see him in full frontal glory."

Daisy shuddered. "Oh. My. God. You did not just say that. You keep your eyes on Dad."

"Nothing wrong with looking."

"Blech! My mom cannot be checking out my..."

Her mom grinned. "Love?"

"My...something. I don't know what he is."

Her mom became serious. "I think it's time you found out."

25

Trav knew he should cool it when it came to Daisy. She'd been depressed for a week now. He shouldn't be so concerned. Ry kept telling him to cool it. Yet he couldn't stop himself from checking in on her every day.

He rang the bell to her apartment.

Daisy opened it. "I'm fine, Trav. You don't have to keep checking up on me."

He stepped inside and gave her a quick once-over. She was wearing clean clothes—jeans and a fuzzy V-neck sweater —and she'd washed her hair. That was a step in the right direction.

"I'm not," he said, slipping off his jacket. "I'm just visiting Bryce."

He didn't miss her eye roll as he headed for Bryce on his blanket doing what looked like baby pushups. "That's new."

She stood by his side, and he breathed in her citrusy scent. "I think he's gonna crawl soon," she said.

He turned to her in surprise and snapped his attention back to Bryce. "Really? Already?" He grinned and pounded his chest. "That's my boy."

"We've got to baby proof everything." She sat cross-legged on the floor. "I mean *everything*. We are in for it."

He sat next to her, imitating her position. "How ya doing?"

"Fine," she said through her teeth.

"I was glad to hear you went back to work. Good to keep busy, be around other people."

"Not when those people stare at you like you're a freak because Jessica Larsen made you sound like a monster on national television."

"No one thinks you're a freak. They probably think you're famous. They're curious."

She scoffed. "Freakishly famous."

"They're probably like"—he spoke behind his hand—"there goes that freakishly beautiful Garner girl."

"That's Liz."

"With that freakishly hot bod."

She smacked his chest and leaned her head against his shoulder. Bryce achieved liftoff and rocked back and forth on hands and knees.

"Oh!" Daisy exclaimed.

Bryce's chest hit the blanket, butt up in the air, and he worked to push up again.

Daisy straightened and clapped her hands. "He's so cute! Go, Bryce!"

Bryce pushed up and rocked back and forth.

They sat there watching Bryce work hard on crawling until the boy tired out and started crying. Daisy scooped him up and held him close, speaking softly to him.

Trav's throat tightened at the sight. He never wanted Bryce to know the pain of losing his mother.

"I'm still getting nasty emails," Daisy told him.

He shook his head. "These people need to get a life. Did anyone threaten you?"

"No death threats," she said, patting Bryce's back. "Yet," she added.

"If someone threatens you, forward it to Ry. He'll track them down, and you can press charges."

She crossed to the sofa and sat down. "Everyone hates me, Trav." Her voice came out small.

He sat next to her on the sofa. "No one hates you."

She nodded. "They do. They really do. And there's nothing I can do about it. I screwed up, and people want me to pay for it." She met his eyes. "If they only knew how I felt on the inside, they'd know I pay for it every minute of every day."

Panic clutched at his heart. He found it hard to breathe. He jumped off the sofa and bolted for the kitchen, where he helped himself to a glass of water. He couldn't let this go on. People were torturing her, remembering only her mistakes, ignoring what she'd done that was right and good. He'd been in a similar place as a teenager. It had gotten to the point where he didn't even have to say anything, his reputation spoke for him, teachers dreaded having him in the classroom. Fathers didn't want him to date their daughters, despite the fact he'd never been disrespectful to girls. He loved women. He loved Daisy.

Geez, he was an idiot. Why had he acted like love was something invented by corporations? He loved Daisy so much it made him hurt when she hurt. When she was happy, he was happy. Wasn't that what love was, caring about someone else as much or more than yourself?

He returned to her side. Bryce was sound asleep in her arms.

"Here, let me." He reached for his son.

She shook her head. "He'll wake up," she whispered.

He ignored her and lifted Bryce from her arms, carrying him to the bedroom, where he deposited him gently in the crib. The little guy curled on his side in blissful sleep.

He returned to Daisy and sat on the sofa. She sat there, mouth agape, staring at him. "How did you do that?"

"Do what?"

"Move him without waking him. I always have to hold him at least a half hour."

He shrugged. "I always do that."

"Wish that worked for me."

"He's probably in heaven in your arms and gets mad when he has to leave."

She snorted.

"I know I would be." He scooted down and put his head in her lap. She stroked his hair. "Daze, I love you."

Her hand stilled, and he read not joy in her face, but pain. She stared across the room, not meeting his eyes. "Don't love me, Trav. I don't deserve you."

He sat up. "Yes, you do. I don't deserve you."

"Don't. Don't just say that because I said it. Besides, you're wrong. It'll be a long time before I can earn anyone's love and respect. I'm bad news."

He took her hand. "I used to have a bad rep, you know."

She shook her head. "It's not the same. You were just a kid."

"Grown-ups make mistakes too. You're human. The important thing is you won't make the same mistake again."

She sighed and leaned her head on his shoulder. "I'm so tired. Can I just rest here, just like this?"

"Yeah, you can." He slipped an arm around her shoulders and held her like that. He wasn't upset that she didn't say she loved him back. He understood her well because she was very much like him. She'd had a shattering blow to her confidence and needed to feel whole again. He couldn't pull her out of her funk alone, but, based on his experience in straightening out his own life, he had an idea of who could.

Daisy felt Trav's absence keenly. He hadn't checked in on her all week, and he'd been brusque when he took Bryce for his usual Sunday daddy-son day yesterday. While she'd been so busy being annoyed with him for checking in on her, she hadn't taken the time to appreciate why he did it. He'd offered his love, and she'd thrown it back in his face.

She grabbed some Sno-Caps from the cabinet and settled on the sofa. Maybe she should call him. No. She didn't deserve his love. She didn't deserve anything. She tossed back the Sno-Caps and chewed.

The doorbell rang, and she leaped to answer it, hoping it

didn't wake Bryce. She swung open the front door. Trav stood there holding a large cardboard box. He smiled. She smiled back, her throat tight. He was here. He hadn't given up on her.

"Hey to you, too." He muscled past her with the box and set it on the kitchen table. "Open it."

She pulled open the folded-over flaps. Letters. Lots and lots of letters. All addressed to her.

"What in the world?" She lifted an envelope and slowly pulled out a letter. In bold letters at the top it read: Why Daisy Garner Kicks Ass…

She read the note from Mrs. Peters, her first-grade teacher, with Trav looking over her shoulder. The shaky scrawl came right to the point:

Daisy was the kind of girl that the boys loved to chase and pull her pigtails. But unlike some little girls, who tattled and cried, Daisy fought back, stealing baseball caps and spitting in their juice as our juice helper. I knew then that this girl was going to be strong and feisty just like the woman she is today.

Rock on, Daisy.

Mrs. Bertha Peters

Daisy clapped a hand over her mouth, torn between a laugh and a cry.

"You spit in their juice?" Trav asked. "I'm glad I never crossed you back then."

Daisy laughed. "I did. And Mrs. Peters never said a word. I thought she didn't know." She pulled out the next letter from Sally Phillips, the town clerk.

The same thing at the top in bold letters: Why Daisy Garner Kicks Ass. Trav must have printed out a bunch of these and went around town gathering responses. She glanced at Trav, who was reading the letter, and her eyes teared up. He chuckled as he read, so she read on to see what was so funny.

· · ·

Now maybe I shouldn't have talked to that reporter about you, Daisy. I'm afraid I got a little excited about being on TV, so I understand perfectly why you might have lied to get on TV too. I'm telling everyone who comes into Town Hall how it was all just a silly mistake; then I remind them of that time when you were ten and sat right outside this very room handing out Vote for Sally Phillips for Town Clerk buttons to everyone who came in since you had newly decided to be a democrat. I didn't have the heart to tell you I was running unopposed because who wanted to stand in the way of all that fiery passion once you discovered your political path? Never lose that fire, Daisy. Hold it close to your heart. The world needs more people like you that act from the heart.

Sincerely,

Sally Phillips, Town Clerk

Her knees went weak, and she slowly sank to a kitchen chair. She pulled out the next letter, and the next, and the next. From everyone in town—Alan Zinkman the mailman, Gary from the health food store, her old soccer coach. Her family, his family, her friends. Everyone. And then she got to the letter from Chief Bailey.

She turned to Trav. "He says we should read it together."

He scooted closer.

Why Daisy Garner Kicks Ass…(And Trav does too)

She smiled at Trav and kept reading.

Daisy and Trav, when I heard you two had a kid, I thought, look out, Clover Park. You both had your fair share of trouble, but you want to know something? I always saw, in both of you, the good in you. I tried to scare you straight. Trav, I think that worked for you. But, Daisy, you don't scare so easily. You're tough, stubborn, strong. That's what's gonna see you through this mess with that TV show. Maybe when you come out the other side, you'll find yourself on a new path. The one that Trav's been walking all this time. Daisy and Trav, you kick ass because no matter what comes down the pike, you just keep going. As for Bryce, all I can say is what goes around, comes around. But maybe you'll remember to see the good in him too.

Chief Glenn Bailey

"Oh gawd," Daisy said. "I'm gonna start bawling."

Trav looked at her with alarm. "This is supposed to make you feel better."

She threw her arms around him. "It does. I can't believe you did this. Why?"

He pulled back to gaze into her eyes. "I've been in your shoes. In fact, I've been *beneath* your shoes. I pulled some crazy shit when I was a teenager, and the people of this town helped me get it together. They believed in me when I didn't believe in myself. I wanted that for you. And I didn't do this to take care of you. I did it because I believe in you." He grabbed a handful of letters. "And all these people believe in you too."

She opened her mouth and shut it. She'd turned her back on Clover Park the very first moment she could make her escape. And now her hometown, her community, was truly welcoming her back with open arms even knowing how she'd screwed up again.

And Trav—the guy she'd pushed away with every word of committed, stable future that had come out of his mouth —was, amazingly, still here. She was so glad he was. He wasn't like Max. He'd never turn on her or abandon her. He'd shown her that in every way he could from that first night they'd been together. She'd listened to those messages he'd left on her cell after she'd skipped town. They were sweet, but she'd been too afraid to give a relationship a chance.

Trav's first message: "Look, I never do bar hookups, but I've always liked you." And the next: "Daze, this wasn't a one-night stand for me. I want to see you again." And his last try: "I don't know what that night meant to you, but... anyway, call me if you want to go out sometime. Take care of yourself."

Now her voice came out choked with tears. "I-I don't know what to say. This is all so..."

He pulled an envelope from his back pocket and handed it to her. "Here, read mine."

With shaking hands, she took it from him.

∼

Trav shoved his hands in his pockets, hoping to hell that she wouldn't judge him, that she'd understand.

He didn't have to read along with her. He had it memorized. It had taken him ten tries to get it right.

Why Daisy Garner Kicks Ass...

Daze, I am so damn proud of you. You've been working your ass off since day one when our son was born. Always putting him first. You're raising him with so much love even though he's a tough kid, always going that extra step to meet his needs. You amaze me. So you stretched the truth a little in a blog. You apologized, and, in my book, that's enough. That's why you kick ass.

Everything you heard about me is true. Drinking, drugs, stealing, vandalism, fighting. It was only a matter of time before I got shipped off to juvie. I hit rock bottom at seventeen when I broke into the high school and set fire to my permanent record. I was sick of everyone judging me the minute I showed up. I know, it doesn't make sense. I did do bad shit. Anyway, I thought the fire was out when I tossed it in the trash, but the embers caught on some other papers, and, before I knew it, the fire had spread. I booked it out of there, hitting the fire alarm as I left.

You probably know the rest of the story. The fire department got there in time to save the school. The main office was damaged but still structurally sound. I didn't come forward like I should've. They came and got me. Turns out a security camera showed me breaking in. I was facing breaking and entering, trespassing, arson, destroying public property. Principal Herzog was going to throw the works at me. He hated me for all the trouble I caused, and I didn't blame him.

It only took a few people to believe in me. That was Gran, Ry, and Chief Bailey. The chief talked the principal down, and the town agreed to let me make up for it with community service. I mowed lawns, cleaned up litter, and weeded anyone's garden who needed it, by hand. Do you know how many weeds grow in the spring and summer around here? I do. Long story short. I loved working outside, and now I'm a landscape architect. So I guess that turned out okay.

Daze, just like for me, this whole town has your back. I'm sorry for pushing you so hard to marry me just because it was best for Bryce. I guess my screwed-up family made me want a better life for Bryce real bad. I did this all bass ackwards as usual. So I will only ask you this. Will you go on a first date with me? We can have dinner at a back booth at Garner's and talk all night about our dreams, our hopes for the future, what we love, what we hate, just like we said we did in the first place.

Love,
Trav

She looked at him, her smile big and sunny, making his heart fill with joy to see that smile again.

"Yes, Travis O'Hare, I will go on a first date with you."

26

Daisy couldn't believe Trav remembered their fictional first date so well, but here she was living it. Saying *yes* to Trav was the best thing she'd ever done. He held the door to Garner's open for her as they left the restaurant. It was late. They'd already been talking in a back booth for two hours, trading horror stories of their teenage pranks and adventures. They vowed to keep Bryce on a tight leash.

"Where to now?" Trav asked.

"Come back to my place," she said.

He grinned devilishly. "Yeah, I'm all over that."

"To talk!"

"Oh, yeah, talk. Of course." He swatted her butt. She jumped and swatted him back. "That's what I meant."

"Yeah, yeah, yeah," she said.

They walked to where she'd parked her car and made the short drive back to her apartment. Bryce was staying with her parents for the night, who were thrilled she was going on a date with Trav.

When they got to her place, she poured them both a glass of white wine and joined him on the sofa.

"Thanks," he said, taking the wine. "So we've covered hopes, dreams, loves, hates. Teenage tales of woe. What else do you want to know about me?"

"Tell me why you love me."

"I love you because you are bright and bubbly, and loving, and fun, and so-oo-oo *sexy*." He waggled his brows and leered at her.

"How can I take you seriously?" she asked with a laugh.

"You want serious?" He set down the wineglass and went down on one knee in front of her.

"No! Don't do it!"

"Daisy Garner, I will love you until the day I die—"

She put her fingertips over his lips and knelt beside him. "It's my turn. I will love you until the day I die."

He kissed her fingers and held her hand.

"I've loved you from the first moment you held Bryce. I fought it because I didn't trust myself not to screw up. But now I do. Trust myself, that is. Travis O'Hare, will you do me the honor of becoming my husband?"

He cradled her face and placed a tender kiss on her lips. "I knew I'd wear you down."

"So what's your answer?"

He rocked his head side to side, considering. "I kinda like this turnaround. Think I might leave you hanging a little longer."

"Maybe you need a little convincing," she said, throwing herself on top of him. They toppled over, and she straddled him.

He ran his hands from her hips up to her breasts. "I do. I need a lot of convincing."

She pulled her shirt off, revealing her black lace bra.

He groaned. "I love you, woman."

She smiled, knowing she had him for life and not because of Bryce, because of them, who did everything backwards, but still found a way to move forward together.

She unclipped the front clasp of her bra. "I love you too, man," she said cheekily, swinging the bra over her head and throwing it across the room.

He laughed. She slowly leaned down, her breasts rubbing his chest, and he became serious as she went in for a kiss. She stopped a breath away. "Did I convince you yet?"

One corner of his mouth kicked up. "I'm afraid not."

She kissed him then, suddenly ravenous for him. He wrapped one hand in her hair, holding her head as he kissed her back, slow and tender, his mouth tasting and nibbling, while his other hand ran down her spine and cupped her bottom. He kissed her like he had all day, and it was making her crazy.

She broke the kiss. "Trav, I want you." She undid the button on her jeans, and his hand stopped hers on the zipper.

"I got it." He pulled her up off the floor. His hands made short work of it as her jeans and thong hit the floor.

She pulled off his shirt and reached for his jeans.

"Slow down there, Speed Racer," he said. "It's called fore-play. And you're first."

He kissed her, and his hand slipped between them to stroke her. She moaned and stroked him over his jeans. He pushed her hand away and moved to kissing her neck, keeping up a slow and thorough massage, touching every-where but where she craved it most.

"My turn," she gasped. "I want to give to you."

"Oh, you will," he told her, moving up to kiss the shell of her ear. "You will."

He increased the pressure and finally reached her center. Her knees buckled, and she surrendered to the rush of sensa-tion. She wrapped her arms around his neck and simply hung on for the ride. Moments later she cried out, his name on her lips.

He kissed her again. She gave him a slow smile and dropped to her knees, unzipping his jeans and pulling them down with his briefs. "Your turn."

She took him in her mouth and heard his sharp intake of breath. Now she was in no hurry, determined to torture him with slow tastes and deep suction, her hands cupping and massaging him underneath.

He watched her, and she felt the moment he started to lose control. She pulled back and looked up at him. "Did I convince you yet?"

He grasped her arms and pulled her up. "This is gonna be

over way too soon if you keep that up." He led her into the bedroom. "And I still need a lot of convincing."

She crawled onto the bed, stopped on all fours, and looked over her shoulder at him. "Take me, Trav," she said huskily.

"Now I see what you're doing there," he said, setting a condom on the nightstand. "And I do appreciate the view, but this isn't gonna be a wham, bam, thank you, ma'am."

"I like the wham, bam," she said, rolling to her back and opening her legs to him. She let her fingers trail down, touching herself. "Are you convinced yet?"

He closed his eyes. "Not yet," he croaked.

Then he was on her, entering her in one swift stroke that had her breath catching. She wrapped her arms and legs around him, bucking her hips, urging him along. He stilled, slowly pulled out and thrust back inside. Again. And again. Forcing her to his rhythm. She stopped bucking and went with it, letting him take the lead, take his fill. She gave him everything she had in complete surrender. He must have felt the moment she was on the edge because he suddenly pumped hard and fast, giving her the release she needed. He went with her a moment later.

Trav rose up on his elbows and grinned down at her. She smiled back, filled with love for this man.

He kissed her again. "I love you."

"I love you too. Does this mean you'll be my husband?"

"I might need some more convincing," he said with a grin.

"Well, we've got all night."

He nibbled at her lower lip. "Yeah, we do."

They spent the night wrapped in each other's arms, their love burning bright and hot. By noon, they got up for lunch. He kept her in his lap as they ate grilled cheese, his hand playing with the side of her breast, her hand running through the hair at the nape of his neck.

She met his hazel eyes and saw love shining back at her. "I've got you now," she told him.

"You always have," he replied.

EPILOGUE

They married barefoot on the beach in July.

Daisy didn't want to overshadow Liz's special day in June —a grand event with most of the town in attendance in a huge mansion that was owned by the town and used for special events. Liz had looked like Scarlett O'Hara descending that grand staircase to her very own Rhett Butler. Their parents had catered, of course.

Daisy dug her toes into the sand across from Trav. Her tulle over chiffon gown was cut high in the front, ending mid calf so it didn't get caught in the sand, while the back trailed full length behind her. Trav looked stunning in a tux with the pants rolled up at the cuffs. Ry stood next to Trav as one of three best men, holding Bryce in a baby tux. Her little guy was officially an O'Hare now. He'd turn one next month and was already walking. He was so much happier now that he was on the move and had settled right in with her at Trav's place. The other two best men, Shane and Rico, stood nearby. Liz was her matron of honor, and her two closest friends, Amber and Zoe, her bridesmaids.

Justice Fleming approached the happy couple as the sun began to set over the Long Island Sound. Maggie had held out hope that her new certificate as a minister of love that she'd printed off the Internet would turn things in her favor, but they'd remained firm in their choice of the justice of the peace.

Daisy took a deep breath. Now that it was real, she was shaking. She'd never gotten married with so much riding on the outcome. Her son's future happiness. She'd demanded so much from Trav. Could she give as much as he gave?

Trav gripped her hand tight, seeming to sense her nerves. "Relax. It's us. We're forever."

And just like that, she felt better. It was the "us." There truly was an us now, living together, raising Bryce together, sleeping together. Her body warmed at the memory.

Justice Fleming, an elderly woman with dyed black hair, looked to her for the go-ahead. She nodded.

"Friends and family, we are gathered here today to witness the marriage of Dorothy—"

"Daisy!" she corrected, her face flaming.

"*Daisy* Garner and Travis O'Hare. On this beautiful beach, we are privileged to witness the love of two young people close to our hearts."

"I've written my own vows," Trav whispered.

Daisy turned to him in shock. "You did?" She'd planned to recite whatever the judge said. Trav was always surprising her. Like when he'd told her he wanted to put an addition on to the house and then showed her an amazing plan he'd designed. She'd have to try to keep up. She looked forward to the challenge.

Trav smiled. "Yeah, I'll go first."

"The groom has prepared his own vows and would like to go first," Justice Fleming announced.

"Awww…" the crowd sighed.

Trav cleared his throat. "Daisy, I promise to be my whole genuine self with you. You'll have to put up with my jokes, and my bed head, and my toothpaste cap problem."

Daisy smiled as the crowd tittered.

He went on. "And in return, I promise to leave the seat down and never, ever, say you look fat in those jeans." His eyes sparkled merrily. "Through thick and thin, good and bad, for the rest of our lives."

She gazed at him, a surge of affection running through her. She just wanted to kiss him right now. "You goof."

He grinned. "Your turn, sweetheart."

"Travis, I promise to be my genuine self with you and give to you as much as you've always freely given to me. I won't be the perfect wife or the perfect mother, but I will always work hard to be my best. You'll have to put up with…" She tried to think of some bad habits that she wouldn't mind sharing with the world.

Trav shook his head. "Really? Can't think of a single thing?"

Everyone laughed.

Just stick with the truth.

"With my messiness!" she said. "I really don't care about cleaning. And I don't cook. And…in return, I promise not to leave feminine hygiene products lying around"—the crowd roared, and she raised her voice—"and to be sweet to you, except when I have PMS, and to never say I have a headache." She grinned. "Through thick and thin, good and bad, for the rest of our lives."

He cradled her cheek and kissed her in that slow and tender way of his that always made her crazy for more. The kiss quickly turned hot, and she threw her arms around him as the rest of the world fell away.

Justice Fleming cleared her throat. "I didn't say you were man and wife."

They kept kissing.

The judge sighed. "I now pronounce you man and wife."

Everyone cheered. Trav pulled away, and they smiled at each other. She liked that when she looked at him now, she saw a man and not just a dad.

"Do I look like Bryce's mom to you or just Daisy?" she asked.

He cradled her cheek. "You look like my woman, who's going to get ravished tonight."

She beamed. It was what she'd wanted all along. Well, not the ravishing part, but…well, yeah, that too.

～

Daisy's Private Journal—No Peeking

Trav wants me to follow my dreams, so it's on to the next adventure. Before all the excitement over my blog, I'd been really excited about the infant massage that worked wonders on Bryce's colic. It absolutely saved my sanity to have a way to soothe him that really worked (except for his nightly pre-bed scream session), so I'm going to an infant massage training workshop in the fall to become an instructor!

I might write a little fiction on the side. About a single mom who demanded more from a guy who gave and gave and gave, until she finally realized it was her turn to give.

I think it will have a happy ending.

Daisy Garner O'Hare

Don't miss the next book in the series, *Bad Taste in Men*, featuring Shane and Rachel in an unexpectedly intimate encounter!

Something's brewing between friends...

Rachel Miller knows opening a café will make her struggling bookstore *the* place to hang out. But when the bank turns her down and her best friend Shane steps in, she vows business will never ruin their friendship.

Gourmet chef Shane O'Hare knows food, not women. To sweep Rachel off her feet, he secretly sells his beloved '67 Shelby Mustang and becomes a partner in her café. And then she sets him up with a friend.

As they build the café together and Rachel learns what Shane has sacrificed for her, she finds herself falling for him. Now way too much is riding on the success of this business venture—her career, her best friend, and her heart.

Sign up for my newsletter and never miss a new release! https://www.kyliegilmore.com/newsletter

ALSO BY KYLIE GILMORE

Unleashed Romance <<steamy romcoms with dogs!

Fetching (Book 1)

Dashing (Book 2)

Sporting (Book 3)

Toying (Book 4)

Blazing (Book 5)

Chasing (Book 6)

Daring (Book 7)

Leading (Book 8)

Racing (Book 9)

Loving (Book 10)

The Clover Park Series <<brothers who put family first!

The Opposite of Wild (Book 1)

Daisy Does It All (Book 2)

Bad Taste in Men (Book 3)

Kissing Santa (Book 4)

Restless Harmony (Book 5)

Not My Romeo (Book 6)

Rev Me Up (Book 7)

An Ambitious Engagement (Book 8)

Clutch Player (Book 9)

A Tempting Friendship (Book 10)

Clover Park Bride: Nico and Lily's Wedding

A Valentine's Day Gift (Book 11)

Maggie Meets Her Match (Book 12)

The Clover Park Charmers series <<sweet and sexy charmers!

Almost Over It (Book 1)

Almost Married (Book 2)

Almost Fate (Book 3)

Almost in Love (Book 4)

Almost Romance (Book 5)

Almost Hitched (Book 6)

Happy Endings Book Club Series <<the Campbell family and a romance book club collide!

Hidden Hollywood (Book 1)

Inviting Trouble (Book 2)

So Revealing (Book 3)

Formal Arrangement (Book 4)

Bad Boy Done Wrong (Book 5)

Mess With Me (Book 6)

Resisting Fate (Book 7)

Chance of Romance (Book 8)

Wicked Flirt (Book 9)

An Inconvenient Plan (Book 10)

A Happy Endings Wedding (Book 11)

The Rourkes Series <<swoonworthy princes and kickass princesses!

Royal Catch (Book 1)

Royal Hottie (Book 2)

Royal Darling (Book 3)

Royal Charmer (Book 4)

Royal Player (Book 5)

Royal Shark (Book 6)

Rogue Prince (Book 7)

Rogue Gentleman (Book 8)

Rogue Rascal (Book 9)

Rogue Angel (Book 10)

Rogue Devil (Book 11)

Rogue Beast (Book 12)

**Check out my website for the most up-to-date list of my books:
kyliegilmore.com/books**

ABOUT THE AUTHOR

Kylie Gilmore is the *USA Today* bestselling author of over fifty humorous contemporary romances. Her series include Unleashed Romance, the Rourkes, the Happy Endings Book Club, Clover Park, and Clover Park Charmers. With more than three million downloads of her books, readers all over the world love escaping into her hilarious feel-good romances featuring strong bonds with family, friends, and community.

Kylie lives in New York with her family, a demanding cat, and a nutso dog. When she's not writing, reading hot romance, or dutifully taking notes at writing conferences, you can find her flexing her muscles all the way to the high cabinet for her secret chocolate stash.

Sign up for Kylie's Newsletter and get a FREE book! kyliegilmore.com/newsletter

For text alerts on Kylie's new releases, text KYLIE to the number (888) 707-3025. (US only)

For more fun stuff check out Kylie's website https://www.kyliegilmore.com.

Thanks for reading *Daisy Does It All.* I hope you enjoyed it. Would you like to know about new releases? You can sign up for my new release email list at https://www.kyliegilmore. com/newsletter. I promise not to clog your inbox! Only new release info, sales, and some fun giveaways.

I love to hear from readers! You can find me at:
kyliegilmore.com
Instagram.com/kyliegilmore
Facebook.com/KylieGilmoreToo
Twitter @KylieGilmoreToo

If you liked Trav and Daisy's story, please leave a review on your favorite retailer's website or Goodreads. Thank you.